Porcelain Posy

Georgene Weiner

Author of:
Rape Seed
Cheater's Choice
A Second Chance

Cover art: Olaf Holland/ Alamy Stock Photo

This work is dedicated to the one I love—my husband, Allen.

I'm about to spill my guts to you, dear reader. Don't judge me too harshly until you have all the facts and understand why I acted as I did.

JAMES PRICE

Chapter 1

After the tragedy, most townspeople were used to Madelaine Frazier's eccentricity. From their storefront and office windows, they'd watch with mild curiosity as she passed by, absorbed, unmindful. Once in a while, if he happened to be outside his antique shop, cranking out the green and white-striped awning with a long aluminum pole, Lester Cox would smile and call a cheery *Good morning* to Madelaine; but she'd just lift her hand and flick off a perfunctory wrist-wave in Lester's direction, her vacant eyes acknowledging nothing in particular. She would lumber down Main Street like an old bear kicking up a fine layer of daily dust that settled on her sensible shoes. During Madelaine's morning strolls, they'd see her: unkempt, stringy blond head skewed slightly so that with one doleful eye she could scan the inscrutable sky for clues—or perhaps, directions. "Her head's in the clouds," is what some had said of her, suspecting that in such a detached state, she could, at any time, trip over her life and not know it. "Such a pity about that kid," they'd say, despite Madelaine's adulthood. Others thought this way about Madelaine, but not I. I knew her better as someone who holds onto an insight as if it were a sacred secret—a talisman, maybe. The flutter of birds' wings high above provoked the faintest flicker of recognition in her eyes; on such rare occasions, the corners of her mouth may have turned upward.

Madelaine had the uncanny ability to leave her mind as anyone else might leave her apartment. She remembered always to close the door behind her but did not bolt it; she needed to assure herself that she could return when necessary and did not want to lock herself out. Having the luxury of leaving her mind at will, she could venture anywhere she chose. Dust balls nestled undisturbed in the dingy corners of her brain and uncleansed memories piled high in the cracked, stained sink of her mind. A brown dullness hovered over the dilapidated furniture of her being like a drab slipcover. But Madelaine paid little heed to the gritty details of her mental housekeeping; she sprayed the interior spaces with a perfume of nonchalance and insulated the vacuum with an air of insouciance.

And oh, the places Madelaine's mind had visited: The Tower of London, the Taj Mahal in Agra, and the Kilimanjaro in Africa, the Catacombs of Rome! She would drift regally along the canals of Venice as if she were the special guest of the Doge, exuberantly waving to the plangent sounds of the ghosts at the Bridge of Sighs. From front row center at *La Corrida de Torros* in Madrid, she would throw flowers to the dying bull—her eyes bulging with fierce passion for the tormented beast. Truthfully, she preferred the style of horseback bullfighting in Portugal; there, it is unlawful to kill the bull.

Sometimes, Madelaine preferred to cruise in a catatonic sleep. Adrift turbid waters, she rocked to the rhythms of her solitude. Rippled waves slapped against the wormy wood of her unconscious. The long sough of distant horns pleaded with her from a blackened shore. But Madelaine surfed her loneliness with a dispassion that deceived even her; she didn't dwell on the substance of her alienation, nor worry about the effect of her detachment. As she judged it, her life was about as full and satisfying as anyone's. Who else could jump ship or derail at leisure?

Thirty years ago, Mrs. Luella Frazier threatened to break the sound barrier at the Waterford General Hospital. A weary E.M.T. patrol unit, alerted to the hysterical, 3:30 A.M. call from Number 8 Eighth Street, responded with the alacrity of frozen fish. Intravenous amphetamine would not have energized them to respond quickly to a neighborhood where misfortune seemed contagious. So, it was with trepidation that Mike Stewart and Jo-Jo Banks answered the frantic call from central dispatch.

"Could you guys get over to Eighth Street?" And then, as an afterthought, "Some guy's wife's in labor. Number eight. Name's Frazier."

After draining his Styrofoam cup of its last drops of black coffee, Jo-Jo eased the emergency van out of the Dunkin' Donuts parking lot. "Whatta 'ya think, Mike? Got us another cracker?"

"Odds are good, Jo. Yeah, damn good." Into the microphone of his two-way radio, Mike responded to the dispatcher, "Copy, central. We're on our way."

"Scenic route?" Jo-Jo smiled, activating the red flashers.

At the hospital, Luella's wails ricocheted off the lime membrane of the corridors like bilious green gallstones; they did not mute the ear-burning blasphemy spewing from her mouth. Flush-faced doctors, nurses and available personnel at Waterford General scurried down the halls; white coats flapping like bird wings, they subdued the flailing woman and quelled the coarse obscenities. Aware that Mrs. Frazier was about to deliver her baby without the assistance of a personal physician, attendants quickly wheeled the woman into an elevator and jabbed the button for the third-floor delivery room.

Madelaine was not so much born as she was expelled, perhaps aided by the hard press of a hand upon Luella's abdomen. Madelaine was propelled like cork from a bottle of warm champagne. A wet and slippery projectile, she was caught almost in mid-air by an unsuspecting resident physician. Young Dr. Abbot was frightened by such a precipitous, explosive entry into this world. "Holy shit!" he blurted. For the rest of her life—either by imprinting or indelible imaging—Madelaine would wear Dr. Abbott's same look of consternation upon her otherwise flat, pale face, never quite relieved of her oval-mouthed perplexity. To this day, heavy-lidded and confounded by darkness, Madelaine falls into sleep as one might slip beneath the frothy sheets of ocean waves.

Luella's birth-rupture did not produce a loud protest from Madelaine; her first comment registered as a plaintive, high-pitched whine. She never saw what all the fuss was about then, and she would come to question what, if anything, mattered—ever. Upon Luella's discharge, she bundled Madelaine up in pink bunting; wisps of blond hair poked out from the margins of her baby's color-matched, crocheted hat, framing a porcelain-fine, nearly transparent countenance. Madelaine's eyes hid behind blue-veined lids and gauzy lashes. Edgar Frazier untwisted his corkscrew mouth and assessed his newborn daughter philosophically.

"No worries here," he declared.

"What's that mean?" Luella asked, quizzically scratching her head. She had already counted for ten fingers, ten toes.

"Just that a beautiful daughter is a worry to her father," Edgar said.

"One day she'll bloom, you'll see," Luella assured him.

"At our dark place?" Edgar asked, his eyebrows arching high on his bony face, dark eyes wide with disbelief. "A flower needs fresh air and sunshine to grow. Nothin' beautiful's gonna come of this milkweed. Why, I can almost see right through her."

Luella, used to Edgar's pessimism, shrugged at his tactless comments. She thought it unwise to bring up once again the matter of Edgar's poor salary as night cashier at the Seven-Eleven. She would have to do other people's laundry for additional income, do piecework garment alterations at home, or baby-sit for other kids. Edgar was not a provider—about that she had no question. But, she did love him; that had to count for something.

The Fraziers rumbled home in a borrowed, red Volkswagen Beetle. Edgar did not seem to mind the cramped, bumpy ride; instead, he savored the opportunity to drive a stick-shift automobile. He thrilled to the power of control that the stick imparted and slyly enjoyed the irritation this ride provoked. Louella did her best to control her mouth, biting hard on her bottom lip to douse the fire that was building, licking at her throat. Like hot lava from an active volcano, Louella's reproach could scald. "The baby's getting carsick, Ed, and I'm ready to puke," she cautioned. Then, "Slow down, you fucking idiot!" Edgar, awakened from his pedal-pushing fantasy, lifted his foot from the accelerator to slow the car. "Sorry, Lu," he said, wishing he could leave his wife and daughter at the nearest intersection and wave goodbye for a few days. How free he'd feel as master of his own life! Just a few days of freedom—the kind of freedom that allows you to dream and deny—that's all he'd need. Instead, Edgar pulled the car up to the curb at Number 8 Eighth Street and then turned off the engine; it rattled for a few seconds before coughing to a halt. Unraveling his long legs first, he extricated his lean body by holding onto both sides of the doorframe. Stiffly, he walked around the back of the tiny car to Luella's side and opened her door. Grunting, she handed Madelaine to Edgar and heaved her own body—still swollen and sore—from the passenger seat. Handing the soft bundle to his wife, Edgar announced, "Gotta' get this thing back to Hank... Be back soon." He closed Luella's door and all but skipped back to the driver's side. Were it not for the look of contempt on Luella's face, he might have experienced twenty minutes of unbridled joy. He knew, however, that his failure to offer his assistance up the three flights of stairs would hang like an albatross around his neck for days. He hoped Luella's choice of punishment would be her silence. He loved that golden silence more than he could think of.

Madeleine was soon ensconced in the bottom drawer of her mother's bureau, cushioned with a puffy pink, quilted blanket. This deep box was placed on the floor by Luella's side of an old, red maple bed. Next to the bed stood a small nightstand, scarred by ubiquitous cigarette burns. To her credit (or to her fortune), Luella had never caused a fire; but Edgar's rants to stop her "filthy habit" did inspire her yearly resolutions to quit.

The Fraziers' third-floor apartment, despite the burns, chips, cuts, and gouges, was clean and tidy. Luella took great pride in having made the cheerful, chintz curtains that hung over the kitchen window. She had shopped the thrift stores with an eye to color and taste—her own—even if the furniture, the rugs, the wall hangings, and the floor lamps seemed a bit tawdry. Her personal touches could be seen in the damask drapes she had sewed, in the velvety seat covers she had upholstered by hand, and in the warm quilt she had knitted for their bed. Luella's mother had been a fashion and fabric consultant at an exclusive shop on Newbury Street in Boston; a caterer of haute couture to the café society, she taught her daughter the fine points of stitching, binding, and edging design, while sowing the seeds of self-sufficiency within her. Had this mother lived to see her daughter's future destroyed by a man of such little ambition, she might have embroidered some reason to prevent the inevitable tear to Luella's heart.

Bland ingredients in the spicy cultural stew at Eighth Street, the Fraziers did not mix well with the cacophony of foreign tongues and exotic garb. Pungent smells from the congested apartments merged into a United Nations of Aromas—spicy scents and garlicky odors permeated the walls and wafted from kitchens on stale, summer night air. Though courteous and cordial, the Fraziers tried to keep to themselves, to live hermetically in a building that teemed with raucous children, multinational music, and marital discord. Every culture seemed to have its own contemptuous word for whore; in every language it was a word that was spat rather than spoken.

Chapter 2

$\mathcal{A}$ lthough life was hard on Eighth Street, we did our best to survive the ignominy of poverty and the incessant hunger for escape. Our street—like an amputated appendage reattached to the body of Main Street by an intoxicated surgeon—resembled a crooked little arm that jutted right, then took a quick, sharp turn to the left for another hundred yards or so where it was supposed to rejoin Main at the hip. Second Street was a half-road, recognized as a mistake, and then abandoned as a dead end. No one lived on Third Street, which served well as a safe, undisturbed place for playing street hockey, basketball, and for Saturday night necking. As a child, Madelaine never mingled with the us, never played ball, never twirled a hoola-hoop around her waist or jumped rope. Instead, she spent her days and nights counting the pennies she kept in a glass jar on the top shelf of her closet; or, she sat with her mother on the springy sofa, folding laundry, mending her father's socks, or reading mail order circulars. For diversion, Madelaine and her mother watched *I Love Lucy* and an occasional *Queen for a Day.* Bob Barker lightened Luella's day with the illusion that luck stood in wait behind one of three curtains and Luella dreamed of one day choosing the right one. The only laughter that filtered through the open windows of the Frazier's apartment emanated from the small, black-and-white-screen television; it crackled and sputtered from the banged-up box perched atop a milk crate in the living room. Of course, the volume had to be set low to avoid waking Edgar during his daytime sleep. Madelaine became quite expert in the game of Solitaire.

Not surprisingly, our childish games did not evoke what we wanted: some sign of penetrability. Whenever the girls played hopscotch or we guys slapped a ball against the side of our building, we sang this made-up refrain:

> *Mad Elaine, Mad Elaine, bound in chain,*
> *Left on foot or maybe train,*
> *Could not locate half her brain,*
> *Found herself in sunny Spain,*
> *Poor Elaine has gone insane.*

I think Madelaine's absence from our childhood playground bothered our mothers a whole lot more than it did Madelaine; but, even then, it was hard to tell. When my mother overheard our taunts, she'd come bounding out of our apartment in outrage. Wiping floured hands on her yellow gingham apron, lips pursed and brow wrinkled in scorn, she'd yell, "Stop, children. Stop!" Then, she'd point her powdery finger at me in reprimand. "Not nice, Jimmy. You're hurting that poor girl. She's got feelings, you know."

"Not so, Missuz Price," Telly Sandakis offered, mostly to protect me and partly to make himself sound smart. With a finger aimed at his temple, Telly drew imaginary circles. "She's got screws missing upstairs. Like you know, light's on but no one's home."

Telly said this to my mother without malice, without rancor; for him, Madelaine's behavior was a bizarre fact of life.

"Keep your big shot opinions to yourselves, boys," my mother fumed, her green eyes as menacing as those on the dragon pin she wore on her Sunday church dress. "Who knows what she thinks of *you!*"

"But she don't even laugh when we're nice to her!" Telly protested.

"Never mind that. Just leave the poor dear be. Hear?"

We'd scratch our heads and watch my mother stomp off to finish making soda bread, leaving a cloud of guilt over our heads. We hadn't considered—even for a moment—that Madelaine might have opinions of us—let alone *feelings.*

Once, moved, perhaps by her maternal instinct, my mother appealed to Father Martineau.

"What will become of this lost child, Father?"

"We will pray for Madelaine," he replied.

So, for years, thinking it more judicious to bow to discretion than to question the Divine, we prayed. We left the child on the doorstep of Fortune.

Sometimes some of the other women in the complex positioned themselves on the sidewalk, just under the Fraziers' open window. They talked in loud voices, wanting their words to rise up three levels and smack some sense into Louella's—*that woman's*—head.

"What kind of mother keeps her daughter cooped up like a dog?" Mrs. Dubicek would ask.

"Yust a shame, is vot I tink," Mrs. Loebelle proffered, patting her ample bosom with self-righteous indignation.

"Dat chile need fresh air, "Mrs. Allen would declare, "ain't fittin' she be in dat house all the day. No way to raise no chile. No way."

Luella smelled their accusations rising up off the concrete as if they were stink bombs. She ignored their "common talk" and responded with a quick, resounding slam of the living room window. She could deal with the stifling heat in the apartment better than she could with the hot air of busybodies rising from below. How dare these women pronounce judgment on her? Who gave them the right to finger point? *I'm a good mother. I'm a good mother. I'm a good mother.* Luella knew how to combat jealousy: just keep repeating what you believe, and you will convince yourself, eventually, of almost anything. To Madelaine, Luella scoffed, "They're just ignorants, Honey, and that's why we don't pay them heed. The Lord knows how much better I had hoped for you—for me." And Luella would return to the crackling reception of the television and stare morosely at the screen, wishing she had paid more attention to her mother's painstakingly precise, delicate stitching.

"Want some iced tea, Mama?" Madelaine would ask.

"Yeah. Sure, Honey. You go get the playing cards, too. Iced tea will be real nice."

By the time we finished junior high school, most of us had tired of playing a conscious role in the drama of Madelaine's real life. We tired of venting our adolescent spleens and raining our cruel idiocies on someone who refused to cry; who failed to run away from our bawdy taunts; who cared little about our ridicule. Madelaine made our wickedness seem boring. Denied the scent of blood, we hounds were confused; we forgot why we tracked her as prey. Madelaine's response was the unkindest cut: she simply would not bleed. She became a niggling itch behind our collective ear, a pesky flea. In high school, we called her "Mad Elaine"—a sobriquet preferable to being dismissed entirely, for we acknowledged her existence and validated her semi-presence. Madelaine's indifference to our efforts, though not meant as effrontery, only bolstered our contention that she was beyond our poor powers to make *ourselves visible to her*, though we certainly did try.

Madelaine's world—however circumscribed, however insulated and out of sync with ours—seemed devoid of purpose; all she had to do was show up for her life. What we learned much later was that to grow up without expectations was to have no one to displease, no one to disappoint. We watched with wonder as Madelaine grew to adulthood with no clear understanding of who she was and no interest in who she might become. Like canned fruit suspended in a Jell-O mold, Madelaine maintained a kind of wobbly persistence. We believed her to be *exempt* from demands and, therefore, free of the distorting guilt that is the child of failure. And the strangest realization for me was how I felt about her. I loved her because I thought no one else did. Yet, my feeling for her was not pity. I loved her because she did nothing to elicit my love; in fact, she considered my love *illicit*. I loved her as a rare and precious work of art, a treasure unearthed from the tomb of a long-lost civilization. I wanted to believe that she was innocent and naïve; that her insufferable detachment was a plea born of neglect. I loved her because I realized that her affection for me did not allow the warm, chaste kiss I once planted lightly on her cheek. "Don't," she warned, wiping the kiss away with the back of her hand. Her dark eyes had hardened to black marbles as she stared at me with apparent disgust. "You have no right," she admonished. I had no idea what she meant by right, but I was sure that I would do no further wrong.

Still, despite our murmured doubts about Madelaine's happiness, no one was surprised that her grades were the highest in our senior class. Nor was anyone shocked when she declined to present the graduation valedictory address. If there was anyone who most deserved our praise and adulation, it was Madelaine, the one who coveted them least. But Madelaine did not show up for Commencement.

We learned, to our horror, how much we had been deceived, how much we had deceived ourselves. Like thousands of random particles that align in a bright beam of sudden insight, the details of Madelaine's sordid existence soon became the subject of our daily discourse. We found out that some people live in a time and space that is contained by different boundaries than those we've known and taken for granted; that some people live in a place that recognizes no imperatives and allows for behavior that is, at its core, untenable. Consequence and accountability are abstracts that have no useful application in a framework of delusion. Like a surrealist painting, Madelaine's world challenged us to understand; it broke our hearts to try to fully comprehend the *meaning*—or the lack of it—in a life of such disorientation and confusion. And what we could not see, what seemed so remotely possible, was there, in our faces, all along. But it was too late.

To this day, Madelaine vehemently insists that the sex between her and Edgar was consensual; that their affair was as passionate as any that may exist between lovers. Madelaine is content with the knowledge that, from the age of ten, she *enjoyed* Edgar's nighttime visits to her bedroom where she would wait impatiently for his late return from the convenient store. Trembling with the anticipation of his slipping noiselessly into her room, into her bed, she'd leave her door slightly ajar and listen for the sound of his quickened breath. She waited for the singular smell of him as if he were a bouquet of freshly picked wildflowers. The stale scent of old bread and day-old coffee, of overripe bananas and cigarette smoke, of rancid luncheon meats well past their expiration dates, clung to Edgar's skin, hair and clothing. However malodorous he arrived at her bed, Madelaine lay content and took him in with all her senses, feeling more alive in this, her real world, as she could ever hope to be. Yes, she did have feelings, and she would give up all else to possess them. Telly be damned.

It had begun as a game Edgar called *Mailman.* First, he needed to "ring her bell to see if she was home." His fondling sent currents of lightning and quivers of titillation coursing through her obliging body. As the years passed, Madelaine learned how to receive a "love letter." Madelaine was to think of herself as a mail slot—just like the one on their front door. Like a fragile, white butterfly on display, wings splayed and pinned to a board, Madelaine lay beneath the weight of her loving father, sucking in shallow breaths that Edgar mistook as ardent pants. "That's just right, my darling," he'd coo. And when he was spent, he would hold her small quivering body to his and rock her gently in a sweaty embrace that spoke to Madelaine as pure, undeniable love. Before he left her room, Edgar would place a candy treat on the nightstand. "For you, my lovely porcelain posy," he'd say, "a chocolate kiss for tomorrow."

"I love you, Daddy," Madelaine would whisper.

"Daddy loves you, too, sweetheart," Edgar said with no concern for being overheard. He was, after all, Madelaine's daddy.

Closing her door behind him, Edgar padded lightly down the hall to his own bedroom and Luella's raspy snoring.

Edgar did not have to report for work on Sundays and was, therefore, most available to Luella. She excused his unwillingness to attend church, preferring to sleep in all morning, cuddling, making love. Luella often could not contain her desire until Sunday, thinking it cruel that she was denied Edgar's physical attentions during the week.

"I miss you, Honey," Luella would often complain, nuzzling his ear and pressing herself to him.

Turning onto his far side, Edgar would apologize. "These night hours at the store are killing me, Love. So damned tired. Sorry. 'Night."

Despite her rejection, Luella would spoon her body to Edgar's and drape an arm over his waist, settling for the curve of his body next to hers. A kiss to her forehead would have been nice, though.

To protract the morning of pleasure for which she dutifully waited, Luella devised a plan: Madelaine was dispatched around eight o'clock to run errands. Her itinerary began at the bakery where she was to buy a sliced egg bread and six powdered crullers, then on to the smoke shop for two packs of Chesterfields and the Sunday paper. Luella could have asked Edgar to bring home three bananas from the convenient store but preferred to add this item to Madelaine's list; she had carefully calculated the time it would take her daughter to walk from Eighth Street, down to Zeke's smoke shop at the railroad station, two blocks east on Main, and then back to their apartment house. This meticulously planned route allowed Luella to enjoy quiet, private time with Edgar, to luxuriate in his strong arms, to be seduced by his mischievous smile. On Sundays, there was nothing she could want more than the feel of his smooth skin on hers, his sinewy legs rhythmically rubbing against hers, his provocative whispers and sensuous touches, his long, hard kisses. Sometimes her teeth hurt from the pressure of his lips on hers and, often, she needed to choose a deeper shade of lipstick to cover the bruise marks he left on her mouth. "With those beautiful, slender fingers you could be a pianist," she once told him. "How you'd tickle those ivories!"

"I'd rather tickle you, my dear," he had said, playfully tapping at her ribs, "the sound of your laughter is music to my ears."

By the time Madelaine returned with her purchases, Luella and Edgar were ready for breakfast. Madelaine would put up a pot of coffee and set three places at the chrome trimmed, green speckled table. Infused with jealousy and frustration, Madelaine could barely down a cup of coffee. Anger burned in her chest at the sight of her mother's reaching out for Edgar's hand and holding it to her swollen lips. Luella did not protest when her daughter wisely excused herself from the table, rinsed her yellow cup and chipped plate, set them squarely on the bleached rubber drain board. and abruptly exited the kitchen.

And so it was, on the Sunday before Madelaine's graduation from Senior High School, a day bright and warm and filled with the early summer smells of damp earth and sprouting dandelions, pungent pork kielbasa and fried kippers, that Madelaine rounded the elbow of Eighth Street and wished that the hand of a vengeful god would reach down and strike her blind. What Madelaine had to take in—not in pieces, but in its entirety, in its enormity, in its unimaginable brutality, were the flashing red lights of two police cruisers parked facing each other at the curb of Number 8. Three officers stood in a semicircle around Luella, their backs to the road; they formed a blue phalanx either to prevent Luella's escaping, or to protect Luella from the crowd of curious neighbors already gathering. Luella sat on the bottom step of the concrete entryway to her apartment building, hugging her dingy white terrycloth robe to her naked body and rocking to and fro in a primitive rhythm of grief. Her sobbing was soft, childlike. Slumped in despair, Luella appeared to be shrinking, crumpled and balled-up like a discarded tissue. Her long, dark hair was uncombed and matted to the left side of her head.

Two brown grocery bags fell from Madelaine's hands, ripping apart and spilling their contents on the sidewalk. Three powdered crullers rolled onto the street, leaving behind a wavy, white trail. An errant gust of wind lifted the edges of the Sunday Chronicle and swirled its pages high into the air, indiscriminately dropping them into trees and plastering them to the neighbors' windows. Madelaine rushed to her mother, parting the officers' blue blockade by hurling her body at theirs. Startled, one of them reached for his revolver. Equally startled, Luella raised her head from her bloodstained forearm. A smear of red colored her cheek and the bridge of her nose; like a paintbrush slap of dried crimson, it streaked across her face and splattered her ear. Madelaine did not speak; she felt her tongue turn to cotton and stick to the roof of her mouth. Luella's feral eyes told her everything she had long expected, everything she believed to be inevitable and fitting.

"Hey, who're you?" the big-bellied officer asked, raising his cap and repositioning it further back on his sweaty head. His blue eyes were gentle but guarded. "What's your name, girl?" he asked again when there was no response.

And then, a voice rose up from the turbid depths of a vile underworld, a deep, guttural voice, anguished and loathing. "My daughter... Edgar's *lovely porcelain posy.*"

Madelaine felt the quick slash, the painful slice of her mother's accusation as it cut through her flesh and ripped her heart into a thousand shreds. She brought two fists up to her eyes and tried to blur the vision of her mother's open hatred. Sinking to the ground, she buried her head in her lap. She refused to bear witness as Edgar's corpse was brought down the stairs in a black body bag, placed on a stretcher and carefully loaded into the waiting ambulance. Silently, she vowed that forevermore, she would shield her eyes from all such murderous truths and testify to nothing more than having once been loved.

Sometime later, when guiltless dreams eluded me, and the terrible weight of conscience robbed me of peace, I sought my comfort in long walks about town. I preferred those brisk autumn nights when, if I didn't keep moving, a reproving chill crawled up the sleeves of my overcoat. If one particular midnight sky had not been so clear nor its moon so full, I might not have discovered where Madelaine sought her own solace. There, just beyond the far corner of Waterford High's football field, in a thicket of scraggly blueberry bushes, young poplars and discarded beer cans, I espied Madelaine Frazier kneeling beside a tiny, unmarked mound of earth. Carefully, she removed each oak leaf that had fallen atop the little swell and began to stroke it with the most incredible tenderness. I stood in the shadows, transfixed by my exquisite anguish. Tears stung my eyes and I had to force myself to look away. It was then that I heard Madelaine's long, wistful sigh—a single melancholy note; it floated high into the supplicating boughs of the stripped oak trees, and like a halo, shimmered overhead.

Chapter 3

After serving twelve years in the state penitentiary for second-degree manslaughter, Luella was released. The anguish of the physical and mental abuse she had endured at the hands of other inmates left her feeling bereft and worthless. What they had called her, and what they had threatened to do to her—and often did—she countered with a disturbing equanimity; she felt she had deserved it. Of course, her submission had only infuriated her tormenters more. She had worn her bruises—both inside and out—as if they were her very own crown of thorns, and however repentant, she knew that she would never be welcomed at St. Peter's pearly gates.

Deposited outside the gates of the prison, she had nowhere to go, nowhere to seek solace, nowhere to reclaim her sense of self. Edgar was dead, the right side of his head bashed in by a chipped-glass paperweight she had kept by their bed. That fateful afternoon, she had whispered her most seductive sighs into Edgar's ears and had snuggled close to his warm, sleeping body. Half-awakened, he had uttered, "Come to Daddy, my porcelain posy." He had reached out toward Luella, who lay there frozen in fear and disbelief. And then, she had reached for the paperweight.

Twelve years in prison seemed a small price to pay for what she had done. But what caused her the most pain was not seeing her daughter, her only child. The wounds of that ghastly day would not heal. Madelaine had never visited her, never once tried to explain to her mother why she did not report, did not complain. For Luella, this behavior suggested Madelaine's complicity, that she had welcomed Edgar's abuse! In fact, her daughter had become her rival, satisfying Edgar as she could not. Did Luella despise her daughter, or did she pity her guileless little girl? Luella would leave prison childless, friendless, and homeless. Who would want a murderess as a friend or neighbor? She, herself, wouldn't want that. Who would hire an ex-con, crazed by betrayal? A desperate plea to her younger brother yielded a lifeline, of sorts. Having refused to be a character witness at her trial, Dwayne offered her a small back room in his home. Like most people, he believed Luella guilty and deserving of punishment. Still, she was his sister, albeit a murderess. Of course, the offer came with the caveat that Luella would have to earn her keep and stay out of sight.

Thinking back on her trial, Luella could not think of one person who would come forward to vouch for her. Madelaine, her only defense, refused to testify, never once admitting to what had fueled her mother's outrage. She did not show up for the trial; the District Attorney pleaded that Madelaine was "not competent," not a "credible witness given her obviously diminished mental capacity." The prosecutors just didn't know how this "challenged young woman" could endure such intense scrutiny under oath. Luella never told the police nor revealed to those prosecutors the truth of what had brought her to the brink of insanity. They would not have believed her. She was convicted on the evidence: a crime of passion

24

and jealousy because of Edgar's infidelity. And I was a coward who did not come out of the shadows. Until now.

I would find out later, that the mother of my school chum, Telly Sandakis, had taken Madelaine into her home, provided meals, had given her shelter and a warm bed. Madelaine's presence in her small apartment, filled the void left by her son's supreme sacrifice as a Navy fighter pilot. Viola Sandakis visited Telly's graveside every Saturday, leaving freshly cut flowers in an urn. Her laments were heard near and far, especially unnerving to those who were new to the old neighborhood in which I grew up. She continued to live on Eighth Street, as lonely and lost as Madelaine, both perpetually fixed to a time and place not of their own making. For twelve years, Viola allowed Madelaine the latitude she required: the freedom to walk the streets of her sullied youth, unfettered by propriety. Except for a few cleaning chores, helping to fold their laundry, and assisting in the kitchen, Madelaine did nothing more to show her gratitude.

Chapter 4

After graduating from Emerson School of Broadcast Journalism, I fled what I considered the provincial world of Boston. I traveled, some by thumbing my way across the country, some by wheedling airfare from friends who were headed for esoteric destinations in Europe. I hiked a lot, staying in hostels or cheap boarding houses. I sowed my youthful oats, then returned to the States both broke and inexperienced. My former roommate at Emerson convinced someone at the Globe to offer me an apprenticeship in the newsroom. It was there that I cut my journalistic teeth, assigned to copy-editing and layout. They paid me, but not enough to live big. I worked my butt off learning all I could from more senior editors and eventually, worked my way up the ladder of success by boldly submitting my own bylines and commentaries. Management was pleased with my work, as well as the flood of "letters to the editor" my columns provoked.

As my stature at the paper improved, so did my appeal to my female counterparts. I dated several, but eventually fell under the spell of Donna Chapman. She is a brilliant, perspicacious woman with an eagle's eye for detail and a fine-tuned ear for phoniness. Short, curly dark hair frames her round face, almost always flushed by her high energy and passion. Her blue eyes sparkle with a gaiety that lends a cherubic quality to her allure. When truth and substance are her targets, however, she pursues them with feline tenacity. She believes that at the core of every misdeed, there must be an underlying provocation.

Donna possesses a passion for certainty that I have sorely lacked. Having long ago abandoned my life on the back streets of Chelsea and the memories of those past turbulent years, I've lived a peaceful, blissful life with my wife, and our four-year-old son, Paul. We are happy in our tree-lined, suburban neighborhood of Cambridge, but constantly reminded that reality and authenticity rarely cross paths.

I remember the warm, Sunday morning in June when the tranquility of my life abruptly ground to a halt. Donna and I were seated at the kitchen table, mugs of our favorite coffee before us, leisurely reading the newspaper. There, on page 7, was a file photo of Luella Frazier being led away in handcuffs; terrycloth bathrobe hanging loosely about her sagging shoulders. Her hair was matted, and blood stains could be seen on her face. I studied the photo for many minutes, my eyes riveted on another figure partially obscured by police and coroner's personnel. My quick intake of breath and the sudden drain of color from my face frightened Donna. She put her coffee mug down with alarm and reached for my hand.

"Jimmy, are you okay? You're pale!"

There was no response from me, other than tears in my eyes. I could hardly breathe.

"My God, you look ghastly!" Donna rose to comfort me, then wrapped her arms around me from behind my chair.

Until that day, I had buried the memories that I had hoped to forget. I suspected, though, that I was not going to be spared involvement in what would surely come next. I couldn't sit there and study the faded image of a young girl—my former neighbor—with dispassion. Part of me wanted to be like all the rest who shook their heads with tight-lipped scowls. The other part of me could not shake off the enormity of the part I had unwittingly played in this drama. Deep in thought, I pulled at the hairs of my beard.

"You seem too affected by that picture, Jimmy. Tell me what's making you so anxious."

I never told Donna that I had come upon young Madelaine Frazier, in a thicket just outside the playing field of our high school; that she had been crouching over a mound of dirt under which I presumed lay buried an aborted fetus. I had kept this secret for so long, it had imbedded itself in my very soul. I had never told my mother, either. I know she would have scolded me and insisted that I tell Father Martineau or that I report it to the police. My widowed mother (my Dad died of a sudden heart attack when I was twenty) lives in Arizona with her sister, Mae. Had I confided in her at the time of my discovery, perhaps I wouldn't be still harnessed to such a heavy load—an ox to his yoke. I had reasoned, at the time, that I was just a kid whom no one would believe. I'm not a kid anymore. But I am still a coward.

Perspiring, I suggested that Donna sit down beside me. "I will tell you a secret," I began, "but you must promise that you won't judge me harshly."

Nodding her assent, she took my hand in hers and whispered, "You're trembling."

Donna listened with patience, squeezing my hand gently to encourage me when she sensed my reluctance to continue. Indeed, I was trembling, traumatized by a memory of long ago, a memory of inexplicable sorrow. With Donna's encouragement, I went on to expose Madelaine's lurid past and the reason behind her "madness."

When I was finished, she covered her mouth to stifle a cry of indignation. The arms of our son's mother were covered with goosebumps. "That poor, poor child," she whispered. "And poor Luella. Jimmy, I think you must reach out to them... somehow. Why hasn't anyone other than Mrs. Sadakis tried to help?"

Donna had shifted into her passion mode of wanting to rectify perceived wrongs; she was already setting her sights on how best to find justice for two defenseless victims. She rose from her chair and poured us each another helping of coffee. I could tell by the flush on her cheeks and the intensity of her gaze that she would not rest until Madelaine and Luella were reunited. How she could imagine accomplishing her goal was beyond me. To break the tension, I suggested taking Paul to the park where he could play and feed the ducks. We would pack a picnic and try to enjoy the bright sunshine with our son. We would try forestalling the demands of a Monday workday.

Chapter 5

*W*eeks after returning to my job and to the paperwork piled high on my desk, I was still consumed by the photo of Luella's release from prison. I continued to feel the niggling effects of seeing her in handcuffs. More to the point, I was troubled by what I discerned to be the outline—blurred, but clear to me—of Madelaine standing aside a police officer. I couldn't imagine the fright that this scene must have created in her being, nor could I imagine what would drive a seemingly decent, however elusive woman to kill her husband. To me and my friends, Luella had been over-protective of her daughter, keeping her indoors and out of reach of our youthful indiscretions. The recent reports of the effects of bullying and scapegoating, however, have shed new light on the victims of this blatant disregard for another human being, no matter how "different" from the rest he or she may be. Did our behavior toward Madelaine lay the groundwork of her undoing? I thought I had acted kindly toward her; I had wanted her to know that we could be friends. I guess I just didn't try hard enough. Madelaine did not fit in and was thus rejected, the object of our thoughtless chiding.

The more I tried to concentrate on my work and my next deadline, the more these thoughts intruded. I was obsessing and couldn't stop thinking that Donna was right about doing something, but what? My eyes scanned the newsroom for my wife, hoping to further explore her suggestion that I write an opinion piece for the newspaper. Would that just make matters worse? Should I just let sleeping dogs lie, as it's said, with the hope that they wouldn't wake up and bite me in the ass?

Donna wasn't at her desk; instead, I could see her sitting on a plush, cushioned armchair in the glass-walled office of our editor-in-chief, Fiona Moran. She was leaning forward and gesticulating with great animation. Like me, Donna is Italian and speaks with her hands, especially when fired-up about some issue. It appeared to me that Donna was either trying to impress her boss with the import of her ideas, or that she was struggling to convince Fiona of their righteousness.

Fiona is a tall, willowy, middle-aged woman who is not impressed by her own importance. Never officious or overbearing, she allows her staff to explore unconventional avenues and to mine the depths of their investigative skills. She demands propriety and accuracy but has been known to bend the rules now and then. She wears her silver-streaked hair severely pulled back into a chignon at the nape of her neck—perhaps for effect—and fashionable black-rimmed eyeglasses perch on her aquiline nose. She is a good, decent woman who does not suffer fools nor sycophants. She eschews designer apparel, preferring her own monogram FAM (the A is for Alice).

As Donna's hands fluttered in the air like birdwings, Fiona's rested on the arms of her white leather desk chair, slightly tilted backwards. I could see her drumming her long, manicured fingers, listening intently but giving no clue as to her disposition.

When Donna finally emerged from Fiona's office, she wore a half-smile—something just short of a smirk of satisfaction. She skipped, rather than walked, to my desk, then planted her butt on it. Fiery Donna meets circumspect me. Perched atop my desk, oblivious to the paperwork, she could not contain her excitement. Her long, shapely legs crossed at the knees momentarily diverted my attention.

"Jimmy, I'm bursting at the seams! Fiona has given me the go-ahead to pursue what I convinced her is a miscarriage of justice for Luella and... to find a way to reunite Madelaine with her mother."

I was stunned, half-believing that my wife would surge ahead without my knowledge or consent.

"Whoa! Slow down, Honey. Where is all this coming from? Why didn't we talk about this together before forging head-first into an improbable plan?"

"I knew that's how you'd see it. Your innate pessimism just doesn't allow for spontaneity." She was grumbling now.

"I call it impulsiveness," I countered. Now I was the one grumbling.

"Well, aren't you at least going to ask me what the plan is, before you brush it off like lint on your jacket?" She leaned in and brushed away the lint on my jacket. "Let's talk over lunch. Okay?"

Donna truly believed that wrong could be made right; she was convinced that good can transcend evil, if only one were willing to try. Her optimism was no match for my skepticism. We somehow managed to meld our two opposing natures and come up with a viable compromise. We were the results of two distinct cultures.

Chapter 6

My grandparents' native homeland was Sardinia, an ever-evolving, yet beautiful historical landscape. It is the second largest island in the Mediterranean Sea, second only to Sicily. The brutal Fascist crackdown in World War II and the ensuing economic crises hastened their departure from the land they loved. Fleeing the oppression and threats to their lives and emigrating to a far-away land, they learned the invaluable tools of survival: closed mouth, open mind. They raised my mother in an atmosphere that could best be described as healthy skepticism and caution. And, yes, I ate sardines often, sometimes finding them in my school lunchbox.

My grandparents landed in Boston, poor but proud. A cousin who had emigrated earlier arranged for their transfer from Ellis Island and generously loaned them enough money to open a small trattoria in an abandoned storefront on Eighth Street. My mother, when she was old enough to remove plates and clean tables, worked long hours in the kitchen with her mother, preparing delicacies from old-world recipes. They cooked and baked until they could barely stand upright, while my father took care of the business' finances. I rarely saw my mother not wearing an apron. They had managed to restore the upper floor—until then used for storage—into habitable living space where I was born and where I lived my first eighteen years. Out of necessity, my grand-folks lived frugally; they were gentle, generous immigrants who worked hard for their subsistence and valued the opportunities America afforded them. They learned to speak English and, studying together, took night classes to pass the tests for citizenship. I remember how proud they were the day they learned that they had fulfilled all the requirements and would be issued their citizenship papers. On that day, every patron who stopped by for lunch or dinner was told, "No charge."

Donna's grandparents are Sicilians. Upon reaching the States, they were helped with an abundance of get-on-your-feet money, and a well-paying job working in Uncle Leo's garment factory in Boston. Granddad's tailoring skills served him well, when years later, he helped Donna's father open an exclusive men's apparel shop on Newbury Street where he custom-fit the wealthiest business men, bankers, and politicians. Both clans, while clinging tenaciously to their respective traditions, feted us with an extraordinary wedding celebration.

The only wrinkle in the festivities came when my grandmother broke down in tears, still mourning the death of her older sister, Rhonda, a victim of the Spanish flu (January 1918-December 1920). That historic, tragic pandemic infected five hundred million people world-wide and caused the deaths of fifty to one hundred million people. Grandma didn't speak much of her sister; instead, she commemorated her passing each year by lighting a memorial votive candle on the anniversary of her passing. It took a glass or two of *Mirto* liqueur to calm her, and not wanting to spoil the party, she respectfully joined her relatives in the tradition of throwing plates at the bride and groom. Each plate is full of grains (abundance), salt (wisdom), rose petals (tenderness), candy (sweetness), and money (richness), and in throwing them at the newly married couple, these qualities are symbolically passed on to them.

In his toast to us, Donna's uncle, Gino, regaled us with stories about his father Leo's business "partners" whom we all knew to be family members—not related, of course, but nevertheless fiercely loyal.

Yes, we were a family of opposites, come together in the spirit of cautious harmony.

Chapter 7

*D*onna and I agreed to meet at a small sidewalk café within walking distance of our workplace. The weather was warm and balmy, richly perfumed by the stands of potted herbs and lilac bushes. Our table was set under an old sycamore tree, more interesting for its layers of shedding bark than for its flowers.

After placing our orders of grilled chicken, Caesar salad and iced-tea, we sat back in our folding chairs; each of us crossed our arms over our chests—a rather defensive posture for a married couple out to lunch on a beautiful afternoon.

Until then, I had hoped, however naively, that I could be like everyone else and just read about Luella's release, then forget. Yet, preternaturally, I sensed that I was not going to be spared involvement in anything remotely connected to the Fraziers. Having read the news article and seen the photos, I could not be dispassionate; I was, like it or not, a part of the story.

"Okay," I began, squeezing a lemon wedge into my drink, "tell me what you and Fiona have conspired, or, cooked up."

I knew my wife would take offense at my choice of words. "Jimmy, we were not conspiring; we were brainstorming. We both feel that we can use the power of the press to reawaken some moral obligation to help that poor girl and her mother." She stopped to take a sip of her tea, then twirled the lemon wedge with her plastic straw. Blue eyes ablaze, Donna stared at me, hoping for some encouragement.

"So, what is my part in this obligation?" I knew the answer; I just needed Donna to present the plan in a coherent, plausible way.

"Fiona thinks that you should write an article about the "incident" (fingers raised to simulate quotation marks), revisiting the shameful way in which all the neighbors, except your mother, treated Luella like a pariah, offering her no solace nor benefit of the doubt. Granted, they didn't know the real reason for her impulsive act against Edgar because they didn't want to know. Everyone just assumed she was a jealous, unstable woman who lashed out in rage. The fact that no one especially liked her didn't justify their disregard for a possible, underlying truth; to them, she was just plain guilty, no excuses."

"But, Honey, she never volunteered the truth, never confided in her court-appointed lawyer, and never asked for a retrial. She was guilty of killing her husband, yes; but she never shared her motivation for doing so."

Our lunch dishes arrived and we each picked up our forks to start eating. Simultaneously, we both pushed the food around our plates, then lay our forks down on the table, our appetites gone.

"If we uncover her true motivation," I argued, "what can of worms will we be opening? What are the chances that Madelaine will come out of her stupors and shed any light on things? The only person Madelaine exchanges any words with is Viola Sandakis, and I doubt she knows anything more than we do."

"But, *you* do, Jimmy." Ah, the *Coup de grace*. The final blow to my resistance. Suddenly, I was rethinking the wisdom of having shared my accidental finding of Madelaine who was wailing to the ether.

"All you have to do is write a piece about the day of the murder... no, don't call it murder, that's too powerful a word." Donna was coaching me, and I wasn't thrilled with her input.

"Luella took a life, Donna; that's called murder."

"Yes, but what about the withheld information that was never submitted at trial?"

"Who knew there even *was* withheld information? It's not like she was led to the gallows without due process!" I could feel the heat rising around my shirt collar.

"You knew, Honey. And that must come out now, like it or not."

"So, now you're telling me that somehow, I was complicit in this deplorable scenario? Give me a break, Donna; I didn't withhold information. I just didn't want to get involved." There, I said it. The guilt that has plagued me all these years finally makes its debut on the big stage, or rather in a short but stunning newspaper article.

Leaning in conspiratorially, I whispered, "I need more time to think about this, Honey."

"You've had twelve years, Jimmy. There's not much more to think about except, maybe, your own hubris."

"I can't accept that," I shot back. "My intention was not to hurt anyone with my suspicions. And that's all they were, Donna, suspicions."

"We all weave our own webs, Love. I'm convinced that yours can be untangled."

Was she right? Had I woven a web of self-deceit? I could feel the first signs of an oncoming migraine.

Donna checked her watch and called for our waiter. "Please, we'd like to take these with us for later," she demurred. I paid the check, leaving a generous tip. My guilt knew no bounds. Together, we made our way back to our offices and, heavy-hearted, got through the rest of the day.

Chapter 8

For a guy who writes for a living, I was at a total loss for words when I tried to dispassionately put down on paper a reconstruction of the Frazier killing. My intent was to revisit the scene as an objective reporter, utilizing my professional skills of objectivity, while obfuscating my real, more personal interests. It was truly difficult to separate myself from my imagined role in the drama that played itself out before me. Was I bestowing on myself too much credence, too much self-importance on my potential role in Luella's future? In short, did I owe her anything more than a reprise of the events that led to her incarceration? Long ago, it was Madelaine who told me that "I had no right," when I planted that chaste kiss on her cheek. Maybe, I had no right to be digging up the past, going somewhere in someone's life where I didn't belong and where I had not been invited.

Donna periodically came into my study to inquire if I was making progress. I was sorely tempted to implore *her* to write the article; but, conceded that she was just trying to keep my nose to the grindstone. Not lost on me, however, was the fact that she was also bolstering her own need to see my article appear in tomorrow's edition of the newspaper. With difficulty, I refrained from telling her that her frequent interruptions were annoying the hell out of me.

Donna's heart was in the right place; she wanted to make life better for people she didn't even know. I, on the other hand, knowing these people all too well, was reluctant to jump head-first into a pool of polluted, murky water. I wanted to mind my own business; yet, my wife had convinced me of my moral obligation to dive in, head-first. "Can I get you anything, Honey? Coffee, something stronger?"

I would have loved a stiff shot of bourbon but didn't want to cloud my thoughts. "No, thanks. Maybe when I'm finished."

I saw her face brighten with this last statement, reassured that I would, indeed, accomplish my task. "All right, I'll join you then."

∞ ∞ ∞

Around midnight, I put the finishing touches on my article, intent on submitting it in the morning to Fiona. Lifting the pages from my printer, I felt queasy just holding them. Sensing that what I had written was just the first wave of a brewing storm, I closed my computer and walked into our living room. Donna was engrossed in a new best-seller, lounging on our faux suede love seat, her stockinged feet crisscrossed and resting on one of its arms. A shaggy white pillow cushioned her head.

"I think I'm ready for that bourbon," I declared. My presence must have startled her, as she bolted upright, dropping her novel onto the carpet. "Didn't mean to scare you."

Seeing the printed copies in my hand, she smiled, adjusted her glasses, and reached for the papers.

"I'll get our drinks," I offered. She had already started reading.

When I returned with two bourbons straight-up, she was totally immersed in my writing. Now sitting Indian-style, the forefinger of her right hand traced every word. Absently, she reached out for her glass. "Careful, there, Honey," I said, placing it on a coaster to protect our high-gloss, birds-eye maple cocktail table. I chose a recliner next to the fireplace and sipped my drink in silence. The only sounds I heard from Donna were several "uh-huhs" and "hmms." As I waited for her to finish, I closed my eyes and rested my weary head against my seat back. I felt like a schoolboy, waiting for the teacher to correct my test and, hopefully, paste a gold star at the top. I valued Donna's opinions, always perspicacious and wise; however, I did not take her criticisms of my writing lightly. I had to silently promise myself that if my ego emerged bruised, I would accept her judgment with deference. This is what I wrote:

The Consequences of Avoiding Responsibility

A few weeks ago, in accordance with the terms of her parole, Luella Frazier was released from the county penitentiary. Luella had been found guilty of manslaughter in the second degree and had been sentenced to serve twelve years behind bars. At the time of her sentencing, it was generally agreed that Luella had discovered her husband's infidelity, and in a moment of temporary insanity, she had killed him with a blow to the head. The murder weapon—a glass paperweight covered with blood from Edgar's fractured skull—was the only evidence submitted in court proceedings.

Luella Frazier was and continues to be a good, decent woman, who, I believe, suffered more punitive sentencing than she deserved. She is not, as some have concluded, a cold-blooded murderess.

As one who used to live on Eighth Street and witnessed the hysterical rush to judgment that ensued, I wish to tell you that I am guilty of having withheld vital, perhaps mitigating information. Had I come forward with that information, there is no doubt in my mind that Luella's sentence may have been shortened. I am talking about a miscarriage of justice, due in part, to my inability to square what Luella may have thought right with what I knew to be wrong; my cowardice may have cost her more years behind prison bars than she merited. Luella is a free woman now; but she will continue to live a life of condemnation and isolation; that is, unless I break the silence I've kept.

My intentions are to not to revisit the events of the fateful day of Edgar Frazier's demise, but to make up for not coming forward when I knew more about Luella's motivation. I cannot change the last twelve years; I can only reach out—assuage my own guilt—and try to restore a good woman's name. I hope to reunite a mother with a daughter lost to her, so that they might cobble a new life together.

I beseech you to reserve judgment until my investigation is complete. At that time, every and all responses will be welcomed.

Sincerely,

James Price

jprice@globe.com

I was holding my breath waiting for Donna to finish reading, then digesting my words. I refused to open my eyes until I heard her verdict.

"Jimmy, this piece is potent. I'm so proud of your sincerity! This is a brave thing you've done, putting yourself out there." Donna removed her glasses, rose from the couch, and plopped herself onto my lap. She kissed me and ruffled my hair. "I love you, Sweetheart. This took so much courage. My one reservation, though, is that you will need Luella's permission to publish this. You can't just put this out there without it. She will still want to protect Madelaine from public ridicule."

"I owe it to Madelaine to try. I owe it to myself to clear my conscience. Hopefully, I can do both without appearing exploitative, or self-serving. Let's just hope that people don't start throwing stones at me."

"Let's just finish our drinks and head upstairs," she said, taking me by the hand and leading me to my reward.

Chapter 9

*F*iona Moran read the Frazier article with satisfaction. She was thinking about the stir of controversy that was bound to arise among the paper's readership, spurring interest and increasing circulation. Disregarding the terms of our agreement, she wasted no time in ordering the publication in the next day's edition. Fiona had never met Luella Frazier and had no serious curiosity about her guilt or innocence. What excited Fiona was the prospective buzz on the street that might elevate the telling of this story to the national level.

Ostensibly, Fiona called me into her office to congratulate me, as well as to commend me for sticking my neck out. This was my expectation; but I would soon discover how wrong I was. When I entered, she was standing by a window that overlooked the courtyard gardens. Hands clasped behind her back, she seemed deep in thought, preoccupied. At five feet, nine inches tall, she stood almost three inches taller than I; she often relied upon her stature to evoke respect and admiration. I cleared my throat to make sure that she knew I was present.

"Yes, come in, James. Make yourself comfortable." Turning to face me, she offered me water; on her desk was a cut-crystal dish filled with wrapped candies. I declined both. She was dressed in a cream-colored silk blouse tucked into a black pencil skirt that accentuated her slender build. The matching jacket hung over the back of her desk chair. She approached me with a fluid motion and extended her scarlet fingertipped hand. She wore no wedding band.

"Good work, James. Your article took guts to write." Fiona's words were always clipped and free of excess embellishment.

"Thank you," I replied, shoving my sweaty hands into my pant pockets. "We have our work cut out for us."

"We?" she asked, her eyebrows raised in surprise.

"Well, I mean, Donna and I." Including Fiona in the "we" was presumptuous, and I wished I could have sucked my words back into my big mouth.

"Ah, yes. Husband and wife working together, hot on the trail of a..." She stopped abruptly, realizing that she was mocking me. "Oh, dear. Didn't mean to imply... oh, never mind," she chuckled.

"No offense." I lied, offended. Her comment rankled me, especially since I was short on sleep.

"You know, James, I was just wondering. Might you be opening yourself up to some legal liability for having concealed evidence, or whatever? I'm not a lawyer, so I don't know what the ramifications of your confession could be."

"Fiona, begging your pardon, but you and Donna decided that my going public was a positive move. You gave your blessings, so to speak, to my so-called 'confession.' Are you telling me now that it was a mistake, that I shouldn't have written it?" *What a goddam hypocrite!* I thought. "Well, for your information, Fiona, I did exactly what you and Donna decided I should do. I did it and I'm not sorry. If there are ramifications, as you suggest, shouldn't you have considered them then?"

I was fuming at her and at my wife, too. I felt used.

Fiona was taken aback by my counter response; she didn't like to be second-guessed, let alone contradicted. Rising from her chair, stiff and apparently riled, she peremptorily dismissed me. "Good day, James," she said through clenched teeth. Turning her back to me, she resumed her previous position in from of the large window.

"Yeah, same to you," I snarled. If I lost my job over this exchange, I'd blame my wife, and me, for being so naïve and malleable. Truth be told, I had not stopped to consider what legal consequences my new-found altruism could incur. Closing the door to Fiona's office behind me, I shuddered to think that I might have made myself a bed of bristles on which to sleep. I returned to my desk feeling compromised and humiliated. Was I to be a sacrificial lamb on the altar of my wife's ambitions? I didn't have to look in a mirror to know that my ears were fiery-red, matching the high color in my cheeks. As a kid, I was often teased; my moniker was "Red." I was ablaze with anger. Having seen my hasty exit from Fiona's office, my colleagues buried their noses in their paperwork; they recognized that I had lost favor with the boss and they didn't want to get involved. Donna looked up at me with tears in her eyes, with such sorrow that I almost forgot that she was the instigator of my problem. I chose to spend the night on the couch.

The next morning, we hardly spoke to one another. We sat at the kitchen table, sipping our coffees but avoiding eye contact. I blew the curls of steam away from my mug, but not away from my angst. Our drawn faces and blood-shot- eyes were proof that neither of us had had much sleep. Donna was the first to break the silence.

"Jimmy, we need to talk. I am so terribly sorry for getting you into this fix. I know your feelings are hurt, but I still think we're doing the right thing."

"*We? We're* doing the right thing? *I'm* the one who's going to take the heat, Donna. I was spitting my words, sour on my tongue. "You sweet-talked Fiona and then you sweet-talked me into going out on this broken limb. Then she hung me out to dry. Just like that." I snapped my fingers right in front of her face.

Donna tried to mollify me. "There are lots of cases where people remember things well after the fact, lots of people who've said that they saw something at the time but didn't come forward. You can't get in trouble for not saying something; you didn't even know what you were seeing. You were just a kid, Jimmy!"

"I should've told someone: my mother, or Father Martineau. You've no idea how this thing... this guilt is eating me up inside. And now Fiona is having second thoughts. Geez!"

"I don't know what Fiona's thinking; I just know that we're doing the right thing for two people who need help."

"We're doing the right thing!" I almost shouted. "I'm the one people will pillory, not you." I got up to rinse my coffee mug in the sink. It was 5:10 a.m. and I could see lights coming on in our neighbors' houses. I heard the familiar sound of the news truck delivering the morning paper and felt a chill run down my spine. In a few short hours, my name would be on everyone's lips. I was going to be deemed a coward or a fool; either way, I couldn't win. After rinsing my mug and placing it on the drainboard, I turned around to say something more to Donna. She had left the room.

I had acted like a petulant child, shouting at my wife in a truly hurtful manner. Calming down, I realized that I had agreed to the plan; that my Donna, always ruled by her heart and not intending to put me in jeopardy, was seeking justice for an aggrieved woman and her disturbed daughter. I could not blame her for wanting to help;

she meant no harm, only good. And, I could not continue to lick the wounds of my injured ego. The water from the upstairs shower trickled down the pipes, emitting a shushing sound that quieted my nerves. I went upstairs to apologize.

Chapter 10

*P*lanting my briefcase atop my desk, I draped my jacket on the back of my chair, loosened my tie, and tried not to make eye contact with my co-workers. I felt diminished, brought down to size, as they might say. At the door of her office, Fiona was hooking her forefinger at me, her way of beckoning me. I feared the worst and, with great trepidation, put my jacket back on, adjusted my tie. For some reason, I straightened my spine and jutted my chin—signs that I was ready for my punishment. I wasn't, but no one had to know that. Who is ever ready for a firing squad?

"Come in, James. Close the door, thank you." Fiona was seated behind her mahogany desk, a wry smile on her lips. "Please, sit down." Her mood was remarkably cheerful, and I worried that her demeanor was a ruse to catch me off-guard. I sat down and folded my hands in my lap; they were shaking, but I tightened my grip until my fingertips were almost white.

"James, I'm sorry about our little tiff yesterday; my intention was not to upset you. You see, I had to know how committed you are to pursuing a difficult quest for justice. I'm satisfied that your motives are as honorable and well-intentioned as I had hoped they would be. I would have been surprised if they were not, remiss if I hadn't questioned you. I had to be sure."

So, I thought, she was testing me. Now she acted as if nothing untoward had occurred the day before. She needed to be assured that I would not chicken out or turn tail and run; after all, she did have her own reputation at stake.

I let out a breath I didn't realize I was holding; my chest caved, and I slumped in my seat. The relief I felt was immeasurable. I didn't know how to respond. I mean, she had almost compromised my marriage, and nearly cost me the respect of my co-workers. Geez. This woman before me was made of tough stuff; no wonder she rose so quickly to the top of the newsroom ladder. Finally, I recovered my equilibrium and found my voice.

"I can assure you, Fiona, that my motives are sincere. Your doubting me was painful, I admit, but I do understand why you had to put my feet to the fire. You were doing your job, I know."

"James, I want to help you and Donna however possible. Follow up on all your leads, keep me informed, and good luck." She rose and extended her hand for me to shake—a sign of renewed, mutual respect.

"Thank you," I said, shaking her hand quickly, before she changed her mind. I left her office with my head held high. Donna smiled at me as I passed her desk and gave me a thumbs-up.

A copy of the morning edition lay on my desk; alongside the paper lay a single white rose.

The other reporters in the room were reading their copies of the newspaper. Some tilted their chairs way back and hoisted their legs up onto their desks—a practice, by the way, that may look good in the movies, but is disapproved of by Fiona. They nodded their heads and absently chewed on pencils held between their teeth. Then, spontaneously, they gave me a round of applause, something like a group hug in my business. I thanked them with a grin larger than the Cheshire Cat's.

I sat down to ponder what our next step should be. We needed a plan, a strategy for how we would begin our mission. Fiona had called it a "quest" much like Don Quixote's, implying that we may end up tilting at windmills. Nevertheless, we had to figure out where to start and how. My thoughts were running in the direction of Eighth Street; a return visit to the old neighborhood and, if we were lucky, finding some of the people who knew Luella and Madelaine. They had never expressed much affinity for Luella, branding her an "unfit mother." Still, I wanted to ask them questions about their antipathy and why their dislike didn't extend to Edgar, as well.

From the corner of my eye, I could see that Donna was doing her own thinking; I was certain that, by the end of the day, we both would have our plans and that we would spend time after dinner figuring out how to implement them. I could feel the juices of anticipation rising in my veins. Or, maybe it was my blood pressure.

We drove home from work both deeply pensive and absorbed by our plans. When we arrived, we discovered that our nanny, Adriana, had already given Paul his supper of macaroni and cheese. For dessert, she allowed him a piece of the apple cake she had baked for him, carefully eliminating any nuts from the recipe. On seeing us enter the kitchen, my son ran straight into my awaiting arms. His squeals of delight were music to my ears, as I lifted him high into the air and wrapped him in a bear hug. Donna thanked Adriana Leone and handed her the weekly check. With our combined salaries, we were able to employ a nanny, refusing to send Paul to day care for two reasons: One, we weren't sold on the idea of day care, pre-school, or whatever they call it nowadays; for us it was a germ-transfer environment. Two, Adriana had six grandchildren of her own; they lived with their parents in different states and she did not get to see them as regularly as she would have liked. We thought she would be a perfect surrogate grandmother for our son. Besides, she is my mother's second cousin and that is about as good a recommendation as I could imagine.

"Paul was a very good boy today, Donna. He took a nice nap after lunch and I took him for a stroller ride around the neighborhood. No problems, um, except for one strange phone call. Someone on the other end of the line was saying nasty things, using very bad words. So, I hung up."

Well, I thought, I expected something like this would happen. I knew there would be people whom I would upset by digging up the uncomfortable past. I suspected that there would be many more phone calls to follow, advising me to mind my own business.

"Thank you, Adriana. If you get any more such phone calls, just hang up right away."

"I will," she agreed, scooping up her handbag and retrieving her sweater from the back of a kitchen chair. Adriana is a short, plump and perky woman with an ample bosom and a jovial manner. Her full head of curly, snowy white hair and rosy cheeks make me think of Christmas and Mrs. Santa Claus. She never complains about anything—just the air conditioner. It was summertime, but Adriana always feels chilled. Blowing a kiss to Paul, she took her leave. "See you tomorrow, Love," she called to him. He waved and smiled, then tightened his grip around my neck. "Hug," he demanded. I was all too happy to comply.

Donna was busy at the sink, washing vegetables for our salads and slicing some left-over chicken breast to add to them. She suggested that I bathe Paul and get him ready for bed.

"Mommy will come to give you kisses, Honey. Will you choose the firetruck jammies tonight, or the spotted dog ones?"

Paul contemplated his choices and decided on the black and white Dalmatians.

Bedtime was always a challenge. We felt guilty being away from Paul all day, and he let his feelings be known by insisting on several story book readings while one of us cuddled with him on his bed. He also insisted on seven "check-ins" after being tucked in for the night, and that every one of his favorite stuffed animals be placed near him. We did not begrudge him this need for the attention he craved and deserved. Love is a salve for little boys and their conflicted parents. But, despite the daytime separation, Paul was thriving and well-cared for. As promised, Donna came upstairs to his bedroom, dimmed the lights, and activated a recorder that played soothing, white-noise. She gave him multiple hugs, promising to return seven times to say, "I love you." By her fourth trip back to his room, Paul was fast asleep, his sandy-blonde head resting peacefully on his pillow, his arm draped around Pinky Winky the rabbit.

Once convinced that he was down for the night, I opened a bottle of Malbec, poured us two generous glasses, then joined Donna in the living room. She sat ready on the sofa, feet propped up on the matching ottoman, notepad and pen in hand. I handed her a glass of wine and sat down beside her. She kissed my cheek and said, "Okay, Inspector, let's make a plan." I assumed she was referring to the Inspector Clouseau of Pink Panther fame and chuckled.

"Okay, Lois Lane. Who goes first?"

"You know a whole lot more than I do about the people who were living in your neighborhood. You, first." She took a sip of her wine.

"Okay, here's what I've been thinking: tomorrow, let's drive over there and knock on Mrs. Sandakis's door. If she lets us in, we'll question her about the Fraziers and why she might think Luella capable of her crime."

"But, Jimmy, you lived there yourself. Surely, you knew how reclusive and different they seemed to others."

"I was just a kid growing up there, Honey. In those days, people cupped their hands over their mouths when they gossiped, trying to keep their buzzing from us kids. We had our own problems with Madelaine, but we just chalked it up to her not liking *us?*"

"What if she doesn't want to talk about what happened. She may not invite us in."

"We'll appeal to her good sense and decency. I remember her as being kindly. If she closes the door in our faces, which I hardly expect she'll do, we'll move on to Father Martineau. I've heard that he's been promoted to Monseigneur now; perhaps he'll have some inkling of what inspired so much antipathy towards the Fraziers. Maybe, like me, he knew something and kept it to himself."

"Not likely, Jimmy; but, let's start from there."

Chapter 11

*L*uella was hard at work in the back room of her brother, Dwayne's small market in Chelsea. Far enough removed from those who might remember her from Revere, she accepted deliveries of goods from various vendors, kept an inventory of all receivables, and signed the bills of lading. She stocked the canned goods on shelves and the perishables in a refrigerated room, taking care to place those items with longer expiration dates behind those which were short-dated. Luella was grateful for the opportunity to work; she wasn't paid but never complained about the long hours or rude deliverymen. She tried to keep out of the way of Dwayne's family, retiring each evening to her small alcove above the market where she had a bed, a shower/toilet, a coffee maker, and a closet for her few, worn clothes. Her sister-in-law, Penny, was tolerant of her presence, though reticent to include her in much of her family's daily activities. Penny visited various thrift shops and purchased some passable clothing for Luella. However much Luella disliked the purchases (often too large, or too small), she did not complain.　Any kindness shown to her, considering her circumstances, was a blessing.

Penny believed that Luella should reacquaint herself with local and world events.　Each morning, she left a copy of the Globe by Luella's door.　On one such morning, sipping her coffee, Luella read my article, saw the printed photos of her arrest, and squeezed her eyes shut to blot out the memory.　She choked, clutched at her neck, then covered her face with trembling hands.　Her coffee cup fell to the floor and shattered.

"Oh, no!" she cried. "Oh, no! no! no!"

Pumped up on adrenalin, neither Donna nor I slept well the night before our planned trip to Revere.　Silently, we rehearsed what we would say to Mrs. Sandakis and how we would entreat her to help us. We awoke early, dressed, and shared our morning with Paul who was happy to munch on some Cheerios until Adriana's arrival.　We would have liked to linger, but we downed the last drops of coffee from our mugs, rinsed them, and were grateful when Adriana rang the front doorbell.　Paul immediately brightened at the sound of her arrival, thus giving us the opportunity to exit without any fuss.

"Good morning, everyone!　And, how's my little sweetheart this morning?"　She immediately donned her sweater, a silent but obvious signal that she was feeling the chill of the air-conditioning.

"Good morning, Adriana," Donna almost sang, grabbing her handbag and giving Paul a kiss on his bed-head locks.　"Be a good boy for Adriana.　We'll see you later, Darling."

"Bye, Mommy," Paul said, releasing us from any further obligations. No one, according to Paul, made better scrambled eggs and buttered toast than Adriana.

"Bye, Buddy. Have a fun day." I ruffled his hair and gently tweaked his little nose. "Love you." I added, as much for me as for him.

Once in the car, we each took deep breaths and exhaled slowly. We fastened our seatbelts and pulled away from our home with nervous anticipation.

"Here goes," I said, feeling the dread of the unknown and what may be lying ahead. I was pretending to be a Fearless Fosdick—that satirical comic strip character with whom Al Capp had entertained me in 'Li'l Abner' comic strips; I could only imagine what obstacles we would face.

We made our way over to Soldier's Field Road and onto Storrow Drive, took Route 1N toward the Tobin Bridge, then to Revere Beach Parkway. Morning rush-hour traffic was heavy, but we made the 11-mile trip in forty minutes. Donna had never been to Revere and was intrigued by the proximity of the triple-deckers. Those boxy homes with flat roofs and tiers of porches were built in the late 1800's to house immigrant workers; they lined the streets of my old neighborhood. Many of the older duplex and triplex buildings were bought by investors, renovated or turned into condominiums. Ever perceptive, she commented, "Having lived so closely, how could they not have known or suspected that something was awry?" Sometimes, hostilities poured out onto the streets, provoking fist-fights and brawls; but these were isolated events, usually caused by too much hard liquor and too little wages paid for hard labor.

"Our parents were all in the same situation, so we tried our best to coexist."

"Well, apparently, the Fraziers were an anomaly." Donna deduced.

I drove slowly through town, wending my way toward Eighth Street. Memories—both good and bad—flooded my brain. I had not anticipated the sudden wave of nostalgia I was experiencing. Total strangers to me were out walking their dogs, children were at school bus stops with their mothers, waiting to be picked up. On the blacktop of the dead-end street where we boys used to play ball and the girls, hopscotch, I saw a ratty basketball net but no chalk-marked squares. I stopped the car and parked in front of Telly's old house. We exited the car, and I locked it. Weeds poked out from between the worn pavers that led to the front stairs and the siding was in dire need of a paint job. The screen on the front door hung askew like a broken arm. I prayed that Telly's mother would remember me. Taking a deep breath, I rang the doorbell. Donna studied her pretty shoes.

At first, we didn't think that anyone was at home, as there was no sound, no answer. I rang again.

"Who's there?" A tremulous woman's voice asked.

"Mrs. Sandakis, it's me, Jimmy Price."

"Who? I don't know no Jimmy Price. If you've come to rob me, forget it; I have nothing you'd want." I could see her furtively separating the curtain on the side panel of the door and trying to peek out without being seen.

"I'm Jimmy, Telly's old buddy and school chum, God rest his soul. My mother used to be your neighbor and friend."

There was an extended pause, as if she were trying to decipher this information and turn it into recognition. The mentioning of Telly's soul must have convinced her. Finally, the door creaked open just enough for her to take in our full measure.

Linking my arm with Donna's, I added, "This is my wife, Donna. We'd really like to talk to you, Mrs. Sandakis. We need your help."

Through her wire-rimmed glasses, her rheumy blue eyes scrutinized Donna up and down; if she could, she would have looked at her from the inside out.

"Pleased to meet you, ma'am." Donna thought by saying "ma'am" she was conferring deference when she spoke to her elders. Maybe she was right, as Mrs. Sandakis smiled and opened the door fully. "Come in," she offered, struggling to push the screen door. I gently swung it wide enough for us to enter. Once inside the dim foyer, she looked up at me, squinted, and lay her hand upon her chest. "Oh, Blessed Virgin, it really is you!" She opened her arms and embraced me with tenderness. "Jimmy Price. You rascal! Who'd believe I'd be setting my poor old eyes on you, again?" There were tears in those poor old eyes. "Please, come in, come in. Can I offer you some tea or anything?" We declined, as she took Donna by the elbow and ushered us both into her parlor. Make yourselves comfortable, my dears." Despite the condition of the outside of her home, the inside was tidy and well-kept. The old brocade fabrics on the sofa and chairs that I remembered so well were worn, but not tattered. There were well-attended, healthy plants on various windowsills and a lovely antique china clock on the fireplace mantel; it still chimed each quarter-hour. As I took in the familiar surroundings (dark green hooked rug, glass-paneled, ornate breakfront filled with curios, and framed photographs of Telly in uniform), I felt such affection for this frail woman, dressed in a pink gingham housecoat and fluffy white slippers. She chose a straight-backed armchair and drew it closer as we sat on the sofa. Apparently, she wanted to create a cozy atmosphere; she was also a little hard of hearing.

"So, what brings you here?" she inquired, getting right to the point—always her way.

Donna took the initiative. "In truth, Mrs. Sandakis, we're here to ask you some questions about Madelaine. Jimmy and I believe there was more to that tragedy than was revealed at her mother's trial. Is there anything you can tell us that would support our theory?"

Mrs. Sandakis looked at us with suspicion. "What do you mean by more," she asked, stiffening and pursing her lips?" How easy it is to betray yourself; all you need to do is answer a question with another question—an avoidance technique practiced by those who have the most to hide.

"We believe that Madelaine was traumatized by something more than her father's death." Donna was intentionally eschewing the word murder, hoping to get a rise out of Mrs. Sandakis. And, that she did.

"It was murder, straight and simple. There's nothing more to discuss what took place twelve years ago. Don't go there, Jimmy," she bristled.

"But, why not, ma'am?" Donna pressed.

"Stop calling me 'ma'am.'" Mrs. Sandakis retorted. "We don't live in the South! I have nothing to tell you because I don't know anything. Madelaine lives here with me. I take care of her needs, give her a place to stay where she feels safe. Please, just leave us both alone. There's nothing good to be had going back. No, nothing good." She had worked herself up and was visibly agitated. I had to wonder why she was being so defensive.

"Mrs. Sandakis, I'm sorry. We didn't come here to upset you. But, you see, Madelaine must have experienced more than just the shock of Edgar's... um, demise. We want to help her get better; we want to help Luella, too."

"Help that bitch? Oh, no, I won't be a party to that, Jimmy. No way. Madelaine has suffered enough; she still suffers. You have no idea what that poor girl has gone through."

"Yes, that's exactly the point," I interjected. "There is more to Madelaine's story that she keeps locked up inside her. I'm certain of it."

"And what makes you such an expert? Look, Madelaine does not confide in me; she doesn't share what goes on in her head. She's sad and lonely. One thing I can tell you, though."

My ears perked up immediately.

"She's not crazy. Some people think she is, but she's not. She's disturbed. But, wouldn't you be, too?"

The pitch to Mrs. Sandakis's voice was now elevated several decibels. She was red in the face and her lower lip was trembling.

Just as she was about to rise from her chair and dismiss us, the front door opened. Madelaine entered and stood rigid before us. Her look skewered me like a steely, red-hot poker. Then, in a gravelly voice straight from the grave, she said, "James, leave."

I was astonished to be confronted with a Madelaine I barely recognized; she, however, knew exactly who I was.

"Madelaine, please wait. We just want to talk with you. Nothing bad is going to happen, I promise."

She did not respond but turned on her scruffy heels and ascended the stairway that led to her room.

I yelled to her to stop but to no avail. She seemed to evaporate before my eyes, an ephemeral being whose presence vanished into a vapor.

"We'll let ourselves out," I told Mrs. Sandakis. "Sorry we bothered you."

"Jimmy," she called to our backs, "stay away from Madelaine."

We closed the door behind us, slipping through the crooked screen door, and briskly walked to our car. Once inside, we looked at each other and let out huge sighs.

"Well, that didn't go very well, did it?" Donna seemed disheartened, but we both had the feeling that we were on to something big. And, we surmised that Madelaine, seeing me, suspected it, too.

It was past noon when we left Revere, so we decided to stop along Route 1 for lunch. We found a luncheonette that featured homemade soups and salads, and sandwiches. Once inside, we were seated at a wooden booth near the window. A pleasant waitress approached, setting down glasses of ice water. To my parched mouth and energy-depleted body, the water was like liquid manna from Heaven. We greedily guzzled our entire glasses and, seeing our empties, the waitress returned to replenish them.

"Wow, I didn't realize how thirsty I was. Feel better, now."

Donna picked up her menu and added, "Yeah, me, too. Let's order; I'm starving."

We ordered the featured vegetable soup and tuna salad, then sat back in our booth feeling exhausted. Our minds were racing, trying to digest the portent of what we had experienced, if not learned. We both agreed that we had, indeed, tread on sacred ground vis-à-vis Madelaine's state of mind. Mrs. Sandakis, obviously, was hiding some crucial information. The question now was how to unlock the box of mystery containing her denials.

"You know, when you mentioned trying to help Luella, Mrs. Sandakis was nearly apoplectic. Clearly, she blamed her for Madelaine's condition. I guess that makes sense, given the guilty verdict and prison sentence."

"Yeah, but I think there's something strange about her reaction to our bringing up Edgar, too."

"I agree. She had no kind words for him, either." Donna twirled the ice cubes in her glass with her straw. "Where do we go from here, Jimmy?"

"Not quite sure, yet. One thing we do know, though, is that our... your initial instincts were correct. Maybe we'll get some leads from my article. By now, I'm guessing someone with information has read it."

Our lunches arrived, and we ate heartily. I gave a thumbs-up sign to the young waitress when she asked for our approval. Donna wiped some mayonnaise from the corner of her mouth and winked at me. I could tell that she was already plotting our next moves.

"My turn to bathe Paul tonight," she said, in-between spoonsful of her soup.

Chapter 12

*L*uella picked up the pieces of her shattered coffee cup and threw them into the bathroom wastebasket. She washed her face with cool tap water, brushed her hair back from her scar-ravaged face and held it in place with a pink ribbon. She had no doubt that Dwayne and Penny had already read the article and she worried that they would question whether to extend their hospitality. She dressed in jeans and a black sweatshirt, typically oversized for her. Haltingly, she approached the back doors of the market, unbolted, then swung the large wooden doors open. Early morning deliveries were due, and she readied herself for the usual commotion they incurred. While she waited for the huge trucks to arrive, she sat down on a yellow plastic stool near the doorway to contemplate what may be in store for her. She shuddered to think what her brother might do. Startled, she heard his voice calling to her from outside the door.

"Luella, you in there?"

"I'm here, Dwayne; no need to shout."

Dwayne mounted the rickety stairs and stormed into the room. A tall, rangy man of thirty, dressed in denim overalls and a checkered, red flannel shirt. He wore his long, dark hair pulled back into a ponytail. He looked down on his sister with a mix of fear and anger. In his hand he held a rolled-up copy of the Globe. "What's this all about, Lu?"

"I don't have the foggiest idea," Luella answered, tears brimming.

Squatting down beside her, Dwayne softened his tone. "Listen, Sis. I don't want no trouble, hear? Is there something I need to know?"

"Dwayne, I'm not in trouble. But, someone is out there trying to make some. I don't know why."

Dwayne took Luella's hand in his. "Sis, who's this guy James Price, the guy who wrote the article? Do you know him?"

Luella had failed to see my name at the end of the letter; if she had, it did not register after so many years.

"Think hard, Sis. Why is he going into that old stuff, digging up dirt? He says that he withheld evidence. Why?"

Luella had no answers, just a terrifying notion that her world was about to spin out of control and land on its head, once again.

"So, whaddaya think we should do? I can't get involved in a scandal, Lu. I love you, but I have a family to protect."

"I'll think of something," Luella promised. "Just please don't kick me out. I'm begging you."

The delivery trucks started to arrive, the drivers blaring their horns to alert everyone at the market.

"Okay, then. Think of something, because Penny is very anxious." He descended the stairs and waved to the truck drivers. "Morning, guys," he shouted.

Deep within the recesses of her memory, Luella did remember my name; she just had not made the association. Some things, however, burrow into the subconscious like a mouse in a woodshed. She remembered that Madelaine had occasionally spoken of me; that I was "nice to her." If I was so nice, she wondered, then what the hell was I doing, trying to cause her more heartache? Why can't people just mind their own goddam business? she asked out loud.

"You talkin' to me, Luella?" One of the drivers had overheard her question.

"No, Mike; just thinking out loud's all. Here, let me show you where to put those cartons."

"I know where they go, Luella. I been working this shift a long time. You sure are actin' mighty strange this morning." He stacked the canned vegetables on their proper shelves, tipped his cap to her, then left.

Luella sat down on her stool, rubbed her chin, and stared into space. An idea had slowly taken root in her mind, an idea that needed time to germinate and flower into deed. This man, James Price, had to be stopped before he could do damage—real damage to her and to her long, lost daughter, Madelaine. Under no circumstances would she allow him to retry her case and uncover the ugly, lice-infested truth. No, there were boundaries that never should be crossed, sacred grounds that never should be violated. She would tell this Mr. Price to fuck off!

While she restocked the storeroom shelves with canned peas, corn, beans, and beets, Luella silently played out in her mind the scenario that she could envision. By the time the dairy deliveries of eggs, milk, cheeses, and butter had been carefully arranged in the cooler, she had devised a plan whereby she would anonymously call that Mr. Price at the Globe, feigning knowledge of the case and refuting any erroneous conclusions that might have been drawn by "publicity seekers." To snuff out all conjecture, and douse the fires of speculation, she planned to rehearse her lines all night, if she had to, and gird herself against any pushback.

Chapter 13

*A*fter our long, first day of the interview with Mrs. Sandakis, we arrived home to find Adriana weeping. Seated at the kitchen table, she dabbed at her swollen eyes with an already saturated handkerchief. Paul was playing quietly with his Legos, looking disconcerted and uncertain. Upon seeing us, he brightened and held his arms up, wanting to be held.

"Adriana, my goodness, what's the matter? Are you ill?" Donna sat down next to the nanny and gently placed a hand on her arm.

Trying valiantly to regain her composure, Adriana explained that during the day, several mean-spirited people had called, spewing invective and insult. She had dutifully done what we had instructed her and hung up. But, the last call came about an hour before we returned, and this one rattled her to the core.

"What did this caller say?" Donna pressed, visibly agitated, as well.

Adriana inhaled deeply and paused to gather her strength. "He said that you, Jimmy, better watch your back; that you've put your family in grave danger. 'Shut up or be shut up' were his words.

Donna, I'm so afraid that something awful is going to happen to you, and to Paul."

"Should we call the police and report this harassment, Jimmy?" Donna rose to pour herself a glass of water.

With Paul's arms around my neck, I felt vulnerable and stupid. Had I, in my zeal to revisit the Frazier case, put my family in jeopardy? I tried to put him down, but he tightened his grip and would not let go. He was sensing the tension in the room and absorbing it.

"Did the caller say anything else?" I asked.

"Yes," she cried, "he says he knows where you live."

Realizing that we had crossed into hostile territory, I seriously had to reconsider the wisdom of pursuing the investigation. My family is most precious to me, and here I was, subjecting them to risk... or worse. I was being irresponsible and nearsighted. Luella Frazier and Madelaine were not worth my family's safety. The caller knew that his threats would unnerve me; he knew how to get to me.

"Would you recognize his voice if you heard it again?" I asked, grasping at straws.

"It was muffled like maybe he was talking through a hanky or something."

"We have caller ID on our phone," I remembered, quickly checking for a recognizable number. All that appeared on the little screen was "Unidentified Caller." I wondered if the call could be traced anyway.

"It's okay if you want to leave now," I told Adriana. She was still agitated, but she was fueling Paul's anxiety, as well. His lower lip was quivering, and I figured he was about to cry. "Maybe a nice warm bath will help to calm you."

Adriana looked at me incredulously but understood my intentions.

"I think I'll do better with a vodka tonic," she said, rising and patting my arm. "Don't worry about me; I'll be okay. Good night, dearest Paul." She pulled her sweater closer to her body and left, her steps a bit unsteady.

Paul settled down and we were able to establish a sense of calm for his sake. We had to appear relaxed and prepare for dinner, as usual. Donna's lips were pressed into a tight, straight line and I figured she was clenching her teeth. She rummaged through the fridge, feverishly extracting ingredients for making hamburger patties and mashed potatoes—another of Paul's favorite foods. We would go through the motions of having a nice family dinner, but neither Donna nor I had much appetite.

"It's okay, Honey. I'll give Paul his bath and get him into his jammies. We'll play some games, so you can see to dinner."

Donna looked at me gratefully, holding back the tears she would allow to fall once Paul and I were safely out of her sight.

Dinnertime was not as peaceful as we had hoped. Paul decided he didn't want or like the hamburger on his plate. He spat the food out onto his dish and said, "Yuk. I want mac and cheese."

I controlled my temper and admonished Paul for his bad manners. "Never do that again, Buddy. Mom made a delicious dinner for us and that's rude."

"What's rude?" he wanted to know.

"Spitting food, that's what's rude. Now, say you're sorry to Mom and eat your mashed potatoes if you don't want the burger."

Defiant, Paul dug in his heels. "I want mac and cheese."

Donna, however annoyed, explained to Paul that what she made was our supper. If Paul didn't want to eat what was served, he could just have a glass of milk and go without eating. With that, our usually sweet-tempered boy swept his plate onto the floor and crossed his little arms across his chest.

I realized that Paul was reacting to the tensions of the day and that he was acting out his feelings. I wasn't in the mood, though, for a confrontation with a four-year-old. Biting my lip to contain my own stress, I picked him up out of his seat and carried him upstairs. "You're tired, Buddy. Say good-night to Mom and we'll head upstairs to bed."

Paul did not resist; instead, he sheepishly blew Donna a kiss and said, "Night, Mommy."

Donna blew a kiss to him in return. "Sleep well. Love you."

"Check on me seven times?"

"You bet. Now go with Dad." Donna began to clean up the mess on the floor, and I managed to get Paul into bed without too much fussing. I headed downstairs to the kitchen and found Donna, sitting beside the strewn food, with the most forlorn look on her face that I'd ever seen. I knelt alongside her and held her in my arms.

"What have I gotten us into?" she wept, her head pressed against my shoulder.

I had no answers; all I could offer was a gentle, rhythmic rocking of our clinging bodies.

Chapter 14

*D*wayne Ricci, a small business owner, was well-known among the East End illiterati. As an ex-cop gone rogue, he was feared, as well. His wife's mother, Rita Sheehan, was a moll for several members of the infamous Winter Hill Gang and was no stranger to their machinations and nefarious schemes. Between them, crime and its cousin, political influence, were no strangers, either.

Dwayne kept his Harley Davidson parked in his backyard barn. Each morning, he cleaned and oiled his motorcycle, revving the engine incessantly to hear the potato-potato sounds he loved. What he also loved was to disturb; disturbing was his forte, his foot-to-the-metal mentality. A former motorcycle cop, he enjoyed cruising around town in his leather jacket and black boots, keeping his handgun hidden in a side pouch—just in case. Once arrested for cocaine possession, Dwayne merely needed to suggest a sexual impropriety of a councilman, a sheriff, or a judge whom he knew to be corrupt; he was never charged for a felony. Indeed, his years on the police force provided him with a wealth of useful information which he stored like money for a rainy day—just in case.

Dwayne's countenance bore no semblance of softness, no sign of tenderness. His steely gray eyes conveyed disdain for most people, but especially for those he considered adversaries, those who would dare to look at him directly. "Don't look at me," he'd warn the unsuspecting. The depths of his contempt for his fellow human beings knew no limits; his fuel was jealousy and ignorance combined: a lethal blend. He took advantage of his sharp, aquiline nose when thumbing it at the law. He was, in every respect, a good, "family man," and had learned at an early age the fine art of intimidation. Several missing or broken teeth attested to his penchant for confrontations. As for his grocery market, it was simply a front for the more lucrative narcotics trafficking he oversaw. Despite his antipathy for his sister, well, she was still his sister... family.

Like Luella, Dwayne grew up in a household filled with violence and bullying. Their father had been a welder during the construction of the Tobin Bridge in Boston. He had slaved under the hands of union bosses and overseers and had won respect for his loyalty to them. He never complained, just listened to the conversations of his co-workers for signs of disaffection. Once, he reported a worker who, on a very hot and humid day, snuck a few sips of beer from a concealed can. The following day, that worker was assigned to a post several stages higher on the unfinished section of the bridge. His tumble to the ground was lamented as "a most unfortunate accident." All funeral expenses were absorbed by the "company" as an expression of their "profound sorrow for his widow and four children." Dwayne's father was granted a promotion.

In a house where physical abuse was a fact of life, Dwayne was slapped, belted, and kicked in the groin. These beatings occurred most often when his father, in a drunken frenzy, had nothing better to do. As a rebellious teenager, Dwayne stood up to his father only once, calling him a scumbag. The ensuing pistol whipping he endured cleansed him of any such recalcitrant behavior in the future. Dwayne was frequently absent from school, staying home to hide his bruises and subdue his demons.

Older sister, Luella, avoided the beatings by pretending subservience; she never raised her voice, did her daily chores without complaining, all the while storing up the hurts for a later time. She hated her mother, an ineffectual mouse of a woman who enabled her husband's bullish behavior, never coming to her children's defense. Her bruises and periodic broken ribs were testimony to her own miserable existence.

Dwayne married Penny Sheehan when she was three months pregnant. Luella ran off one starless night with a meek, innocuous guy named Edgar Frazier. He had eyed her for several months as she exited the movie theater where she was employed as a night-shift usherette. He took note of her purchases whenever she stopped in at the 7-11 store where he worked. Eventually he mustered the courage to ask her out on a date. He couldn't afford much on his salary but convinced himself, and later, Luella, that his love for her was pure.

Now, all these years later, Luella had become a virtual hostage under the watchful eye of an unpredictable, violent man, her brother. Somehow, she would have to evade his scrutiny as she began to mentally unfold her plan. She had seen my name at the end of the article inviting readers with any knowledge to contact me. She would try to reach me. Little did she know that Dwayne already had.

We had the weekend off from work and decided to take a trip to Cape Cod. It was too late in the season to obtain ferry tickets to Nantucket or Martha's Vineyard, so we found a small but comfortable resort in Yarmouth. There had been a last-minute cancellation, therefore, were able to secure a room. We hoped that getting away from the city would afford us some quiet peacefulness and much-needed distraction. We packed our bags, loaded the car trunk with beach chairs, water toys and "arm swimmies" for Paul, and, of course, a few bottles of wine for when a day in the sun and water left Paul wanting an early bedtime. We locked up the house, armed the burglar alarm, and set out on our two-hour drive. I hadn't anticipated the long delays and congested roads that were a staple of Cape traffic. We weathered the hour- long backup and arrived at our destination with plenty of time for some fun by the ocean. We checked in at the front desk, were given our magnetic "keys," and found our small but clean and neatly appointed room. On our porch that faced the water were a bistro table and two chairs. Hastily, we changed into our swim suits, grabbed some towels, and proceeded to the white sandy beach. Paul giggled with delight as he went back and forth to the water's edge, collecting buckets of water to pour over Donna's feet. "Feels good, Darling, even if it's a bit cold!" Paul and I built a sandcastle, shoveling and molding the wet sand until it looked fit for a king. When we finished, Paul jumped atop the castle, leveling it. I had not had this much fun as a child; trips to a resort on the Cape were not within the budgets of those who lived in my old neighborhood.

There's something to be said for the restorative powers of a room by the ocean, especially at night when the receding tide tugs at the shoreline and leaves a seductive "kiss" behind. After a leisurely stroll along the nearby jetty that poked the ocean like a pointing finger, we relaxed on the restaurant's outdoor patio and ordered our dinners "al fresco." Donna and I indulged and ordered fresh lobster tail, while Paul, as content as the region's celebrated clams, scooped up a huge bowl of mac and cheese. By 8 p.m. his eyelids grew heavy, indicating, as we had hoped, that he was ready for bed. The promise of another fun-filled day was all the incentive he needed; he was nearly asleep when we said our "good nights."

We kept our sliding, screened porch door partially ajar so that we would hear Paul if he awoke or needed a drink of water. On the patio, we toasted the stars with several glasses of wine. Then, we went inside and made love as we had done as newlyweds.

Had Paul not awakened us at 6:00 the next morning, we could have slept until noon. He, however, was up and ready for the promises of more sun and play at the beach. Rubbing the last vestiges of sleep from his eyes, he climbed into bed with us and poked us awake. We cuddled for a while, then, reluctantly threw off our comforter. Donna attended to Paul in the bathroom, while I checked for emails left on my phone. I scrolled through the ubiquitous SPAM, deleting as I went, until I saw a message from Fiona Moran; it had come in sometime late yesterday when I was trying to forget about the real world back home. With great trepidation, I opened the email message and read: Anonymous phone call received asking for you. Caller said she had information you might want to hear. I suggest you get your ass back here ASAP. Could be important development. FAM.

Paul emerged from the bathroom sporting his red and blue checkered swim trunks and Spiderman T-shirt. Donna wore her favorite black bathing suit, low cut in the front with straps that crisscrossed in the back. She had put on a lacey cover-up.

"Your turn," she called to me. I was still in my pajamas, perched on the edge of the bed.

She took one look at my facial expression and the cell phone in my hand. "What's wrong, Jimmy?"

I showed her Fiona's message, closed the cover, and scratched my head. "Don't know, Honey. Don't know."

"Look," she said, earnestly, "we've got one day left on our getaway. Let's not spoil it by disappointing Paul. We'll leave tomorrow, as planned, and deal with whatever this is all about on Monday. Okay?"

I knew Donna was right. Why ruin our good time for one anonymous phone caller? I decided to forestall my reply to Fiona until later in the day. Unfortunately, Fiona called me directly around noon. We were enjoying our lunch poolside when my phone rang. Recognizing Fiona's number on the screen, I hesitated.

"Go ahead and answer it," Donna insisted. "She wouldn't be this intrusive for something trivial."

"Hello, Fiona," I said with some irritation in my voice.

"Didn't you get my email? I truly believe it would be in your best interest to come back, James." The implied threat was duly noted.

"All right, Fiona; we'll head out as early as possible *tomorrow* morning."

"Have it your way, James. But, don't say I didn't warn you." She hung up without saying "good bye." She didn't have to; she was my boss.

We stayed the day, but our moods were dampened by these recent events. Paul looked at us quizzically when, our tempers running short, we scolded him for kicking up sand all around us. Dinner time was not as light-hearted and relaxed as it had been the day before, and, sensitive boy that he is, Paul started to pout.

"Paul, Honey, let's go for a little walk and let Daddy finish his drink. Okay?"

Paul brightened, slipped his hand into Donna's and skipped off with her; he didn't look back at me once.

Damn! Now I have to worry about losing my job! I'm getting tired of this whole confession thing. Still, I had to admit that my curiosity was piqued. Who could this mysterious caller be and what could she possibly know? She couldn't know what I know, for sure. I was getting the creepy feeling that I was being suckered; that someone wanted to flush me out, expose me as a fraud. Or, perhaps the caller had more criminal intentions in mind. I was letting my imagination run away with me. I finished my glass of beer, already turned warm, signed for our dinner, and left the patio. When I returned to our room, Donna was packing our suitcases and trying to keep Paul distracted with a kid's show on T.V. She didn't often allow Paul to watch television; tonight, though, she made an exception. She did not look up at me but continued bunching up our clothes and shoving them into suitcases. I could not determine whether she was terribly unhappy about our abbreviated stay, or that she was incredibly anxious about what lay ahead of us on Monday.

I approached her from behind and wrapped my arms around her waist, drawing her close to me. "I'm so sorry, Honey. I'll try to make it up to you. Please, let's make the best of the evening. We still have an opened bottle of wine!" I was doing my damn-well best to assuage her apprehension.

She turned around and kissed me gently. "I'm scared, Jimmy," she whispered in my ear.

I wasn't succeeding.

∞ ∞ ∞

The ride back to Cambridge on Sunday was eerily quiet, periodically punctuated by a police or ambulance siren. There were delays, but we made it home in decent time. I pulled our SUV into the garage, deactivated the burglar alarm, and then helped Donna get Paul into the house. He was irritably awake. I unpacked our belongings, returned the beach chairs to their hooks on the garage wall and lugged the suitcases into the foyer. We had stopped at our local supermarket for a few items to tide us over until Monday: milk, bread, yogurt, a few bananas and a pint of blueberries. Paul could have a grilled cheese sandwich for dinner; we weren't hungry.

"I'll check the mailbox," I called over my shoulder to Donna. Saturday's mail was usually inconsequential, unless one of us were celebrating an occasion. Opening the hatch door of our street mailbox, I extracted a water bill, an unsolicited issue of Golf Digest (I'd never once played the game), and some flyers from local merchants seeking our interest in mattresses and home goods. As I closed the mailbox door, I heard, then saw, a late model black Cadillac as it started its engine and pulled out from a parking spot across the street. Its windows were tinted, and I could not see the driver. For sure, it wasn't one of our neighbors, as I was familiar with their cars; no one I knew drove a Cadillac with tinted windows. I watched the car drive slowly down our block, then turn left. I shuddered at the thought of being watched. Could that car have belonged to a neighbor's friend or relative? I reentered the house agitated but said nothing to Donna about my fears. At that point, that's all they were: unfounded fears. But, I had been spooked, probably intentionally. What ran through my head were those words that Adriana had heard on the phone: "I know where you live."

Chapter 15

As expected, Fiona lay in wait for me in her office early Monday morning. On her desk was a Starbuck's "Grande" coffee and a half-eaten raisin bran muffin; an errant raisin rested on the glass desktop. I watched her pace in front of the window overlooking the courtyard below. When she saw me arrive, she glared and pointed a hooked finger in my direction. I knew I was in for it. Donna busied herself at her desk; peering over the rims of her glasses, she cautioned, "Easy."

I entered Fiona's lair feeling meek and vulnerable.

"Sit down, Price," she ordered. So, now I was Price, not James. I obeyed and sat down uncomfortably rigid opposite her desk. She took her seat and faced me."

"Look, Price. Let's get one thing straight. When I tell you to do something pertaining to your work ASAP, I mean, As Soon As Possible!" She was shouting, accentuating her words while slamming her fist down on the desk. "Not tomorrow, not the next day, but AS SOON AS Possible!" Again, she slammed her fist down on her desktop. "Do you understand me?" Her face was redder than a Veteran's Day poppy. Her eyes riveted me with the power of her superiority.

I started to reply, but she didn't want to hear it; she cut me off. "Don't even try. Your actions were insubordinate, and I won't tolerate insubordination."

I zippered my mouth shut.

"Don't even attempt an apology, Price. I'm so angry I could fire you this very instant."

I waited for the gallows blade to fall on my neck, but she retreated.

"But, I won't. You know why? Because there's something much bigger, much more important at stake here."

My breathing became more regular, as I then remembered to exhale.

"I want you to connect with that woman caller. Whatever information she may or may not have, she's a lead—perhaps down a dead end; who knows? But she made it abundantly clear that she would speak only to you, James. This was my reason for calling you back here; and, this is why I'm upset."

Well, at least I was back to being James again. I should have told Fiona about the ominous phone call to our home and the appearance of the black Cadillac but didn't feel that the moment was right; she would have become apoplectic over my withholding... again. I let myself out without further exchanges with my boss. I was on thin ice and knew it.

As instructed, I sat by my desk waiting all day for the office phone to ring. I scribbled notes to myself as to what I might say when given the opportunity. I played word games on my computer but stayed at my desk, delaying any trips to the bathroom. Donna brought me a turkey club sandwich for lunch; I ate it, remaining invisibly chained to my chair. I do not like potato chips, but, hey, they came with the sandwich and they gave me something to chew on other than my predicament. By seven o'clock, I hadn't heard from my mysterious caller. Donna and I left for the evening; Fiona stayed on, hoping.

We drove back to Cambridge mentally exhausted and stressed. I put the radio on to hear anything but my own sighs; Donna turned it off. Adriana had agreed to extend her day with Paul and we were grateful to find him fed, bathed, and ready for his nighttime routine. Adriana informed us that nothing new or untoward had occurred all day, a report we were all too relieved to hear. After Adriana left for home, Donna spent some time reading to Paul; I decided to check the mailbox. Inside, were a few bills, a sporting goods catalog, and an unaddressed, unstamped envelope. As I tentatively retrieved the envelope, my eyes and ears were trained on any signs of the ominous black Cadillac. At first, there was no movement, but as I started to close the lid of the mailbox, I heard a motorcycle engine rev and saw a bright headlight suddenly coming toward me. The Harley rolled past me very slowly, as I stood, paralyzed with fear, my hand on the mailbox, as if it had been soldered to it. I hurried into the house and locked the doors. I drew all the curtains closed and told Donna to lower the lights in the living room. I was trembling and still holding the envelope.

"Jimmy, what in Heaven's sake is the matter with you?" Donna had come downstairs to investigate the commotion I was making.

I sat down at the kitchen table, away from the windows that looked out onto the street and stared at the envelope. "I found this," I croaked, my throat feeling like sandpaper. She stood behind me, looking over my shoulder, as I opened the letter; her rapid breathing unnerving me even more.

I extracted a folded piece of dingy yellow paper. Written in bold red magic marker, it read:

DON'T DO NOTHING STUPID!

I stared, transfixed by these ominous words. I was speechless. Then, Donna noticed what I nearly had missed.

"Jimmy, there's something else in the envelope."

I opened the envelope wider and shook out a horrible surprise; it was a photograph of Paul strolling with Adriana the week before our trip to the Cape. Suddenly, I heard a thud behind me. Donna had fainted, banging her head on the kitchen floor.

I rushed to the kitchen sink and soaked a dishtowel with cold water, then applied it to her forehead. She revived, massaging the back of her head where a bump was rising. I sat with her on the floor until she felt able to stand; I pulled out a chair, so she could sit down. Pale and trembling, she ordered me, "Call the police. Right now."

Chapter 16

 rs. Sandakis was in a frantic dither. She paced in circles around her living room, wringing her hands, not knowing how she would be able to console Madelaine. She paced and paced, until she could think of no way to soften the impact of our visit. Finally, she gave up and went upstairs. She found Madelaine lying face-up on her bed, her eyes vacantly staring into a netherworld of space and time that only she could understand. Her arms lay close to her sides, fingers rolled into fists. Still wearing her old, shabby shoes, her toes pointed upward, she lay there motionless, in a torpor. To Viola, Madelaine appeared dead. Slowly, she approached the bedside and gently sat down. She reached for Madelaine's hand, but it was too rigid to lift. She returned her hands to her lap, bowing her head, repentant.

"Madelaine, dear," she said, "I did not ask those people to come here; they showed up at my door uninvited. I've done my best all these years to protect you, to let you be. I'm sorry you feel betrayed." She waited for a reply, a flicker of recognition in Madelaine's eyes to indicate that her message was getting through. No such signs were forthcoming, so she just sat there, bewildered and sad. Madelaine had been out, once again traversing the streets of her childhood, stuck in a place Viola could not imagine. She had not expected Madelaine to return early, nor had she bargained on Madelaine's stone-cold words to her once, long ago friend. But, she felt that she had, somehow, let Madelaine down. What could she possibly do now to win back her trust? After several more minutes of waiting, she rose to leave. With her hand still on the knob of Madelaine's door, she said, "I'm going downstairs to make some tea; if you'd like some, too, please join me."

Not surprisingly, Madelaine did not join her for tea; nor did she come down for her dinner. At midnight, she remained in her room where she lay as she had all day. In the morning, when Viola opened the door to Madelaine's room, there was no sign of her. The comforter was smoothed and the pillow puffed up, as if she had never been there. As if she hadn't existed. Cupping her hand over her mouth, Viola moaned, her eyes filled with tears, as she leaned on the doorpost for support. She had to wonder then, if, by chance, Madelaine had read my article in the Globe and seen the pictures of her mother's release. Surely, this would have upset her greatly. More upsetting was seeing me, the author of that article, seated in the house where she lived. She rarely spoke, but when she did speak to me during that *intrusion*, her words seem to have originated from a chasm of grief.

The chill of guilt creeps into the fibers of your being; it permeates the spaces under your skin, and then, penetrates your soul. Feeling woefully responsible for Madelaine's disappearance, Viola decided to search for her. It was raining heavily, so she donned Telly's old yellow slicker that she kept hanging in her foyer closet, slipped on her rubber rain boots, and went out hoping to find the girl. Given the inclement weather, few people were out and about; there were large puddles to avoid and visibility was poor. Still, on her aching, arthritic legs, Viola Sandakis plodded on. She stopped to ask Lester Cox if he had seen Madelaine. "No, Viola, ain't seen a soul this morning; weather, you know. I'll let you know if I do."

Viola walked several blocks, stopping periodically to catch her breath and to wipe her wire-rimmed spectacles. She stopped at the bakery, continued on to Zeke's smoke shop at the railroad station, then two blocks east on Main. This was the route Madelaine walked along every day, reliving each step she had been instructed by Luella to take each Sunday morning. The rain was not abating, and Viola could hear distant thunder. Still she forged on, hoping against all odds that she would find Madelaine. Just as she turned the corner at the high school soccer field, she spotted her, lying on a bench, rolled up like a beach towel, soaking wet. She appeared to be asleep, but when Viola approached, she recoiled, drawing her arms even closer to her body. Undeterred, Viola sat down, wrapped her arms around Madelaine, and held her close, cradling her as if she were a baby. Madelaine was shivering, her hair matted to one side of her head, her lightweight jersey clinging to her body. But, she let Viola hold her, allowed herself to be enveloped by a warmth she could feel, emanating from under the wet, yellow slicker. And, then, she began to cry—sounds of raw emotion that Viola had not heard before, rising from deep within the canyon of Madelaine's being. Viola held her, encouraging Madelaine to cry, to wail, to scream, if it came to that. And so, years of pent up, buried emotions came gushing up from the geyser of pain deep within her.

"Let's go, Luv. Get you some warm, dry clothes and a hot bowl of soup." Viola helped Madelaine up from the bench, put her arm across her shoulders, and led her back to her house.

$\mathcal{C}hapter\ 17$

$\mathcal{L}$uella stood in the storage room, telephone in hand. She had waited until after work, knowing that Dwayne and Penny would be attending a school play in which their daughter, Bella, had the lead role. She had not merited the coveted part, but, as Dwayne's daughter, could not be denied. Intimidation works even in the third grade; had she not been chosen, he would have hung the principal out to dry. Knowledge of the principal's extra-marital affair with the third-grade teacher was Dwayne's ace-in-the-hole.

Perspiration collected on Luella's palms, as she clutched the receiver, wanting to dial the number at the Globe, yet, questioning the wisdom of her action. Finally, after several anguished minutes, she dialed. As luck would have it, Donna and I had stayed late. Fiona still in her office, watched us while checking the wall clock. Luella's call came to her desk phone first and she nearly stumbled over a chair, rushing to hand the receiver to me. Eyes wide with anticipation, she kept pointing to her receiver as if it were the President calling. After last night's terrifying events, we were not ready for more intrigue. I took the phone from Fiona, sat down at my desk, and answered calmly. "Hello, this is James Price. May I ask who is calling?"

The prolonged silence on the other end irritated me, my nerves already taut and straining. As I was about to return the phone to Fiona, I heard a small, childlike voice.

"This is Luella Frazier, Mr. Price. I read your article in the paper and, quite frankly, I'm not happy with it."

"Hello, Mrs. Frazier." What does one say to someone just released from prison? Saying "how are you?" seems fatuous. "Do you remember me?"

"I know perfectly well who you are, James. What I don't know is why, after twelve years, you wannna' reopen my wounds and pour salt on them."

"Mrs. Frazier, I assure you, that is not my intention."

"James, I've spent twelve years in jail for murdering my husband. There's no dignity in what I've endured. Call me Luella."

"Okay, Luella. Here's the thing: I want to help you."

"I am not a woman who cries easily these days; I shed all my tears in prison. You can't help me now. All I want is to be left alone; do you get that?" I could detect a crack in her voice, as if she had so much more to tell me but couldn't.

"Your daughter needs you," I ventured, not sure whether I was speaking with a forked tongue or not.

"You didn't know my daughter well; she loved her father more than me." She still was not ready to give up what I already surmised.

"And your husband loved your daughter a little too much, right?"
Luella's gasp was my response.

"If you want to see your daughter, I can help you, Luella."

"I'm an ex-convict, okay? Do you have children, James?"

Considering recent events, her question rattled me. I was afraid to answer.

"A mother's supposed to protect her kid, keep her from harm's way. I guess I didn't do that. So, I doubt Madelaine will wanna see me. She wouldn't come to my trial, never visited." Her voice had softened now, more a lament than a complaint. "I failed her."

"Madelaine has been severely traumatized, Luella. She does not function as a normal person. She needs your help if she is ever going to be well."

"How do you know that? What is this so-called *confession* you write about?"

"I'm not prepared to tell you that yet. I'm going to need you to *cooperate*."

"Cooperate? Geez!" Her voice was fraught with fear. "I don't think my brother is going to go for that. He wants me outta sight and outta mind, if you know what I mean."

"No, I don't Luella. Are you in danger?"

Instead of answering my question, she deflected, "Do you know where she lives?" Luella's inquiry was giving me hope.

"I do. Still on Eighth Street. Viola Sandakis has been caring for her."

"Oh, her. Well, that's a kicker."

"Why do you say that?" My curiosity was stoked.

"She never liked me much. Thought I wasn't a good mother. But, then, most of them old hags thought that of me."

Her bitterness was mixed with sorrow. Just then, Luella heard the sound of tires rolling across the gravel driveway leading to Dwayne's garage.

"James, I must go. My brother has returned and if he finds me on the phone, he'll... well, it won't be pretty." She hung up quickly, almost as if her life depended on it.

I had set Fiona's mobile phone to SPEAKER so that she and Donna could hear the conversation. Donna had chewed her thumb nail to the quick, causing it to bleed. Fiona had removed her eyeglasses and was pinching the bridge of her nose.

"You handled that well, James. We'll just have to wait and see if anything comes of this. You gave her a lot to think about, including your own knowledge of Madelaine's abuse."

"Thanks, Fiona. While we're waiting, there's something Donna and I need to share with you, privately."

"Let's go into my office," she offered, leading the way.

Once ensconced, Donna and I took seats opposite Fiona's desk.

"You two look preoccupied with other weighty matters; am I right?" Straight to the point, as always.

My throat was parched, my shoulders bent from the weight of last night's episode.

Donna spoke first. "Fiona, someone or somebodies are following us; they've threatened us in a phone call to our home and sent us a warning letter. In that letter was a picture of our son, Paul, out strolling with his nanny, Mrs. Leone.

"Oh, my God! What did the letter say? Was it mailed or placed in the mailbox?"

"It said, 'Don't do nothing stupid.' And then, we discovered the photograph. We were going to call the police but knew that they can't help us if nothing has happened."

"It's a federal offense to put letters without postage or unsolicited flyers in a mailbox. People do it all the time, and there is rarely an arrest for that violation. I suspect the perpetrators could care less about the law, but this may be a case where you should alert the postal service."

"Fiona, there's also this black Cadillac with tinted windows that drives by me each night as I retrieve the mail. It rolls by me in a predatory, menacing way. I'm sure whoever it is driving that car is the person who left the letter and made the phone calls to my home.

Whoever it is, the intimidation is working; we're both nervous wrecks."

Fiona became pensive, leaning back in her chair. She removed her eyeglasses, rubbed her forehead, then closed her eyes. For several minutes, the three of us remained immobile, reluctant to breach the silence that enveloped us.

"Look," Fiona said, at last. "It's getting late and I know you need to go home. I do have one idea I'd like to leave with you, though. I have a good friend who is a private detective. Any obvious police presence at your home would draw unnecessary attention. Perhaps, he'd be willing to find out who the creep in the car might be. Do you want his phone number?"

Donna and I looked at each other, not knowing what to do. Fiona jotted down a name and a number on a scratch pad and slid the paper across the table. I took it, folded it in half, then stuffed it into my shirt pocket.

"Thanks. I can barely think straight right now. All I want is to go home, have a stiff drink, close my eyes and wonder who would want to punish me for trying to help two sorry souls."

"James, I think you've just put your finger on something important, something we've been overlooking. Who, indeed?"

Nodding our good-byes, we left. We were half-way home before either Donna or I spoke. We relished the spell that simple quietude casts.

My wife, Donna, has always been a woman of certitude; she waits for facts to convince her and never jumps to hasty conclusions. She is deliberate and decisive, never one to venture into the swampy underside of speculation.

Clearing her throat, she shifted in her seat and sat stiffly upright. "I'm guessing that Luella's brother has something to do with the threats. Don't go out to the mailbox tonight, Jimmy. We can wait until morning. Okay?"

We pulled into the garage and closed the door behind us. Adriana was playing games with Paul, both sitting comfortably on the living room carpet. She leaned on the footrest and hoisted herself up.

"Thanks again for staying late, Adriana. We wouldn't impose on you like this if there weren't a good reason."

"I know, Jimmy. Not to worry. Paul and I always have fun. Right, Paul?"

Paul nodded his head in agreement and smiled.

"Well, then, I best be going. There's some left-over casserole in the fridge if you're hungry." With that, she buttoned her sweater and wished us a good night. As I opened the front door for her, I heard a car engine revving. Loud, then louder; fast, then faster.

"I'll walk you to your car, Adriana," I offered. She did not refuse. Sweating, I hurried back into the house. The car remained, engine revving.

I collapsed onto the sofa, my heart synchronized with that car's engine. Paul crawled up into my lap, lay is head on my chest, sensing that I was upset. His sensitivity to my feelings is extraordinary; he knows when to be quiet. In his shy way, he comforts me. We sat there, cuddling and I held him close. Then, I reached into my shirt pocket and extracted the note paper that Fiona had given me. I looked at it long and hard, knowing that I had no alternative but to call the private investigator. I remembered what Luella had said so prophetically, "A mother's job is to keep her children safe...

I failed."

Donna was standing in the kitchen doorway, watching me. "Call him, Jimmy; we can't afford not to. I'll get Paul ready for bed."

I gave Paul one last squeeze, playfully ruffled his hair, and kissed him. "Have a good night, Buddy." My heart thumped with dread.

Before dialing the detective's number, I poured myself a generous serving of bourbon and drank half of it.

My call went to voicemail, instructing me to leave my name, number, and phone number where I could be reached. Detective Marty O'Brien promised to return my call as soon as possible. I had no idea how long I'd have to wait, so I finished my drink and ventured into the kitchen. I hadn't eaten much all day and the booze went straight to my head. I remembered what Adriana had said about a casserole in the fridge and found it neatly wrapped in aluminum foil. I was starving and didn't have the patience to reheat it. Grabbing a soup spoon from the utensil drawer, I scooped up the cheesy chicken dish and ate it cold. I left a portion for Donna, hoping that she would decline; I wasn't disappointed.

"You can finish it, Honey. I'll just make myself a sandwich. I wouldn't mind a glass of wine, though. Did you make the call?"

I filled her in on what had just happened outside, then went to uncork a bottle of Chardonnay. I began to pour the wine when my cell phone rang. I answered immediately.

"Am I speaking with James Price?"

"You are," I replied, trying to sound convincingly calm.

"This is Detective Marty O'Brien. I'm returning your call. How may I help you?" His was the voice of confidence and authority—no nonsense, no beating around the bush with niceties. He must have spent many hours hiding in bushes, but I tried to dismiss this thought from my mind.

"Thank you for returning my call, Detective. Your number was given to me by my boss at the Globe, Fiona Moran. She thinks you could help us."

"Oh, yes. Fiona is a friend; she possesses strong instincts. What is it you need help with, Mr. Price?"

By this time, Donna had joined me in the living room. She sipped her wine and listened intently as I related the facts of our real-life nightmare to Mr. O'Brien.

"Okay, Mr. Price. Um, can I call you James? I'm just Marty from now on."

"Yes, yes; of course. No formalities. Good."

"Can you meet me at Zoe's Diner on Mass. Avenue tomorrow morning, say at seven o'clock? Take a corner booth. By the way, their breakfast menu is super good."

"We can do that. How will we recognize you?"

"Oh, I'll find you; that's my business, you know."

"Right. So, tomorrow at seven."

I closed my phone and stared at it. The reality of what we had just gotten ourselves into struck hard. If Marty thought it was necessary to meet so expeditiously, then who was I to second guess him?

"Jimmy," Donna said, wrapping her arms around her body as if to ward off a chill, "I don't have good vibes about all this; but, we don't seem to have options. I, more than you, have created this problem and I'm truly sorry. If only I had not been so aggressive in pushing the article... well, I did, and I regret it. I'm going to get ready for bed: you should, too. But my guess is that neither of us will sleep much tonight."

I agreed to print that confession, so don't blame yourself. We thought we were setting out on a mission of good. Who knew it would turn around and bite us in the ass. I'll be up in a minute. Just want to think a bit more."

I sat there marveling at what a mess we had created with our good intentions, thinking that yeah, no good deed goes unpunished. I drained the last drops of bourbon from my glass and placed it in the dishwasher. I kept asking myself, what if we **can't** protect our child?"

To my way of thinking, fear is the result of unanticipated events that upset the normalcy of our lives; it disempowers us, makes us feel vulnerable to what we cannot imagine. Worse, it makes us feel incapable of halting those dynamics that spin out of our control. The infusion of fear into our psyche is meant to inculcate even more fear; hence, its effectiveness. Later, lying in bed, I listened to every creak, every normal contraction and expansion of the house, and considered them ominous. It was windy outside, enough to cause a slight rattling of the windows. No, I wouldn't be sleeping much this night.

∞ ∞ ∞

Donna was out of bed before 5:00 a.m. Judging by her restlessness all night, I assumed that she was plagued by the same fears as those that haunted me. In my mind, I pictured her showering, the hot water beating down on her taut muscles. It appeared that she was taking her time toweling off and getting ready to blow-dry her hair. I knocked on the bathroom door and heard no response. Knocking again, I pushed the door open and found her crumpled onto the tile floor, trembling and whimpering. My steadfast wife—my rock that kept me grounded—was having a meltdown, dissolving into a puddle of panic. I wrapped my arms around her, held her close, and let her cry until spent. She would recover quickly—I knew that about Donna—and would pull herself together. I had no words of comfort for her, only sadness.

Paul was still asleep when we quietly descended the stairway and entered the kitchen. Morning sunlight was filtering through the curtains over the sink and I could hear our neighbor's golden retriever barking. Soon, the streets would fill with dog walkers and early morning road bikers. I prepared two mugs of coffee and sat down next to Donna at the table. She had recovered, as predicted, but there wasn't a trace of a smile. We drank in silence, each of us deep within our own thoughts which were nothing more than vacuous dwellings. Adriana was due to arrive shortly, and we heard

Paul call out for assistance on the toilet. Donna hurried up the stairs to help and I welcomed Adriana into the house. I worried that I had inadvertently put Adriana at risk, too. Would the fearmonger outside my home target her, as well? Once she was inside, she slipped into her sweater, placed her handbag in the hall closet, then smiled warmly at me.

"I hope last night's events didn't upset you, Adriana."

"I have to be honest, Jimmy. There's something rotten in Denmark, as they say."

"If you'd rather not stay until dark, we'll certainly understand. Please, just let us know if you don't feel safe."

"Jimmy, you look like sh... Oh, good morning Paul, my sweetheart!"

Adriana rarely resorted to expletives, so I gathered that I looked as haggard as I felt. Donna greeted Adriana with a hug and a wan smile. Adriana studied her, stepped back, and pursed her lips. "I didn't sleep so well myself," she admitted. "Couldn't get the sound of that car out of my head."

"We know, Adriana and we're so sorry to worry you. But, instead of taking a walk with Paul today, maybe you should let him play in the backyard on his swing set or in his sandbox."

"Okay, I understand," she said, shaking her head. "It may rain today, anyway, so we'll find indoor things to keep us busy."

With that assurance, Donna and I kissed Paul and promised him three stories at bedtime if he were extra good. Then we left, heading for Zoe's Diner.

As instructed, we found a corner booth in this retro, quintessential fifties diner; all chrome and red vinyl seating, and a juke box. Once seated, we perused the extensive menu. Had either of us been hungry, we would have been hard pressed to choose from among the tempting specialties. Perhaps, on another day, we would return. Today, however, we would have some difficulty keeping food down.

At exactly seven o'clock, Marty O'Brien walked through the front doors of the diner, wished the waitresses a hearty good-morning, and waved to the cooking staff behind the counter. For a tall, broad-shouldered man with considerable girth around his middle, Marty moved with a smooth, graceful stride down the aisle to where we were seated. He wore black jeans and a starched, white shirt rolled up at the sleeves, exposing forearms thick with muscle. White curly hair peeked out from his open collar; his ruddy face and broad smile added charm. Effortlessly, he slid into our booth and extended his hand in greeting.

"Beautiful morning, wouldn't you agree?"

"How did you know us?" I asked, impressed. His handshake was warm, energetic. Mine felt limp in the grip of his large hand.

"Ah, yes. Tools of the trade, my friends. Growing up in Southie has its advantages. Let's just say that law-abiding citizens don't cower in the corners," he chuckled, not at all concerned about being overheard. "And, a lovely morning to you, Mrs. Price. I've come to help you, so please, try to relax."

I could see the muscles in Donna's shoulders slacken, as she fell under the spell of this charming man.

Marty reached for a menu and studied it carefully. You know, the pancakes here are to die for."

I decided that we would not order pancakes. I bristled, and Marty noticed.

"Listen, guys, you've got to trust me. Lighten up. I'm going to find your troublemaker, and, when I do, he'll pay big."

A soft-spoken young woman approached our table and asked for our orders. Without our consent, Marty said, "Three orders of those luscious blueberry pancakes, Abby, and three coffees." Abby departed, leaving me both speechless and perturbed.

"Really, Marty, we're not very hungry. All we intended to order were scrambled eggs."

Marty leaned forward and folded his hands on the table. With indisputable confidence, he said, "Now, tell me more about how you got into this jam."

Sighing, we took turns describing the reason for the confession, our meeting with Viola Sandakis and Madelaine's eerie demand that I leave. We reiterated the warning phone call and the threatening letter in the mailbox, as well as the previous night's surveillance when Adriana left our home. By the time we finished our stories, three orders of pancakes had arrived. Abby presented our dishes with a flourish, then filled our coffee cups to the brim with a steeping hot brew. Marty rubbed the palms of his hands together and cheerfully said, "Dig in, my friends. Best flapjacks this side of Texas."

We were beside ourselves with disbelief. After all that we had just relayed to him, how could Marty be so cavalier, so nonchalant, so dismissive? Marty looked us straight in the eyes and said, "I don't collect a "finder's fee" until I've nabbed the culprit. Now, can you pass the cream?"

"With all due respect, Marty, there's been no offender yet; there's a menace out there, though."

Marty lobbed off a chunk of his pancake, shoved it into his mouth, and chewed, as if ruminating on an answer. He swallowed, took a sip of coffee, then leaned in; speaking softly this time, he said, "Look, you've come to me as I am the professional here. You're right about there not being an offender, yet. But, yet is a really big word in my line of work. Yet means it's just a matter of time. And my job is to prevent that from happening." He leaned back into his red vinyl seat, dabbed the corners of his mouth with a napkin, then asked, "Do you want my help, or not?"

"I apologize if I insulted you, Marty. It's just that we're scared, and the word "culprit" scares us more, especially since we can only speculate on what he might do."

"I understand," he nodded. "That's his game. Please, leave the speculation to me; don't fantasize. The modus operandi, as you've described it, is classic intimidation. He may try to up the ante; but, he won't succeed, believe me."

"What do you mean by upping the ante? How much danger are we in, Marty?" Donna's shaky voice betrayed her calm exterior. "I mean, are we to play like sitting ducks and just wait for him to do something dreadful?"

"You won't be sitting ducks, Donna. Just do as the note demanded and 'don't do nothing stupid.'"

"Like what?" she pressed, defiantly folding her arms across her chest.

"Like call the police. Like inflame him with more signs of intrusion into the world of Luella Frazier or her daughter, Madelaine."

"Okay, Marty," I agreed. No more articles and no more visits on our part. Maybe things will calm down." My fingers were crossed under the table.

"Maybe yes, maybe no. Just don't do nothing stupid."

Changing the subject, I asked Marty how much his fee would be.

"A retainer of $500.00 is all I need right now to seal the agreement. Then, as I said, the rest will be due when the culprit is apprehended. Not to worry; my fees won't break the bank."

Donna pulled her checkbook from her handbag, fished for a pen, then wrote the requested retainer check. Sliding it across the tabletop, she wistfully told Marty that her quest for redress for Luella and Madelaine would be temporarily terminated, but not abandoned indefinitely.

Marty knew a determined mind when he encountered one; but however much he thought to squelch Donna's misguided intentions, he allowed her to hope.

Folding the check and placing it into his wallet, Marty concluded the meeting. "Okay, folks: I think we're all settled here. Just go about your business as usual and try to stay calm. Breakfast is on me. Great pancakes, right?" He left fifty dollars on the table—more than enough to cover our meals and a tip that would ensure him the allegiance of his minions. "You guys leave first," he suggested. "I have a date with the men's room." We left him still seated at the booth and made our way to our parked car. Leaning with one foot bent up against the façade of the building and leisurely smoking a cigarette, was a young man. Dressed in black jeans and a white shirt, he smiled at us, snuffed out his cigarette against the heel of his sneaker, and then walked away. There was no doubt in our minds that the young fellow worked for Marty and that he was stationed there to guard our car. We exited our parking space and headed for work. We both tried to look calm when we entered our office, walking briskly to our desks, patting the shoulders of a few colleagues. We waved to Fiona; she did not wave back, as we were late. She stayed in her glassed-in office for a while, then approached Donna, ostensibly to discuss news-related business.

"Another call came in for James," she whispered. "I believe it was that same woman, Luella Frazier; but, she said she'd call again later."

Donna slumped in her chair and shot me a glance of utter dismay. She lay her head down on her folded arms and muttered, "Shit."

Chapter 18

The call to Fiona's centrally connected phone line came around six o'clock. We were getting things wrapped up at our desks when she motioned for us to join her in her office. Bowing to her own premonitions, she ordered that this call be monitored and traced. She handed the receiver to me. Donna sat beside me, hugging herself for support.

"Is this James?"

"Yes, this is James. Who is calling, please."

"It's me, Luella. I've been thinking."

"Go on," I encouraged.

"As hurt and angry as I was with Edgar, I shouldn't have blamed Madelaine. She was just a kid, a different kind of kid. You remember? All those other kids in the neighborhood made fun of her and all that. Edgar, that bastard, ruined her whole life; she was too young and naïve. And that's what's so sad, Jimmy. She had no idea; she thought it was love. Mine wasn't enough, not the same, I guess." After a long, painful pause, she continued, "So, I'm gonna try to find my daughter, Jimmy, and tell her we can forgive each other. You know what I'm sayin'?" She had been talking non-stop and rapidly. When she stopped to take a deep breath, I felt I should be giving her moral support, encouraging her; but, in no way, could I cross Marty O'Brien. I couldn't share information with Luella for fear that she might implicate me in some way.

"Listen, Luella, this is all up to you. Do what you think you must do. Go for it. Just be, well, careful. Don't be obvious."

"So now you're cuttin' out on me, Jimmy? After all your promises to help? Well, I should've expected this. In prison, I learned a few things, like never trust anyone. At least you told me where to find my daughter. Yeah, thanks."

"Luella, please understand. There are extenuating circumstances now. I want to help you as much as I can, but, my hands are tied."

"It's okay, Jimmy. I get it. First you offer to help; I stick my neck out; and then, you say your hands are tied. Swell. So, just to let you know, my brother, if he finds out that I'm looking for my daughter, well, he'll beat the crap outta me. Yeah, you heard me right. The loving brother who took me in keeps me caged in like a wild animal. As if I could hurt somebody again. Really! So, don't worry about me. I'll be careful." She hung up before I could respond.

Beads of perspiration clung to my upper lip, as I handed the receiver over to Fiona. I was on a guilt trip that would take me places I didn't want to go. Donna reached across the desk and held my hand.

"You see, my suspicions were correct. It's the brother. He thinks he's protecting his sister. Funny way of going about it, I admit; but, there must be more to his overprotectiveness than meets the eye. Maybe he's protecting himself more."

"But, from what? Fiona, can we get a recording of this conversation? I want to be sure that what I said can't be misconstrued as abetting. Can we get a trace on the number? We've got to keep our hands clean. And that makes me very, very sad." I hung my head in shame.

"I'll get you a copy in the morning, James. Right now, I think you and Donna should go home and... hope that whatever Luella chooses to do will be seen as positive. My guess is that every mother out there, regardless of her prejudice against Luella in the past, will understand her actions."

"Don't be so sure about that, Fiona," Donna cautioned, "this is about more than motherhood."

"Oh, right. I almost forgot, I don't have kids, so I must be wrong." I'd never heard Fiona so defensive. She realized her impetuous remark and sat back in her chair; then, she turned toward the windows, looking at nothing in particular. "I'm sorry, Donna. That wasn't called for."

"It's okay," Donna reassured her, "we're all under a lot of stress. What I meant was that women out there may be empathic toward Luella; her brother—or someone—may not be so understanding toward her or us. There's a bigger reason for the threats and surveillance. Maybe Marty O'Brien will find that out for us."

"So, you've been in touch with Marty. Good. He's a good man to have on your side."

We all rose in unison, weary from this albatross we had voluntarily hung around our necks. Turning back to Fiona, I smiled weakly, "See you on Monday."

Fiona nodded, then lingered at her window, gazing at the darkening sky. She wondered how long it would take before she got over her father, Felix Moran, and their ignominious past. Her heart still ached because of him; but, she would never concede that; she still had her pride and what was left of her dignity. No one knew about Felix; it was none of their business. Slowly, she cleared her desk, shut the lights, and went home to be alone.

Chapter 19

Things remained quiet over the next few days; there were no further threatening calls, no signs nor sounds from the mysterious black Cadillac. I thought better than to get my hopes up; but, I did. We didn't exactly relax; we just didn't jump or quake each time the house creaked, or the windows rattled. I wasn't complacent, just a tad less jittery. Donna used this respite to get her hair styled and her nails manicured. I was glad she had those diversions; she always seemed more good-humored after her beauty parlor appointments.

I spent Saturday with Paul, out in the backyard, pushing him on his swing set, helping him climb his mini-monkey bars, and watching him frolic in his wading pool. Paul is a happy child, though sometimes given to demanding stubbornness; I wouldn't necessarily characterize them as tantrums, but he was beginning to exert his independence/autonomy. Most often, he was a calm, diffident four-year-old boy. His fifth birthday was coming up in September and I wondered if, despite our reservations, it was time to reconsider the benefits of enrolling him in pre-school. Adriana had been a godsend, a doting, loving caregiver to whom we entrusted our only child. I watched him play, amusing himself with his water and sand toys. Still, I had to admit, he needed social interaction with other children his age. The neighborhood youngsters were older than he; and although they were never outright mean to him, they thought him too much of a "baby" to play with. There were no young cousins to invite over. As he watched the other children playing ball or off with their moms to soccer practice, I often noticed the longing in his eyes for a playmate. He also needed a daily routine and structure that an interactive environment could provide for him. Guiltily, I thought that Paul was losing out on real life experience; that his world was too circumscribed. He rarely was asked to deal with obstacles or challenges—all part of the growing up and making decisions. In short, his was not the real world in which he would have to learn to survive. I was so deeply engrossed in my ruminations, I almost didn't hear my cell phone ringing.

"Hello?"

"Well, hello to you too, Mr. James Price. How've you been, you son-of-a-bitch?" I didn't recognize the caller's voice and nearly dropped my phone in the water of Paul's wading pool. The voice was not friendly, not jocular as it would be, say, from an old college roommate. No, it sounded ominous, daring, taunting. I didn't respond, frozen in place.

"Just wanna let you know that your wife's new haircut makes her look even more stunning. Oh, and her pretty painted nails are awesome."

I could hardly breathe, listening to this unknown person talk about my wife in this salacious way. "Who is this?" I demanded.

"It's just me, Jimmy boy, lettin' you know that I'm out there. Keepin' you covered." I then recognized the voice of Marty; he was keeping his promise.

"You scared the living bejezzes out of me, Marty. Don't do that to me again. But, thanks."

"Just doin' my job. Didn't mean to make you wet your pants, he-he!"

"Had a new development at work yesterday. Luella called me to say that she planned on searching for her daughter, maybe confronting her, I don't know."

"What did you say to her?"

"I shamefully told her that I couldn't help her do that; she did not take kindly to my excuse of having my hands tied. And, she was right to be angry with me; I essentially lied to her."

"You did the right thing, Jimmy. Let's see how her plan works out."

"She said her brother—the one who took her in after her prison release, keeps her caged in; that he would beat her if he found out what she intended to do."

"That might be a lead for us. I'm going to investigate this brother. Tell me his name again."

"Dwayne. Dwayne Ricci. Lives in Chelsea or Revere, not sure which."

"Okay, Jimmy boy. Looks like I'll have to find out more about Luella Ricci/Frazier. I'm on it. Sit tight and remember, don't do nothin'..."

"Yeah, I know. Stupid."

I closed my phone and looked down at my feet. Paul was covering them with sand from his box, busily burying my toes. Donna returned from her day of beauty looking refreshed and relaxed; she had treated herself to a full-body massage and felt the relief of unrelenting muscle spasms in her neck and back. She was smiling when she joined us in the backyard, a smile that had been absent from her face for weeks. She sat next to me and laughed at my sand-covered toes. "Well, that's one way to hide those bunions!" I hadn't known that my bunions bothered her; so, I dug my feet deeper into the sand. When I told her about the phone call from Marty, she was initially discomfited. "So, now more people are watching me!" she lamented. "But, on second thought, it's reassuring to know that someone is looking out for me." She seemed content with that analysis, but her smile had disappeared.

To change the subject, I shared my thoughts about enrolling Paul in pre-school for the coming year. It was late to be thinking about it; applications for Play and Learn are requested a whole year in advance. "I'll think about it. You're probably right," Donna concurred. We considered the possibility of a cancellation or an open spot for Paul and agreed to call on Monday. "In the meantime, Jimmy, let's not say anything to Adriana... just in case." It was nearing supper time and Paul was showing signs of boredom.

"Let's go inside and wash up, Buddy. While Mommy makes us dinner, I'll read you three stories. How about it?"

Paul was already scampering toward the house, delighted with the prospect of being the center of our attention. Sand clung to his wet bathing suit, as he ran to the back stairs. He reached behind him to brush it off, not caring much for the gritty feel on his little bottom. "Dirty," he complained.

I scooped him up and carried him into the kitchen, gave him water to drink, then whisked him upstairs for a bath. Donna's smile had returned. "Who wants mac and cheese?" she called out.

"Me!" Paul squealed. "Me, too!" I agreed. I had a feeling that Donna had stopped at the market and bought steak to grill, as well.

A semblance of normalcy had returned to the Price family and we embraced every moment, trying hard to dispel the notion of how fleeting it might be.

Chapter 20

L uella's phone conversation with me was unsettling; she felt abandoned by my sudden withdrawal of support now that she had agreed to *cooperate*. A part of her felt suckered into a trap; the other part tapped into a deeper desire to see her daughter. She kept thinking about what I had said regarding Madelaine's mental health, her suffering, and the need for intervention. She just wasn't sure that Madelaine would or could tolerate seeing her again. In all honesty, she questioned her own interest in seeing Madelaine again. Anguished nights of deliberation kept her awake for hours; sometimes, she just barely missed arriving at the storage facility on time for the deliveries. She made several mistakes in the ledgers and bills of lading, as well as in misjudging the quantities of supplies needed to restock the shelves and cooler. A few of the delivery men gently pointed out her mistakes and quietly corrected them; others, put off by her lack of focus, complained to Dwayne that she was not on top of things; that she seemed preoccupied. A visit from him was not unexpected; Luella braced herself for a stiff reprimand and plenty of browbeating. She would take his carping attacks in stride, remembering how she was able to deflect her own bullying father. She prayed, however, that he would not strike her or send her away. She had neither money nor a vehicle in which to escape. Wayne denied her request for a driver's license. "If you're not going nowhere, you don't need a license," he had sneered. "And, you don't need money to buy stuff you won't use." It took Dwayne a day to peruse the paperwork Luella was not keeping in order. It took him five minutes to bolt out his back door and stomp over to the back of the stock room. He found Luella sitting on her yellow stool, daydreaming. Had she been dozing, he would have smacked her awake.

Storming into the shed, he stood with his back to the driveway, his arms pressed against the doorframe. His imposing figure blocked the morning sunshine. "Okay, sister of mine. What the fuck is goin' on with the books? The guys have been complaining that you're not doing your job."

Luella looked up into the eyes boring into her with disgust and meekly said, "Dwayne, I've been having um... female problems. I need to see a doctor. I might even have cancer."

The wind had been momentarily knocked out of Dwayne's sails. "What kind of problems?"

"You wouldn't understand," Luella demurred. "Things were done to me in prison that I can't talk to you about. An angry woman can do unspeakable things; I was an angry woman, too; remember? I just need to see a doctor. Is that too much for me to ask?"

For the first time in his life, Dwayne felt himself soften. He didn't want Luella's potential illness on his conscience; nor did he relish the idea of having to take care of a dying sister.

"You'd better be telling me the truth, Luella. You know I don't deal good with liars. Daddy taught me that. Anyway, I'll tell Penny to make you an appointment with her doctor in town."

"No, no. I want to see the doctor I always went to in Revere. He was always so kind to me and knowing how little money I could afford, he rarely charged me for my visits. I trust him, Dwayne." Here, she began to weep, lowering her head onto her chest and covering her eyes with both hands. She had learned how to fake that move in prison, too. It was her mother who taught her the fine art of embroidering lies... the one's Daddy couldn't distinguish from the truth; the same ones he didn't deal with so kindly.

Relenting, Dwayne agreed. He liked the idea of not being charged. "Okay, Penny will call your doctor, make the appointment and drive you there."

Luella looked up at her brother, rose, and attempted to embrace him. Dwayne stepped aside, avoiding an uncomfortable moment for him. "Now, now, none of that."

"Thank you, Dwayne; you're a good brother." For affect, she swept away her fake tear with her right forefinger.

Luella returned to her loft above the storeroom feeling confident and more determined. That night, she planned her strategy for visiting Dr. Abbott and getting herself down to Main Street. She had great hesitation about how she would arrange going to Eighth Street where she knew her daughter lived and might be out and about. The memories of that street were still so painful to revisit. First things first, she reasoned. She would proceed with a plan and hope that her plant of wishful thinking would blossom.

That night, assured that Dwayne had weakened, Luella fell into a deep sleep. She dreamed of the better days, when she believed she had Edgar's devotion and desire; she fooled herself into thinking that his ardent love-making more than compensated for his lack of ambition for a better income. She dreamed that they had agreed on having another child—preposterous given her initial disinclination to have children. Her brow-beating father and shallow mother had seen to that. But, oh, how treacly sweet Edgar had been! How sickening to think of what might have been!

Sometime in the early morning hours, she awakened to gruff voices emanating from below. She could not distinguish whose voice she was hearing, so she noiselessly crept out of her bed and put her ear to the floor. Through the rafters, she could hear directives being issued.

"Listen guys, you know what you gotta' do. There's a 'shipment' due in tomorrow. Take care of it, as usual. And, don't let Luella anywhere near the drop."

What Luella heard was a female voice—Penny's voice—as best she could guess.

"I don't care what you have to do; just don't screw up. Dwayne's hoping to score big- time on this one."

She understood that her sister-in-law was conspiring to conceal a delivery of something more than groceries. Her thoughtful, caring sister-in-law who bought her clothes and brought her left-overs from the family dinner, was, in fact, an accomplice to something illicit. She, Luella, would have to be carefully "managed." Perhaps, that was why Dwayne was so amenable to Penny's driving her to Dr. Abbott's office. A ripple of caustic bile rose in Luella's throat and she had to muffle the cry that it produced. Disheartened, she reminded herself to trust no one.

It was necessary now to reevaluate her strategy. How was she ever going to see her daughter? Penny had not questioned her about the absence of her monthly bleeding, assuming that Luella was experiencing early menopause. Well, the odious reason was what she had endured at the hands of the malicious women who did not like her, who thought her meaner and uglier than they. Like them, Penny had learned from her mother the advantages of artifice, the usefulness of cold-heartedness. Apples do not fall far from the tree; rotten ones fall closer to it.

If her every move was to be observed, how would she slip out the back door of Dr. Abbott's office building and onto Main Street? She could not think of a way to escape from Penny's scrutiny.

Disheartened, she crept back into bed and, instead of counting sheep, she counted the stockpile of stones in her mountain of miseries.

∞   ∞   ∞

Late the following morning, Penny visited Luella in the back-storage room. Luella carried out her duties, paying more attention to the groceries and less to the disparaging remarks of some of the delivery men. She ignored their crudeness and answered their catcalls with silence. Some, however, conveyed their concern. "Feeling better, pet?" "A bit off-mark were ya'?"

Luella just nodded and went about her business, wondering if any of these so-called delivery men were involved in last night's discussions with Penny.

On a scrap of paper, her sister-in-law had written Dr. Abbott's phone number, address, and time of the appointment she had secured for Luella.

"It wasn't easy getting' an appointment, see. He's booked for weeks ahead; but, I sweet-talked the secretary into getting you in sooner—told her you were in awful pain."

"Thank you, Penny; you're a dear. What would I do without you?" What indeed, she thought.

"Don't mention it," Penny brushed off any gratitude. "Just be ready to leave from here tomorrow morning at 9 o'clock. She's squeezing you in; now, ain't that a funny way to put it! Chuckling, she left, amused by herself.

Chapter 21

Detective Marty O'Brien had been no stranger to fast women, expensive booze, and strong cigars. Growing up in Southie, Marty learned first-hand about the chasm between an ideal world and the real "underworld" of gang violence and political corruption. His own father, a decorated soldier who had fought in the Korean conflict and wore his battle scars as if they were medals, was gunned down in a drive-by shooting. He had earned the rank of Chief and had become head of the Drug Enforcement Unit. He had devoted his life to the force, believing that he could make a dent in the proliferation of drug trafficking and gang violence. Despite his feelings, he tried to dissuade Marty from following in his footsteps. Marty had been an excellent student who had the potential for success in many other fields; but his penchant for understanding people and their motives for committing crime had won out against his father's wishes. At the Police Academy, he had stood out as a sagacious, aspiring cadet with a great future. Like his father, he rose quickly in the ranks and deeply felt the strong bonds of brotherhood. Until one fateful night, after leaving a floral shop, his father was shot dead. He had just purchased two dozen white roses for his wife of thirty years. Chief O'Brien's 9mm Glock was reported missing. Although some suspects had been rounded up, they were eventually freed; their lawyers claimed that there was circumstantial, inconclusive evidence of the shooter's identity. Outwardly, Marty endured the infamy, the indignation with the stoicism of a seasoned cop. Inwardly, however, his loss became an abyss of grief from which he could not crawl out. Eventually, he spiraled out of control, damning everyone to hell, acting out with fits of liquor-fueled fury against everyone once dear to him: his mother, his younger sister, and his wife. He refused counseling or antidepressants; he just wanted to be angry and he did not want to cry. After six months of his outbursts and belligerence, his wife left him. He seemed not to care and quit the force. He had no mechanism for stanching the flow of bad blood that coursed through his veins. Justice was not only blind; it could be bought.

One December evening, having no Christmas shopping to tend to, he stopped for a drink at a local watering hole. He took a seat at the bar next to a well-dressed woman, quietly nursing a scotch and soda. He ordered the scotch straight up, then asked the woman if he could buy her next drink. Whatever he had in mind for that evening, she didn't. But, she accepted his offer gracefully.

"As long as it doesn't come with strings attached," Fiona Moran stated bluntly.

"No problem, Miss. Just don't like to drink alone." Marty was not used to being turned down.

They spent some time making small talk and discussing the messy state of affairs in our city streets. She told him about her job at the newspaper. On the television screen that hung above the bar, came news of a policeman ambushed while sitting in his cruiser. Marty pounded his fists on the bar, then began yelling expletives. Then, suddenly, he put his head down on his right arm and sobbed uncontrollably.

"Marty, whatever is the matter? Are you all right?" She dared not touch his trembling body; intimacy was not her specialty.

Marty raised his head and reached for a napkin to wipe his eyes and nose. She waited until he regained his composure. Haltingly, he told her about his father.

"Marty, in my business, one doesn't get angry; one gets even. Find a way to avenge your father's murder instead of taking it out on yourself."

Fiona did not offer this advice with rancor, but with the wisdom that comes with having personally dealt with self-destructive anger. She rose to leave, paid for both of their drinks, and said, "Only you have the power to change yourself. *Illegitimi Non Carborundum*: Don't let the bastards wear you down."

It was that singular exchange with a woman he barely knew that altered the course of his life. That night, he decided to become a private detective and to renew his license to carry a gun. A month or two after their meeting, Fiona received a letter from Marty; in it, he thanked her profusely for her advice and included a few of his newly printed business cards. Since then, he gave up the fast life and the booze; he did not give up the cigars.

Each night, as he sat in his dark blue Mini-Cooper, the engine and lights turned off, Marty recalled those moments of deep reflection and the repurposing of his negative energy. Hidden by the tall oak trees that lined the area, he watched and waited in the darkness for any signs of mischief. Two weeks of regular surveillance yielded nothing. Several nights later, as he prepared to leave, he heard the sound of an engine idling. Two occupants of the vehicle lowered their tinted windows to flip their cigarette butts into the street. One got out to relieve himself, and Marty was able to make out the figure of a tall, thin man dressed in a black leather jacket and motorcycle boots. Marty watched as the man leaned against the front fender, his right leg bent behind him for support. Shortly, the driver of the vehicle emerged, lit another cigarette, and joined his partner. Marty could tell by the swagger in this man's walk that he was younger, bolder, more likely prone to impetuousness, though, most certainly, a lackey. He wondered if today's young people understood the meaning of respect; their admiration was bestowed upon high-profile rappers and sexy performers. What did they know, he wondered, about values, about human dignity? What did they care about world crises or about the number of innocent lives snuffed out in a street fight over a pair of sneakers? Today's youth disgusted Marty; he held them in contempt. They thought they were above the law, took everything for granted, never thought about what good they could contribute to the society that catered to their every whim. All that truly mattered to them was their need for immediate gratification. If he indulged in these thoughts for too long, Marty's cynicism overtook his reason. He laid the blame at the feet of the politicians who benefited most from keeping these youth alienated, under their scale-tilting thumbs, with promises they would never keep. The protection game was an old one; he had seen it first-hand.

He recognized the figure leaning against the headlights of his car. He knew who he was, and how he had gotten away with murder. Dwayne Ricci was one of the thugs implicated in the ambush of Marty's father. He had been brought in for questioning, then released. *Insufficient, circumstantial evidence* was what his lawyers argued. Gripping the wheel of his Mini-Cooper, Marty remembered Fiona's words: "Don't get angry; get even." *You bastard*, he thought, *I'll get you yet.*

Dwayne Ricci reentered his Cadillac, revved the engine several times, then sped down the street. Marty followed from a safe distance, hoping that Dwayne would lead him to his lair.

Chapter 22

$\mathcal{L}$uella was up early and ready to leave at nine o'clock. She showered and dressed in clean clothes, combing her hair back behind her ears and securing the loose, thin strands with bobby pins. She looked pale, but that was a plus for someone who alleged her extreme pain. Penny was waiting for her in the car, using the rear-view mirror to apply bright red lipstick. She saw Luella approach, righted the mirror, and lowered the side window to say, "You can sit in the back seat, Luella."

Luella did as instructed, opened the back door, and slid into the back seat. She had never before ridden in a luxury automobile, let alone a sleek, black Cadillac with tinted windows. The interior smelled of cigarette smoke, but she didn't complain.

It had been years since she last saw the sights and sounds along the roadway from Chelsea to Revere. Not much had changed in the physical landscape of Route 16; the fast-food eateries, gas stations; but, there was evidence of some gentrification: a few condominium complexes, strip malls, funeral parlors and medical facilities. Penny drove with her arm resting on her open window, a cigarette dangling from her red lips; it bobbed up and down, as she inhaled, exhaled smoke through her nose, and cursed the drivers who weaved in and out of her lane. "Goddamn idiots," she grumbled, "gonna' get someone killed." Luella did not respond; she wasn't expected to.

Penny drove Revere Beach Parkway to Beach Street; then, to Ocean Avenue. On July 12th, 1896, Revere Beach became the first public beach in the nation; some 45,000 people showed up for opening day. Over the years, Revere Beach held many attractions: restaurants, dance halls and ballrooms, roller skating rinks, bowling alleys and roller coasters, including the well-known Cyclone, a wooden roller coaster, the tallest one ever built until 1925. The beach suffered a decline in the 1950's and, in 1978 was destroyed by a large blizzard. Reopened in 1992, it was designated a National Historic Landmark, sporting new landscaping, parking, and restored sidewalks. Penny found an on-the-street parking meter, tossed an hour's worth of coins into it, then opened the back door to the Cadillac.

"You go on inside, Luella. I'm gonna' sit on that bench over there until you come back out and grab me some rays."

Luella walked into the medical building, ran her forefinger down the list of names, stopping at Jason Abbott, M.D., Suite 3B. Turning around, she saw the elevator doors open; several people exited, and a tanned fellow who wore his sun-bleached hair in a pony-tail, held the door open for her. She thanked the young man and pressed the #3 button. Three dings announced her arrival, the doors opened, and Luella stepped out into a long, hallway with polished tiles and muraled walls. The smell of antiseptic hung in the air. She hurried down to Suite 3B, entered a room of disgruntled-looking patients, then proceeded to the reception desk to sign in. She did not have insurance, nor any other formal identification. Penny had made the appointment, pretending to be her. The receptionist asked for her name and address, handed Luella forms to fill out, then excused herself to consult with Dr. Abbott. Minutes later, she returned, smiled at Luella, then informed her that the doctor would see her. Breathing a sigh of relief, hoping that Dr. Abbott did, in fact, remember her, she completed the paperwork. When she approached the front desk, the receptionist looked up at her and said, "You look sooo familiar, Mrs. Frazier. I know I've seen your face somewhere."

Luella doing her best to ignore the girl's gum-chewing; she just smiled and returned to her seat in the brightly decorated waiting room. Light wood armchairs, upholstered in shades of blue and green, lined the walls—all occupied. Penny had told her the truth about being "squeezed in." Sun streamed in through the windows facing the ocean, reminding her that Penny was down by the beach sunning herself. Wedged between two young girls in advanced stages of pregnancy, Luella felt old and bitter. Tragedy had stolen her only child, as well as what were supposed to have been the best years of her life. To distract herself, she fished through an assortment of magazines; most of them featured the joys of motherhood, recommendations for how to get your new baby to do this, do that, do whatever. She sat back in her chair, folded her hands on her lap, and waited to be called. One by one, the other women were summoned by a nurse to follow her into an examination room. One by one, they filed out, some beaming, others, looking worried. Finally, she heard her name.

"Mrs. Frazier?"

She rose and accompanied the tired, but cheerful young nurse down the hall then followed her into an exam room. She was instructed to disrobe, then, to slip on a johnnie and tie it in the back.

"I'll be right back to take your vitals and weigh you, Mrs. Frazier."

Mrs. Frazier, she thought. *How strange to still think of myself that way!*

How did I get here? Who am I? Does anyone know or care about me?

Luella looked around the examining room, noting the doctor's diplomas with degrees from various well-known institutions hanging on the walls, framed testimony to his worthiness. She waited for what seemed like an eternity, wondering what Dr. Abbott would say about her mutilated insides. As she waited, Luella contemplated what she would ask of the doctor. Of course, she should have thought about all this before the appointment.

"Ah, Mrs. Frazier," the doctor said, entering the room and going directly to the wash station. "How are you?"

"Do you remember me, doctor?" Luella challenged him.

He was now several years older, balder, filled-out through the mid-section. He wore his years of having seen both joy and suffering with an appropriate gravitas.

"Yes, indeed. I remember the night you delivered your daughter. That was some night, don't you agree? I was just a young, inexperienced intern at the time. Have to tell you, I'll never forget it. Now, what is the reason for this visit?"

"I've been having very heavy and painful periods, Doctor. I'm not a complainer; but, sometimes the pain is unbearable."

Luella was impressed by the fact that he didn't mention what she knew he knew.

"Okay, then, let's give a look-see."

He was both gentle and kind. The inserted speculum was cold and extremely painful, but Luella did not cry out; she had endured much worse.

After his examination, he slid his chair backwards and said, "Luella, from what I can see, you've had some pretty bad times." He didn't mention prison. "I see a lot of scar tissue and what must have been um..."

"Doctor, you can't imagine what was done to me. However, that is not why I'm here."

He peeled off his examination gloves and said, "Please, join me in my office after you're dressed."

Presenting herself in Dr. Abbott's private office, Luella tried to calm her nerves; she did not know how to ask him if he could help her find her daughter, let alone free her from the bondage under which she lived.

"So, Luella," Dr. Abbott began, sitting down at his desk, opposite her. He bridged his fingers across his nose and said, with great compassion, "What I find is consistent with scar tissue, abrasions, and insults to the vaginal wall. Your physical symptoms are treatable. I worry, however, about the psychological implications. My God, what kind of people would do this to you?"

Hearing Dr. Abbott's words, Luella crumbled and began to sob. "Not people, Doctor—animals." Between labored intakes of breath, she pleaded, "Doctor, you have to help me. Please! I'm being held captive by my brother and his wife because of my... history. I can't bear it any longer... I'm afraid he'll throw me out into a world that already hates me."

Dr. Abbott did not expect this sudden outburst; his thoughts were focused on a surgical intervention. He did not want to be dragged into a family quarrel.

"Luella, I'm a doctor, not a lawyer. I don't get involved in domestic disputes, unless my patient is in imminent danger."

"Doctor, I **am** in imminent danger. There is an investigative reporter who has written an article claiming that he knows more about my... case. I tried to protect my daughter; but I can't get to her." Luella had perfected the art of lying convincingly. She wasn't being completely truthful with the doctor; in fact, she was lying through her teeth.

He closed his eyes and shook his head. "Luella, I so much wish I could help you. I'm guessing that the jury did not have all the facts."

Luella remained silent for a few seconds, then whispered, "No, no. I withheld some vital information, true. She loved her father. Now, this reporter is threatening to expose some awful truth. I know this guy means well, but my brother will do anything to prevent that from happening." Exhausted, Luella slumped in her chair and wiped away her tears with a sleeve of her sweater. "He won't let me even look for her."

Dr. Abbott came around from his desk, knelt beside her chair and offered her tissues.

"Madelaine is in despair, unable to function normally."

"How do you know all this?" Doctor Abbott asked, skeptical.

"A reporter from the Globe, an old school chum of Madelaine's wrote a letter; he said that he had something to confess about withholding evidence that may have helped me at my trial."

"I remember reading that piece; at the time, it seemed exploitative to me. The pictures of your release may have prompted his reporting something... forgive me, scandalous. Stories like that sell newspapers, Luella. What is this reporter's name?"

"James Price. He's been after me to "right things," as he puts it. He's threatening to uncover things about my... past."

"Jimmy Price? Geez, I know that guy. He married my wife's cousin." He rose and opened a cabinet behind his desk. He extracted a trial sample tube of ointment, sat down at his desk and wrote out a prescription for that medication, and another for an antidepressant. "Try this ointment twice a day. Fill these scripts." He slid the prescriptions across his desk, hesitated, then added, "I remember the night of your daughter's birth; it was one of my first assisted deliveries, one I will never forget. I remember you and... I remember your husband who did not seem happy. His face was full of disgust. I'm so sorry, Luella; my hands are tied. Do you understand?"

"I understand that you won't help me. Can I leave now?" She hadn't meant to sound so caustic to someone who was trying to be compassionate towards her.

"Yes, of course. On your way out, schedule a follow-up appointment with me and tell Gretchen there'll be no charge for today's services. He rose, extended his hand to Luella; she accepted his handshake with tepid response. "Thank you for your kindness," she said. She appreciated his caring; but she was irritated by his unwillingness to help her. She had confided in him; but it was too late now. She knew about doctor-patient confidentiality; she had not revealed the truth about Edgar; that secret had to remain buried in the darkest recesses of her mind. She had decided then, hoping to save Madelaine from inevitable ridicule and from becoming the object of sordid accusations which she knew to be true. She realized now, too late, that she had made the wrong decision. She scheduled a follow-up appointment, knowing that it was unlikely that Penny would take her here again. She put the prescriptions in her pocket and walked down the three flights of stairs to street level. She looked for Penny who was supposed to be sunning on the beach bench. Shading her eyes with her hand, she scanned the area. She found Penny stretched out on the sand, asleep; her blouse was unbuttoned, revealing her bare chest, now quite sunburned.

"Penny, wake up! Get up, you're burned." Luella bent over her sister-in-law and shook her by the shoulders. Penny woke with a start.

"Holy crap, Luella? What time is it? You took such goddam time in there, I got tired and fell asleep." She looked at her exposed breasts and quickly buttoned her shirt. "I got hot," she sheepishly explained.

"Okay, Penny. You're just lucky someone didn't come around and ..."

"I get it; now drop it. No talk of this to Dwayne, right?" She gathered her things and steadied herself on Luella's arm. "Let's get outta here."

Little did Penny know that Marty O'Brien, hidden behind a short stone wall, had taken several photos of her with his long, telephoto lens. He also was able to photograph the license plate of the Cadillac he had tailed since the night before. His nighttime vigil had paid off and he smiled with the satisfaction of knowing that he had "ammunition," should he need it.

On the windshield of the Cadillac was a parking ticket for a time violation. Penny whisked it from under the wiper blades, tore it up, then threw the pieces into a nearby trash receptacle. "Let's go," she ordered. I need a soda."

Once inside the car, Luella said, "Penny, I have to fill two prescriptions at the drug store. I don't have the money. Will you cover me?"

Realizing that she owed Luella something for keeping her mouth shut, she said, "Sure. Where's the nearest one?"

The only one Luella remembered was located near her old neighborhood. "There's one not too far from here. I'll show you the way."

Penny eased her way out of the parking space; her cheeks were flushed, and she felt dizzy. She followed Luella's directions without the bluster of having been made to wait too long. "How much further is this place?" she asked, testily.

"Just a few more blocks," Luella informed her, noticing how erratically Penny was driving. Nervous about being near Eighth Street, she tried to stay calm. *Try not to think about it; try not to think about him.* At the next intersection, Penny stopped for a red light. It was then that Luella caught sight of her daughter, Madelaine, lumbering down the street. Her eyes were cast downward, and she did not take notice of anyone or anything around her. On seeing her daughter, Luella's heart seemed to leap into her throat. She gasped, impulsively swung open the rear door, and fled the car, leaving the door open behind her. She could not believe how fast her legs were carrying her towards the one person in the entire world who meant anything to her.

Quickening her step, she shouted, "Madelaine, stop; it's me, your mother."

Madelaine did not slow down; she accelerated her pace. Luella caught up with her, out of breath, beseeching her to stop. Madelaine had no intention of doing so. Planting herself directly in front of her daughter, Luella raised both arms in front of her, attempting to thwart Madelaine's forward movement.

Madelaine stopped short and raised her head so that she could see who this intruder into her nether-world might be. Her piercing look bore through Luella like a hot knife. If there were a flicker of recognition, Madelaine's eyes did not betray it. With her mother standing before her, feeling trapped, she took two broad steps sideways. Her attempt to evade Luella wrenched her mother's heart. "Please, Madelaine. We need to talk; we need to make peace. I love you, dearest. Please, just give me a chance to...." Luella was able to grab hold of Madelaine's shirtsleeve.

Madelaine ignored Luella's pleas; her vapid expression had turned to panic.

Feeling like a mouse cornered by a feral cat, she darted sideways then quickly lunged forward. Luella chased after her; pulling at her sleeve. "Madelaine, please."

Madelaine tore free of her mother's grip, abruptly stopping in her tracks. With words that seemed to come from a deep well, Madelaine turned toward her mother and uttered, "Go away." She then resumed her onward quest to the nebulous place where she felt most comfortable. Luella stood there, not able to move, not able to comprehend just how damaged her daughter was. Something was ripping at the seams of her heart and she could not contain the anguish.

Penny pulled up curbside, fiendish. "Luella, get in this car immediately. I'm not kidding. And, who the hell is that freak you were yelling at?"

Luella's fists, already balled and ready to strike, hung at her side like unexploded ordnance. She could, and would have punched Penny square on the jaw, but held back, knowing that the last thing she needed was another arrest. Tears were streaming down her cheeks as she confronted her sister-in-law. "That so-called "freak" is my daughter! Please, let's just go home. To hell with my prescriptions."

"But, I'm dying of thirst." Penny protested.

"You'll make it home; trust me." Luella's own mouth was parched; her tongue clung to the roof of her mouth. Such was her incredible thirst for love from a daughter who despised her; she had murdered the man who violated every fiber of Madelaine's being, and yet, it was she who remained the villain.

"Okay, then." Penny agreed. But, I'm stopping at the first gas station; I need to pee, and I need a Coke."

All the way back to Chelsea, Luella fingered the prescriptions from Dr. Abbott. *Why bother?* she asked herself.

"Sorry for what I said," Penny contritely told her.

Luella did not respond; she just sat in the back seat, wiping away the tears that trickled down her cheeks.

Having followed the women from Revere Beach, Marty had witnessed Luella bound from the back seat of the Cadillac and chase after a young woman. He was able to video-record the confrontation on his cell phone, knowing that he had captured a moment of singular importance.

When the women arrived home, they scurried to their respective bedrooms. Luella threw herself onto her bed, crawled into a fetal position, and cried. The sight of her daughter after 12 years of separation, was like a blow to her solar plexus. Even with her eyes closed, she could see the image of Madelaine, disheveled and far removed to a world of her own. Behind those vacant eyes, however, there was fright and fear. Her cruel invective to "go away" had hit Luella broadside. Still, that small concession of recognition gave Luella hope. Madelaine may be living in her insulating, self-spun cocoon, but there had to be a way of unraveling this chrysalis. She fell asleep trying to convince herself that twelve years in prison were enough punishment.

Dwayne was out buzzing around town on his motorcycle, making sure that he was noticed. He smiled at the pretty girls on the street, revving the engine for affect. When Dwayne was out of sight, Otis Pillsbury, the high school football coach, saluted him with a raised middle digit.

Chapter 23

We lucked out. Play and Learn Daycare accepted Paul into their program starting the second week in September. Paul's birthday falls out each year around Labor Day weekend and, this year, we decided to host a Barbeque for the neighbors, inviting their young children to help celebrate. Donna wrote a guest list which also included Adriana, Fiona, Marty, and her cousin, Laura. Although they live only a few miles apart, they don't see much of each other. Laura's husband, Carter, is a psychiatrist who doesn't talk much; he's a laid-back academic who smokes a pipe and makes his observations through tortoise shell half-glasses worn low on his pointed nose. He raises his bushy white eyebrows whenever he hears something he doesn't agree with while he keeps his thoughts to himself. We don't care much for Carter's lack of enthusiasm for mundane events—barbeques, for instance—but, he does oblige his wife's requests with wistful compliance. It's not that he's a bad guy; he just rubs me the wrong way. Maybe it's his polka dot bowties or his sport jackets with leather-patched sleeves that make him seem so cliché. Although Donna and Laura keep in touch pretty regularly by phone; we limit our social engagements with them. I have the impression that he enjoys analyzing me, an investigative reporter. I toy with the idea that he might share some insights into Madelaine Frazier's odd behavior. No doubt, he'd pounce on the opportunity to expound on his encyclopedic expertise.

With few exceptions, our neighbors and friends accepted our e-mailed invitations. Paul chose Superman for his party theme, urging Donna to shop for a costume at the Party Store. Of course, she approved and ordered a custom Superman-decorated cake. I was put in charge of purchasing the food items that Donna listed and refilling the propane gas tank for the grille. Beer for the guys, wine or sparkling water for the women. She would take care of the plastic ware, paper plates, napkins, balloons, and tablecloths, all emblazoned with the iconic image of Paul's superhero.

On the day of the party, Paul was up at dawn, eager and lively. He spread his arms out wide and zoomed around our bed, pretending to fly. "Get up, Mommy and Daddy. Party today!" His exuberance was contagious; we both hopped out of bed, filled with excitement. It was a glorious day, full of bright sunshine and low humidity. After a quick breakfast, I got to work setting up our backyard with folding chairs and a six-foot aluminum buffet table. I tidied Paul's sandbox and filled his wading pool with fresh water, then readied the grille for the hotdogs, hamburgers, and spicy chicken wings. Donna set out bowls for chips and nuts, potato salad and coleslaw, as well as trays for pickles and condiments. All was ready by noon; we had an hour in which to shower and dress.

Our guests began arriving at one o'clock, as specified in the invitation. Their children, ranging in age from four to six years old, appeared to be well-behaved and curious about their young neighbor. Paul, dressed in his Superman T-shirt and red cape, greeted them tentatively, at first. Then, as children are wont to do, they relaxed and settled into a companionable group. We were delighted to find

Paul so readily accepted into their inner circle, feeling better about starting him at Play and Learn. When he spotted Adriana, he dashed up to greet her, wrapping his arms around her waist. "Happy Birthday, Sweetness," she said, hugging him to her. She handed him a gaily wrapped present. "Hope you like this," she winked. Paul took the present and put it on the card table we had provided for all of his gifts. Adriana proceeded to the kitchen to help Donna fill the salad bowls and trays. My next-door neighbor came over to me and heartily shook my hand. "Well, finally, we get to do more than wave to each other in the morning! I'm Jeff Peterson."

"Glad to meet you, Jeff," I replied, my hand still in his strong grip. "Can I get you a beer?"

"Sure, great. And, can I talk to you in private?" Jeff was about my age, muscular and tanned; I guessed that he spent a lot of time at the gym. "Let's talk after we eat; Donna's motioning me to get things cooking."

Jeff smiled and agreed. "It's about something that's been bothering me for a while. I just thought I should share it with you."

"I'm all ears. Just give me time to get everyone settled." As much as I wanted to hear Jeff out at that moment, I couldn't just walk off for a chat.

He accepted his can of beer and joined his wife, Elise. I worried about what might have him 'bothered.'

Fiona came late, excusing her tardiness on traffic. Despite her straight-forward, no-nonsense exterior, I knew that she was intrinsically shy and uncomfortable in crowds. She disdained small talk and social niceties; the pretense of strangers set her hackles on edge. She had come to help celebrate Paul's birthday, of course; but she did not like to hob-nob with whom she labeled "social climbers." Her lips were pursed, and although she managed a weak smile, I knew she was uncomfortable. I greeted her warmly, offered her a glass of wine, and tried to ease her tension. There was definitely something on her mind. We chatted for a few minutes; then, unexpectedly, she told me about another phone call she received from Luella. "James, she's had a confrontation with Madelaine. She's distraught and has nowhere to turn for help. She's begging you to intervene somehow. Marty can confirm what she said. Remember that tracer we put on her first call to you? Well, Marty was able to come up with a telephone number. He'll tell you what he found out."

"Marty can confirm? Isn't he working for **me?** Why hasn't he shared this information with Donna and me?" I was beginning to suspect that Marty and Fiona had more than a superficial relationship. I also suspected that Marty was the kind of guy who liked his bread buttered on both sides. "Where is he? He was supposed to show up for the party."

"He'll be here later, James. He needs your full attention in order to share what he's been able to piece together. He also did not want to spoil Paul's celebration."

"All right, I can wait. Will you stay on?"

"No, I'm afraid I don't do well in group-talk. Never learned the flight patterns of social butterflies." A wry smile crossed her lips.

"I'll bring you a slice of birthday cake on Tuesday. Please, though, say your goodbyes to Donna."

"I'll be gracious, James. If nothing else, I understand protocol." She left me standing there, bewildered and anxious.

The party was progressing nicely; all the children and their parents were enjoying the food, and most importantly, Paul was relishing having new-found friends. People were scattered about, some talking politics, others discussing the results of the last golf championship tournaments. I was glad to see Donna at ease with the women, animated and gratefully distracted from our recent concerns. Her cousin, Laura, was by her side; Carter sat by himself, observing, fingering his ubiquitous bowtie. I sought out Jeff Peterson and motioned to him to join me by the fence that separated our houses.

"Listen," he said, skipping a preamble. "I've been noticing something um, unusual going on for a while. Seems there's this big car coming around at night, parking for long stretches, maybe casing the neighborhood. Last time, I saw two guys get out of the car; they were smoking and not saying much to each other. I'm concerned they may be up to no good and thought maybe I should call the police." He took a long draught of his beer.

"I'm aware of it too, Jeff. It's just that they haven't done anything yet; the cops can't and won't patrol the area on a suspicion; they're short-handed as it is." I felt a knot tighten in my gut and wanted to end the conversation there, but Jeff had other ideas.

"I'm not going to just sit back and wait for them to do something. I'm getting spooked and I'm concerned for my family. I know the difference between loitering and intimidating." He was getting worked up; his voice rising a few decibels. Two men turned and glanced in our direction, eyebrows raised. I had no argument. Jeff was experiencing the same fears as I. However, if he decided to speak to the police, my proverbial goose might be cooked.

"Okay," I said, laying a hand on his shoulder to calm him. "If it happens again, call the police. Let me know what they say?"

"Why wouldn't you call the police, too? I mean, they park closer to your house than to mine. Aren't you as unnerved as I am? Two complaints would lend more weight to the situation, I'd guess. And, oh, by the way," he added, "I read your piece in the Globe. Forgive my saying so, but shouldn't you just let sleeping dogs lie? I mean, maybe you've stirred up a hornet's nest." He was proving himself to be a master of cliché.

Instantly, I hated this pompous ass. He was connecting two, ostensibly disparate happenings, drawing conclusions that made my chest tighten.

"I'm a reporter, Jeff. I call them as I see them." Now, it was I who was sounding pompous. "Let me know what the police have to say if you do call them. Okay?" I had promised him nothing and felt incredibly guilty for putting both his family and mine in jeopardy. I just couldn't get the warning letter and Paul's picture out of my head. I was the reason for the ominous parked car on our street. Perhaps, I wondered, I **should** print a retraction of my article, wash my hands of what was clearly developing into a nasty situation, and leave Luella Frazier to her own devises. With the news that Fiona had just delivered, I could not find a way to extricate myself and Donna from this bind. I heard Donna's voice calling from across the backyard. "Time for cake and ice cream! Watermelon, too!" After we sang "Happy Birthday" to Paul, he made a wish and blew out the candles. The children came scrambling to the dessert table, paper plates in hand. Donna served each of them a slice of birthday cake; I placed a scoop of vanilla ice cream on top and handed them forks and napkins. I heard several "Thank you–s" as they hurried to sit at the long party table. Adriana served each of them a cup of fruit punch, then sat down next to Paul. He allowed her to wipe away the frosting from around his mouth. She did not mention how sad she was feeling, knowing that she would not be spending her days with him anymore. She kissed his forehead, rose, and went into the kitchen to dry her eyes.

By five o'clock, some of the neighbors began to filter out, thanking us for a lovely party, others helped dump the dirty plates, tablecloths, and plastic ware into large trash bags and recycle bins. Jeff and another guest, Lenny, helped take down the tables and fold the chairs. Invitations to get together again were extended by the wives and we agreed that we would. We had decided ahead of time not to open Paul's gifts at the party and he was standing by. waiting for the moment he could tear into them. Donna had asked Laura and Carter to stay later for coffee and drinks. As we made our way into the house, I heard Marty's voice calling to me from outside.

"James, come on out here. Beautiful evening. Let's sit a while."

I joined him, showing my disapproval for his having missed the party. "You missed the celebration, Marty. Why so late?"

"We have to talk, Jimmy boy. Things have been happening that you should know about." He extracted a pack of cigarettes from his white shirt pocket and offered me one. "Sorry, we're smoke-free here," I reminded him.

"Oh yeah; sorry." He stuffed the pack back into his pocket.

"All right let's have it, Marty. Fiona has already prewarned me about Luella's distress call. She said you could confirm things, not wanting to share more than that."

Marty leaned back in his lawn chair, extended and crossed his long legs at the ankles, began his detailed report on what he had been observing. From his back pocket, he produced a note pad with names, dates, times, and places. "I know the origin of Luella's phone call; got it traced back to her brother's place in Chelsea.

"So, what about this confrontation with Madelaine," I asked with foreboding.

"I witnessed it, Jimmy. I saw it all... terrible scene. Madelaine shook Luella off as if she were a pesky mosquito, then continued walking past her mother, as if she wasn't there pleading with her."

My heart was beating fast and I had to take a few deep breaths to calm myself. "Then what happened?" I prodded.

"Well, and this is the most interesting part, she got into the back of that black Cadillac and was whisked away by her sister-in-law, Penny Ricci."

"How do you know whose car it is?"

"I've been following that car everywhere it goes. Tailed it from here one night right up to Dwayne Ricci's grocery store. Ha! What a laugh. That so-called grocery store of his is nothing more than a front for his drug dealings. Luella lives in a room above the store and has no freedom to leave, unless supervised. There must be a phone in the back-storage room."

"How do you know about the drug operation?"

"I know Dwayne Ricci; he's as unsavory a character you'll ever meet. I know him because he was part of a mob hit that killed my father."

My brain started to hurt; I couldn't take in all this information at once and process it. I needed Donna to ask the questions I was afraid to.

"Excuse me for just a minute, Marty; I want Donna in on this conversation, if you don't mind."

"Not at all, Jimmy; in fact, I was going to suggest it myself."

Want a beer?" I offered, sensing that my personal feelings were interfering with Marty's good judgment.

"Nah, I'm good. I'll just wait here and enjoy the sunset."

How he could appear so relaxed, so nonchalant, baffled me. I walked away, scratching my head.

"Donna," I called from the back stairway, "can you come down here, please?"

"What's up? She called back, "Carter has us in stitches with one of his jokes."

Carter telling jokes? I was amazed that he knew any.

"Can you come down to the backyard? Marty's here and needs you to hear about his latest findings." I really hated to break the spell of the day for her, but her input was essential. Within minutes, she was by my side, worry lines creasing her forehead. She sat down tentatively and folded her hands in her lap. She remained quiet, contemplative for a while, then asked pointedly, "Are we in over our heads here, Marty? This whole thing is getting blown way out of proportion to our original plans. Maybe we should just walk away from it."

"I think you should wait for Luella's next call. See why she called. Having seen the revolting state her daughter is in, perhaps she can offer up a deal."

"What could she possibly offer up?" I interjected. "She's being held captive in her brother's house."

"She can find out details about Dwayne's business; she could tip us off about future drop-offs, descriptions of 'customers,' that sort of thing."

"But, what does that have to do with helping her with Madelaine, assuming that she'd be willing to put herself in danger. If Dwayne finds her snooping into his so-called business, there's no telling what he might do to her."

"Timing is everything, Jimmy. What would you say we fake a 'kidnapping' of Luella? We'd keep her safe and cared for. In the meantime, we'd get a good look at his drug operations, which would set Dwayne into a frenzy."

Donna's hand shot up to her throat in disbelief. "Good heavens, Marty. This sounds like a cloak and dagger operation. Why?"

"Well, news people would be all over the story; they'd be asking questions; they'd be tracking Luella down to where she had been living. And that's where you two come in. First, you write a story about the girl you grew up with; then..."

"Are you really serious? We'd be the first ones he'd come after." Donna couldn't take any more of Marty's dramatic plot. "Absolutely not!" she blurted, "I won't be a party to this absurd idea. Excuse me, I have guests to tend to." She walked briskly back to the house and I could tell by her gait that she was fuming.

"I guess she didn't like my idea, huh?" Marty didn't appear to be offended, although I assumed that he was. "Okay, back to the drawing board, as they say." He got up, clapped me on the shoulder, turned around, and walked back toward his car, hands thrust deep within his pant pockets. Seconds later, he returned, grim-faced.

"You know what, Jimmy boy? My work is done here. You know whose been watching you; you know who owns that black Cadillac, and you know where he's keeping Luella captive. Now, go get yourself some other fucking P.I." He turned his back to me and left.

I stood there in stunned silence, trying to blink away what felt like a bad dream. I was no psychiatrist, but I knew one. Maybe he'd have more palatable advice. I returned to the house and joined Donna, Laura and Carter in the living room. The half-filled bottle of bourbon on the coffee table beckoned me. Carter eyed me as I poured a generous amount into a glass; my hands shook, and my legs felt leaden. All conversation ceased when I sat down, a dreadful quiet hung in the air like an oppressive, dark cloud. Donna was staring into her empty glass, Laura rummaged through her purse, and Carter was busy cleaning his pipe. He was the first to speak.

"Jimmy, Donna has told us about what you two have been dealing with since your article appeared in the newspaper." It wasn't an accusation, but I flinched. "She's told me about this young woman, Madelaine, and her odd behavior. I'm sure I know what she suffers from, and I'm pretty sure I can help you—that is, if you want my help."

I looked up at my brother-in-law in disbelief. All these years, I had misjudged him. I would have been a fool to turn down his offer. "Carter, I, I don't know what to say. Yes, of course, your help could prove invaluable."

Donna looked up at me with gratitude; the tears she was holding at bay spilled down her cheeks. Laura stopped rummaging. Leaning forward, his arms resting on his knees, Carter shared his conclusions.

"Please understand that I've not had the opportunity to personally evaluate Madelaine; but I would venture to say that, based on my experience, as well as on what you've described, she exhibits symptoms consistent with Post Traumatic Stress Disorder, possibly coupled with a touch of Borderline Personality Syndrome."

"Can you explain what all this means, Carter? Can Madelaine be helped? To be honest, she was always strange, always distant. We thought she was aloof because of her superior intelligence." Combing my fingers through my hair, I almost whispered, "She was sexually abused by her father, but we don't know for how long." I was breathless, remembering how, when I planted that chaste kiss on her cheek, she scolded me, "You have no right, James."

"There's something else, Jimmy; isn't there? What are you holding back? Is there something you need to confess, but can't?"

I wasn't ready for this... not yet; but, somehow, I found the strength to divulge my secret. "Madelaine was pregnant with Edgar's baby. She must have miscarried after witnessing his corpse taken down the front stairs and into an ambulance; her mother was covered with Edgar's blood, pointing at Madelaine and humiliating her. Days later, in a thicket by the high school field, I accidentally came upon her hunched over a mound of dirt. She was keening while her hand traced the buried image of her child."

"Oh, sweet Jesus!" Carter exclaimed, crossing himself not once, but twice. "Jimmy, this young woman is lost to herself; she has no idea who she is anymore. Her pain must be so excruciating that she has sought refuge in another self, another interior self."

Saddened beyond belief, I asked, "How can we help her?"

"If this was what you eluded to in your confession piece, I humbly suggest that you abandon that idea completely. The damage to Madelaine's psyche is severe, make no mistake about it. But, with medication and appropriate intervention, we may be able to reach her before she can no longer stand the pain."

Chills ran up and down my spine. Donna hugged her knees and rocked back and forth in her seat. We had begun this journey into the lives of Luella and Madelaine, naively believing that we could right things; that we could reunite them in perfect harmony. Our naivete was driving us to the brink of calamity.

"What do you suggest we do next, Carter?" Donna had regained her composure and, characteristically, was thinking ahead. "Madelaine is living in Revere with an older woman who looks after her and provides for her daily needs. She's very protective and proprietary, doing her best to shield Madelaine from the demons that plague her. We tried to visit them but were rebuffed. Madelaine herself forced us to leave. Oh, I'm just so confused and conflicted!! Let's call it a night, all right?"

"You're also exhausted," Laura added. "We'll go now; but please, count on us for support." She rose, kissed us both, and helped Carter out of his chair. "I'll drive home," she declared, fishing the car keys out of her husband's pants pocket. He didn't resist. Holding onto his wife's arm for stability, he left us with one more thing to ponder.

"Madelaine needs her mother now more than ever. She just doesn't know that yet."

We saw them to the front door, left the unwashed plates and bowls in the kitchen sink, and climbed the stairs to our bedroom. Adriana had seen to Paul's bedtime needs, bless her heart. She had helped Paul unwrap his birthday presents, lining them up for him to inspect again tomorrow, his first day at Play and Learn. Evidently, she had left quietly, not wanting to disturb us. We folded, exhausted onto the bed. Ironically, I remembered that I had promised Fiona a slice of birthday cake; there was nothing left to save. There was nothing left of our crusade to save, either. We pecked each other on the cheek and said, "Love you." We did not add our usual "sleep well." It was clear that neither of us would.

Chapter 24

That same night, Viola Sandakis died in her sleep. Madelaine would not have suspected that anything was amiss; she hardly paid attention to what went on around her, anyway. But, that morning, she felt a strange foreboding of aloneness, different from that which she had chosen for herself. In her bones, she detected a shift in the alignment of her stars. Perhaps, it was the absolute quietude, the total absence of morning sounds, that quickened her heartbeat and alerted her senses to something unspecified, but, clearly unusual. She did not hear the voices of the T.V. newscasters whom Mrs. Sandakis followed each morning. She did not hear the sounds of dishes rattling or of pans clattering as breakfast was being prepared. It was too preternaturally quiet—even for Madelaine. Despairing of what she may be encounter, she threw off the thread-bare nightgown that Viola had gifted her twelve Christmas eves ago, and dressed slowly, forsaking what may have matched in color or print. She did not shower; nor, did she brush her teeth or hair. Still straining and hoping to hear even the slightest sounds of familiar activity in the kitchen, she slipped into her worn out moccasins and cautiously opened her bedroom door. One clumsy, stiff step at a time, she approached the kitchen, willing Viola to be sitting at the green-speckled Formica table sipping her morning tea. Madelaine's heart fluttered like hummingbird wings. Viola was nowhere to be seen. Had she left unexpectedly? No, she would have informed her. Maybe she had a doctor's appointment. No, she would have told her that, too. Could she have slept late? No, Viola was an early riser. Madelaine's panic began to rise as acid, burning her throat. She sat down at the table to wait. For what, she was not sure.

By noon, Viola still had not appeared. Madelaine fought off hunger; fear tightened its grip around her throat. What if she were dead... like Edgar? Dead like her, except she was alive and breathing. Rising from the kitchen table, Madelaine took a napkin from the holder Viola kept on the table and wrote this: "Mrs. Sandakis is gone. Went to Heaven. She's with Edgar." Then, she ran out of the house as if pursued by blood-thirsty demons.

A day later, concerned neighbors rang Viola's front doorbell. They had not seen her on her back porch, hanging laundry on her clothesline. They had not smelled the lovely aromas of the baklava, moussaka, and spanakopita she made with regularity. When no one responded, they called the police who, after entering and investigating, found her peacefully dead on her bed.

Madelaine disappeared like dissipating gas. She understood that there was nowhere to go; no one to take her in again. No one to care. Wandering aimlessly through the back streets of her youth and now her adult life, evading the main streets and ducking into the shadows, Madelaine's legs followed wherever her broken heart led her. The police put out an All-Points Bulletin for her.

Marty was the first to alert me to the latest development. "They don't know where she might have gone, Jimmy." He no longer sounded wounded or prideful.

It took me fewer than ten seconds to guess Madelaine's destination. I was in my car within minutes, heading toward the abandoned athletic field, toward the tiny grave of her miscarried baby.

The sun was setting when I arrived at the high school. In an effort to conceal my presence, I parked around the block and walked the short distance to the thicket, now littered with trash, beer cans, and discarded needles. I walked slowly, deliberately avoiding broken tree branches. An eerie hush hung over the improvised burial ground. I approached Madelaine from behind. She was lying on her side, stroking the small mound of dirt, clearing away stray leaves, trash, and nut shells left by squirrels and rodents. I watched her rebuild the mound, scooping the surrounding dirt with her hand, then patting it down. It appeared to me that this was a regular activity for Madelaine, as the elements—rain, wind, and snow—most certainly would have destroyed her makeshift shrine by now. I stood absolutely still, drawing shallow breaths. From the looks of things, she had been here for at least a day.

"I know you're there, James," Madelaine whispered, not turning to face me, nor ceasing her reverential rebuilding of the mound.

Dumbfounded, I tried to speak but no words escaped my lips.

"You've always known," Madelaine added.

"But how did you know it was me? How did you know it was me who kept your secret?" I dared not approach; I stood as if rooted to the spot.

"I saw you hiding in the bushes. Moonlight betrayed you."

On a leap of faith, I asked, "May I sit by you, Madelaine?"

After a long pause, she relented. "Yes; just don't get too close."

Carefully, I circled around and sat down opposite her. The grave was between us like a statement of fact.

"Is she dead?"

"Yes, passed in her sleep."

No tears, no emotion. Wherever Madelaine safe-guarded her feelings, they were locked away beyond access in a vault of anger.

Madelaine stopped scooping dirt, wiped her hands on her red flannel shirt, and looked up at me with such anguish I had to look away. She was ghostly pale, more specter than real. Then, I met her gaze with kindness, not with the pity I was feeling, nor the sorrow my heart was desperately trying to hide.

"I've been a coward, Madelaine." Saying those words uncorked something bottled deep within me, and I felt a strange release of tears.

"You protected me."

"And your mother did, too, Madelaine. She didn't even know about the..."

At the mention of her mother, Madelaine cupped her hands over her ears and vehemently shook her head left and right, again and again. "No, she wailed, "she killed Edgar because he loved me better."

I was treading on thin ice and knew it; but, I had to persist. "What Edgar did to you was wrong, very, very wrong. Do you understand me?"

"No! He loved me! He said so!" Madelaine was screaming at me now. How could I tell her that Edgar was an immoral predator—a beast? She was convinced otherwise. As I rose to leave, Madelaine stopped her ranting. Perhaps, what she needed most was to rave, to scream... anything that would crack open that impenetrable façade she hid behind.

"I can get you help," I ventured, waiting for another outburst of protest. "That is, if you want it." I knelt beside her and said, "Madelaine, I care about you."

I expected her to sear me with one of her steely stares and tell me that only Edgar had cared about her. I straightened and turned to leave. If she didn't want my help, well, at least I had tried. Madelaine was sobbing. I was beyond hope that I could reach her in her twisted, alternate reality, where no one else was allowed in. I started walking away. Madelaine having gotten to her feet, followed after me. She grabbed my shirt sleeve, pulling me back. "James, help me."

Daringly, I took her trembling hand. "Will you ride home with me?"

Through her tears, she glanced back at the tiny mound of earth, beneath which lay the seed of the devil incarnate. "Yes."

"We'll figure something out," I said, not convinced of my own words.

She was quiet and sad the entire ride back to Boston. My mind was racing; who, indeed would take Madelaine in? I then remembered that Carter had offered to help. He had said, "Madelaine needs her mother now more than ever. She just doesn't know that yet." Time would prove him wrong; but we didn't know that yet, either.

Chapter 25

*D*onna had gone to the ladies' room when I had precipitously fled the office. When she returned to her desk and discovered my absence, she immediately called to Fiona. "Where's Jimmy? Has he left the building?" Her concern was matched by her curiosity; she didn't like being left out of the loop.

"Call came in from Marty," Fiona explained, "cops have an APB posted for Madelaine. Jimmy flew out of here like the proverbial bat out of hell."

Donna was nonplussed; her dander was up.

"He just ran out of here without telling me? Where could he possibly have headed?"

"No idea, Honey. He just high-tailed it out as if his pants were on fire."

Donna pressed, "What's this about an APB? What's going on, Fiona? I deserve to know."

"Viola Sandakis was found dead in her apartment. Police were alerted after neighbors reported that they had not seen her. By the time she was found, rigor mortis had set in."

"Oh, my God! Where was Madelaine? Does she even know?"

"Good question. She left a cryptic note on the kitchen table to the affect that Viola was "gone." (Here, she made quotation marks in the air with her long fingers).

"You mean, she knows Viola is dead... not just missing?"

"Marty's call was received like an electric shock to James's body. As I said, he bolted without a word to me or to anyone else."

"He didn't even ask where I was?" Donna's wounded ego registered on Fiona.

"Listen, when men smell blood, they behave like the hounds."

"What do you mean by blood? Was Viola killed? Do they suspect Madelaine?"

"No, Madelaine may very well want to kill herself, not Viola. James instinctively understood that, and that's why he rushed to find her."

Donna wasn't satisfied with Fiona's explanation; instead, she felt short-circuited, left out of the action. She packed her briefcase, shut off her desk lamp, and started for the door. Suddenly, she realized that Jimmy had their car.

"Fiona, can I get a lift home?" Thankfully, she had prearranged with a neighbor for Paul's pick-up at day school.

"Sure, no problem. I was hoping that Luella would call back today. Looks like that ain't gonna happen."

Chapter 26

On his police scanner, Dwayne had heard the same news about the All- Points Bulletin for Madelaine. Should he tell Luella? He lit up a joint and stretched out on his white leather sofa. Reason told him that he should tell his sister after all, like it or not, Madelaine happened to be his niece. But, he also knew that the police would be coming around asking him questions, asking Luella questions, too. The last thing he needed was to have those *snoops* finding out more than what they would be looking for. Luella didn't know about his other *business* and he needed to keep it that way. So, the smart thing for him to do was to show up at the police station, acting concerned, but ignorant of her whereabouts, which, of course, was true. He'd have to tell Luella, and she would be so grateful that she'd do whatever he asked. Yes, that was a plan he could visualize. Pinching off the tip of his reefer, he hurried to the back-storage room to find her. He checked the refrigerated room, checked her loft bedroom, but could not find her. She had been there earlier in the morning when the food deliveries arrived; there were invoices with her initials on them, dated this day. Her personal belongings—however little she had of them—were all there, but she was not. Panicking, he ran to his house and called for his wife.

"Penny! Penny! Where are you?"

"I'm up here, in our bedroom, Dwayne."

"I'm looking all over for Luella. Have you seen her?" He called from below.

Penny hesitated, knowing that if she lied, she'd pay for it. Dwayne was not averse to hurting her; he had punched her and pulled her hair more than once during their marriage. "She's up here... with me," she answered nervously.

"What the ... She's up there with you? Are you kidding me? Why on earth is she with you?" Dwayne was ascending the staircase, two steps at a time. When he reached the bedroom, he kicked open the door with his steel-tipped riding boot. What he found astounded him. Luella, sitting on the small chair of Penny's pink chiffon, mirrored vanity table, did not look like his sister. She was showered, smelling of lavender soap; her hair was washed and styled; she was wearing one of Penny's white, ruffled blouses and a pair of black slacks. She wore makeup that covered the dark circles under her eyes and rendered color to her ashen cheeks. For all he knew, she could have been someone else, posing as his sister.

"Well, if it isn't my little sister of the chains! A glamour-puss!"

"Stop your gawking, Dwayne. I've been wantin' to do this for Luella for a long time. She's a woman and needs to feel pretty."

Dwayne stood in the doorway, mouth agape, eyes wide. His mind scrolled back in time to when she **was** pretty; how the two of them used to play and find refuge in each other when their daddy was on one of his rampages. He had taken pity on her and allowed her to stay in the back-storage room; but, he had been treating her like an animal. He approached his sister and crouched down on the shag carpet. His look was not menacing, as Luella had anticipated.

Instead, Dwayne broke the news of Madelaine's disappearance gently.

"Luella, I've heard some news about Madelaine."

Hearing her daughter's name, Luella shot upright. "What? Tell me!"

"There's an All-Points Bulletin issued for her; she's gone missing."

"No, that can't be!" Luella shouted. "I just saw her the other day!"

Dwayne snapped. "What do you mean you saw her? Where was she?"

Trapped, Luella knew that she was about to implicate Penny for not watching her carefully. So, she became creative.

"It was from a distance, Dwayne. I was in the back seat of your car and we were going to a pharmacy so's I could fill a prescription. I saw my daughter wandering down the street."

"Did she see you?" Dwayne was not sure that he believed the story he was being told but held back.

"No. I'm sure of it. We just drove on past."

Penny was sitting on her bed, feigning disinterest.

"Penny, why didn't you tell me about this?" His temper was in check, but he had fire in his eyes. "Did she get a look at our car?"

"My eyes were on the road; couldn't tell you."

"Don't get sassy with me, Darlin'; just answer my questions." Dwayne turned his attention back to Luella.

"What were you doing in her neighborhood, anyways? There's plenty of drug stores around here."

Luella grabbed Dwayne by the shoulders and pushed him backwards; he fell on his butt. A look of total incredulity washed over his face.

"You're being an ass, brother. Madelaine is my kid; she's your niece. Doesn't that mean anything to you?"

On the defensive, Dwayne stood up and smirked. "Call me that again, Luella, and **your** ass will be out the door."

"We have to find her. Please, Dwayne, help me find her."

"I have a plan," he said, settling down. "You and me are going to show up at police headquarters and tell those idiots that we're worried sick; that we have no idea where she is, or who took her."

"You mean like in *kidnapped*? Do you think someone kidnapped her?" Frantically, Luella began to pace the bedroom. "Why would someone want to kidnap my daughter?" If she described her daughter as compromised, Dwayne would want to know how she came by that knowledge. She couldn't let on. Maybe the person who told her—James Price—had taken her! Oh, wouldn't that be a relief! But, she kept those thoughts to herself and agreed to go with her brother's plan.

"Don't want them creeps snooping around here poking into my business. So, we go to them, instead. See?"

"All right, then. Can we go right now? Truth is, Dwayne, we **don't** know where she is; we've got nothing to hide. Won't they want to know why she hasn't been living with me? My stomach is in knots, though; have to tell you that."

"Well, don't unknot it. Show them how upset you are so's they don't suspect you—or me. Ask them if we can help in the search, anything that would convince them that we're not involved."

"Okay. Can we go now? Can Penny come?"

"No, Penny will have to stay here and mind the store. Right, Darlin'? Take care of my *customers*; they rely on me." He winked at Penny and she got his implication: his drug dealers would be showing up, expecting to do business. Penny knew how to handle *exchanges*. And, Luella knew to keep her knowledge of Dwayne's other *business* to herself.

Chapter 27

Fiona had dropped Donna off at our house within minutes of my pulling into our driveway. Seeing me drive up, she remained planted on the front walkway. Madelaine had fallen asleep in the back seat of our SUV; she had not uttered a word from the time we left the thicket. I had tried to reach Donna on her cell phone, but apparently her battery had run out and she never received my calls. She stood on the brick walkway, hands on her hips, anger written all over her face. When I turned off the engine, she approached, ready to tear into me. Donna did not often lose her temper and I could tell that this was going to be an historic moment for her. I lowered my window and sat back, waiting for the diatribe that I most certainly deserved.

"Jimmy, before we go into the house, I want you to know that..." She stopped cold when she saw the prone figure of Madelaine in the backseat, soundly asleep and oblivious. "What the... how... I mean, where...?"

"I tried to call you, honey. I'm sorry, truly am. I couldn't leave her out there alone. I had no choice." I tried to sound repentant, but my heart wasn't in it."

"Of course, you had a choice! The police are looking for her everywhere and you just drive up here so nonchalant. Have you informed them? Where does she go from here? Surely, you don't think..."

When I didn't respond, she stepped back away from the car. "No, James. She can't stay here." She was looking at me as if I had gone mad. Donna's high-pitched voice awakened Madelaine; she blinked several times, trying to figure out where she was. She sat upright but said nothing; she hung her head to avoid making eye contact with Donna. Then she wedged her body into the side corner of the seat, as if anticipating some physical harm.

"Don't come into the house until I've had a chance to talk to Adriana and Paul." She stalked away, trying to suppress her anger.

While waiting for her to return, I turned around to Madelaine, scrunched into the seat corner. "No one's going to hurt you," I promised her. "You can stay with us for the night. Okay?" I couldn't promise her any more than that and felt the guilt of how this new development was going to impact on my family. Madelaine remained silent.

When Donna entered the house, she found Paul at the kitchen table, working carefully on his new Superman coloring book. He looked up, scrambled down for hugs. "Where's Daddy?" he asked. Adriana was drying the last of their supper dishes. Folding the dishcloth and hanging it on a peg next to the sink, she smiled warmly.

"Did you have a great day at Play and Learn, sweetheart?"

"Yeah. But Tommy Ballard pushed me in the playground and I fell.

"What did you do then?" Donna was especially incensed with bullies.

"I pushed him back and then we were friends."

Oh, the logic of five-year-olds, she mused. "That's great, Paul. Now, I have something very important to tell you and Adriana." Adriana's smile weakened as she sat down at the table.

"Okay. Tonight, we're going to have a house guest. She doesn't talk much and doesn't answer questions. I need for you to be kind to her and not bother her."

"But why, Mommy? I don't think I'm going to like her."

"Just because, Paul." That answer has never been enough for any child, but she could not think of a better one. There are moments in time when there are no sufficient answers.

"Okay. But she better be nice to me, too." Our five-year-old's concept of social justice was just forming.

"Just let her be. And don't say anything about how she looks—or smells. I'll take care of that later." Turning to Adriana, who, by now had the look of consternation, Donna asked, "Would you help me get the guest bedroom set up? And, let's put out several bath towels."

"I can do that," Adriana, began, "but..."

"We'll talk more after we get her settled."

Donna signaled from the front door that it was all right for us to come in. At first, Madelaine stiffened and whimpered.

"Don't be afraid, Madelaine. No one's going to hurt you, I promise."

I helped her out of the car, and she allowed me to guide her by the elbow up the walkway and front stairs, then into the house. The whole time, she cast her eyes downward, shuffling like an old woman.

We walked past Paul who stood in the hallway taking his measure of Madelaine. His grimace spoke louder than words. I winked at him and he smiled, but after we passed and made our way up to the bedrooms, he held his nose as if his fingers were a clothespin. Donna and Adriana were preparing the guest bed with clean sheets, pillows, etc. Clean towels were stacked in the bathroom, as was a fresh bar of soap. I guided Madelaine into the bedroom and waited for a response. None came. She stood impassively, wondering what all the fuss was about. To her, a bed is a bed is a bed; put a pretty coverlet over it, and it's still a bed.

Donna turned to Madelaine and explained that she was welcome to join us for dinner; first, however, she'd have to shower, shampoo her hair, and put on some clean clothes which she would find hanging on the door.

"We'll not bother you, Madelaine; relax a bit and come down when you're ready. Do you like mac and cheese?"

Madelaine had no idea what she meant by mac and cheese but nodded in the affirmative. What she did understand, on some level, was that I was making good on my promise to keep her safe. We left her standing by the window, looking out at nothing in particular, arms wrapped around her body to keep the chill of fear at bay. Homeless, parentless, and self-less, she was in no position to argue with kindness. Slowly, she peeled off her foul-smelling clothes, letting them drop into a heap on the bedroom carpet. Naked, she passed a full-length mirror that hung on the backside of the door and gasped; her reflection alarmed her; it reminded her of herself— the one she used to know—before Edgar. Like an automaton, she entered the shower and turned on the spray. She stepped into the soft pulsations and soothing rhythm of the hot water, reached for the soap, and began to lather her violated body. Her tears comingled with the water, each washing away layers of the filth that had piled high in the apartment of her soul. Tentatively, she turned her back to the water and let it penetrate her stringy, blond hair. Nothing so cleansing had happened to her in twelve long years. Mrs. Sandakis had not made demands of her, tolerating her unkempt state without judgment. Now, Viola was dead, and Madelaine had to decide if she wanted to be dead, too. But to be alive meant accepting life; she didn't know if she could or wanted to engage in the sordid facts that brought her to this junction. Disassociation had been her comfort, her refuge. How would she tame the yellow-eyed demons that spoke to her at night, taunting and braying like wolves? Who would understand why she retreated into the steep caverns of oblivion?

Madelaine dried off with the soft, plush towels hanging on a warming rack; then she dressed in the jeans and sweatshirt that Donna had left folded neatly on the bed. A pair of cotton socks lay alongside the jeans. The softness of the towels against her rough skin made her cry once more; reminding her of Edgar's touch.

After an hour's wait for Madelaine to come downstairs, Donna went back upstairs to check on her. Madelaine was fast asleep; her hair was still damp, and she lay naked, wrapped in a soft towel. Jimmy's voice rose from his study where he was heatedly engaged in a phone conversation.

"Yes, she's here. Staying for the night. Tell the cops to call off the search. Tell them she had just wandered away. And don't let anyone else know where she is. Please."

Marty could not believe what he was hearing. "You gotta' be kidding me! You've gotta be fuckin' kidding me, Jimmy boy!"

"Stop calling me that, Marty. Just keep this quiet- until we can figure out what to do next!"

Donna tiptoed out of the bedroom, closing the door behind her. She descended the stairway and joined me in my study. "She's fast asleep. I guess we'll just let her be."

"Yeah, probably a good idea. Did she wash up?"

"She did. I found her lying naked wrapped in a towel. What does that mean, Jimmy?"

Jimmy ran his fingers through his hair and shook his head. "I guess it's time to call Carter."

"Ask him to come over ASAP tomorrow. We can't do this without his help; it's way beyond the point of righting Luella's prison sentence. We're in over our heads, Jimmy, and Madelaine needs professional help."

"I'll call Fiona and tell her we need the day off tomorrow. She's still waiting for Luella to call me back at work. She knows about the police search, but I can't put Madelaine in danger right now."

"Just so you'll know, Jimmy," Donna warned me, "She can't stay here beyond a day or two. If word gets out about where she is, I worry that Luella's brother will come after us."

"Okay, Honey. I agree. Maybe with Carter's help, we can get her into a treatment facility."

"Do you think Marty will keep this quiet?"

"Hard to say. Nothing would give him more satisfaction than going after that punk brother. I think he's still sore at me for not liking his kidnapping plan."

Donna was clearly upset. "She came willingly, but, we've basically kidnapped her. That's not going to sit well with him."

"Or," I mused, "he might see it as an alternative way to flush Dwayne Ricci's drug dealing out into the open."

"But how?" Donna was not mollified.

"Marty knows his way around these things. He'll come up with something."

"After you call Fiona, let's have our dinner; it's probably cold by now." She called out for Paul, and he came scampering into the kitchen.

"Where's the funny-looking lady?" he asked.

"Paul, I told you not to be unkind. No name-calling, remember? She's not funny-looking, just very sad."

"Does she still smell bad?"

"No, darling. She doesn't. Please mind your manners in the morning if you see her."

"Isn't she gonna' eat with us?" He seemed disappointed.

"No, she's sleeping; so, we'll try to be quiet and let her rest."

Paul was intrigued by the strange person brought into our house without explanation. Donna expressed one more worry to Paul.

"Honey, it's very important that you not tell anyone at school about our guest, not even your teachers. Daddy and I trust you to keep our secret. Okay?"

Now, feeling included in the machinations of our keeping Madelaine's presence at secret, he said, "I won't, promise. Let's hook pinky fingers and shake."

Chapter 28

arty O'Brien had both motives and a plan for flushing Dwayne Ricci out into the open, exposing his past, as well as his nefarious drug dealings. From his weeks of surveillance, he knew that Dwayne manned the grocery store, taking care of customers, putting his best face forward. Although gruff in nature, he seemed well-liked and above-board. He joked with them, sometimes telling ribald stories to the men, while courting the ladies with the charm of a snake. His produce was always fresh and artfully arranged, the dairy products, never date-expired. In short, his customers trusted him.

Marty visited the storefront early on a Saturday morning. Silver chimes hung on a string over the front door; they tinkled as he pushed it open. Casually, he took a shopping basket from the stack by the entryway and strolled through the aisles. The store was immaculate and well-organized. Shelves of canned goods were stacked in orderly fashion and bottled drinks were meticulously lined up like liquid soldiers. The wood-planked floor, clean and recently swept, creaked under his weight. On the check-out counter, stood a tall glass collection bottle; a picture of a sick child needing medical care was taped to it. Donations of five, ten, and twenty-dollar bills half-filled the jar. Marty placed a jar of peanut butter, a loaf of white bread, a can of tuna fish and a few Roma tomatoes into his basket. Whistling softly, he appeared to be enjoying his shopping venture.

"Hi there," Dwayne called out to him from behind the check-out counter. His short-sleeved shirt was as black as his ... suspicious eyes. Dwayne's muscular forearms were fully tattooed— "sleeves" of skull and crossbones, black roses, and cryptic letters, most likely gang-related. "Can I help you find anything?"

"Aw, no, I'm good; but thanks." Marty's insides were roiling with anger. He would have forfeited his pension for a chance to strangle this punk.

"You new to town?" Dwayne asked, eyeing Marty suspiciously.

"Been here a bit," Marty answered, obliquely. Name's Rudy. "Heard you have the very best mozzarella and decided to get me some."

"I'm Dwayne, the owner of this here place." Extending his hand, he shook Marty's. "Pleased to meet you, Rudy. You'll find that in the cooler by the wall there." He pointed to a refrigerated case to Marty's left. How about some fresh pizza dough?"

Marty understood the reference to pizza dough; it was a term used by the drug dealers he'd known, and he knew he was being tested.

"My mom makes her own, oh so good, and I thought I'd bring her the cheese. Might you have some pepperoni?"

"No, don't carry meat, sorry. But, would you like me to get some for you? A friend of mine owns a deli."

The references to pizza were actually code words; they sounded innocuous, but, in fact, communicated the availability and interest in Dwayne's drug business. Marty had learned this language from his dad.

"Well, sure, maybe the kind with cracked hot peppers?"

"Come back in a few days; I'll see what I can do, Rudy. Ready to check out?"

"Yup, ready. How much do I owe you?"

"That'll be ten dollars and forty cents."

"That's all?" Marty knew what was coming next.

"The cheese is on me, Rudy. Hopefully, you'll come back for more." His smug smile betrayed a duplicity that made him feel clever.

"See you in a few days, then. My mom is going to be so pleased!" Marty started for the door wearing an equally smug smile, knowing that he had captured the entire conversation on his cell phone. As he reached for the door knob, however, he heard a woman's voice.

"Dwayne, I've been waiting. Aren't we goin' down to the police station?"

Dwayne spun around to find Luella in the doorway.

"What the fuck are you doing? Didn't I tell you to never come in here?" He bolted toward her and back-slapped her face with such ferocity that she stumbled backwards and fell to the floor. Immediately, he straddled her, pinning her shoulders down with his knees, then grabbed handfuls of her hair and pummeled her head against the floor. Luella screamed as Dwayne reached for her wrist and began to fold her fingers backwards. Marty could not stand the sight nor the sounds of this abuse and edged closer.

"Stop, Dwayne!" he shouted. "Get off her, or I'll call the police!"

"Mind your own goddam business and get outta here if you know what's good for you." His eyes were ablaze with a fury not unlike his father's when he saw fit to "teach him a lesson." He rose, but as his last statement, kicked Luella in the ribs with his metal-tipped boots. Her howl made Marty cringe.

"I told you to get outta here," he thundered, his reddened face just inches from Marty's nose. "You ain't seen nothin' hear me? Not if you want that pepperoni." His sneer would have frightened other men, but Marty was not cowed. He left, glancing one last time at a sobbing, broken Luella. Fortunately, his cell phone was still recording. Closing the door behind him, he heard Dwayne say, "No, we're not goin' to the police station, you fool." And then he gathered a wad of saliva and spat at her terrified face.

As soon as Dwayne stormed out the door and she could hear him revving his Harley. Leaning on one elbow, she struggled to her feet. Her head was pounding, and she felt dizzy. Nevertheless, she grabbed the edge of the counter and hoisted herself up, holding on for stability. Her left eye was already swollen and partially closed. Standing alone in the storefront, she felt the same desolation, the same degradation she thought she had left behind in prison.

Penny's voice penetrated the loud ringing in her ears. She turned to find her sister-in-law in the doorway, tears in her eyes.

"Luella, you've got to run. Get outta here as fast as your feet will carry you. Run like the devil himself is chasin' you... and he will."

"But, I have no place to go, no money, no nothing. He'll find me, Penny, no matter where I run to."

Penny unfolded her hand and showed Luella a fist-full of cash. She stuffed the money into Luella's bra, then snatched a water bottle and some cookies off the shelf. Handing them to Luella, she implored, "Go now. Run for your life. I'll find a way to distract him. Just go."

Luella could not believe the kindness Penny was demonstrating. "How can I thank you?" she cried, embracing her. Penny turned Luella toward the back door and pushed her outside. "Go!" she ordered.

Luella had never experienced being a fugitive before; she knew only captivity. With no sense of direction or awareness of her surroundings, she chose side streets, back alleys and lesser traveled roads, stealthily avoiding passersby. She then became aware of a blue Mini-Cooper driving slowly beside her. She recognized the driver as the customer in the shop; he stopped, rolled down the window, and said, "Let me help you, Luella. I'll get you to a safe place."

"How do you know my name?" she asked, disbelieving her good fortune, yet wary of a stranger who knew her by name.

"Let's just say, I never forget one. Now please, get in before someone notices."

Luella obeyed and got into the back seat of the car, crouched low, and held her throbbing head in her hands. By then her left eye was almost completely shut . She didn't ask where Marty was taking her; she didn't care, as long as she was far away from another beating. When they were safely out of Chelsea and heading towards Boston, Marty asked Luella if it would be all right for him to call me.

"You know James?" she whispered hoarsely.

"You might say that." What he wanted to add was that Mr. James Price was the self-same person who got her into this mess.

"I've been tryin' to reach him but keep gettin' some boss lady. Yes, call him, please. He said he wanted to help me and Madelaine."

∞ ∞ ∞

The search for Madelaine had been called off. I had called Carter, and he agreed to stop by in the morning. Fiona was livid that we were not coming into work the next day, still hoping that Luella would call. Donna and I were just sitting down to our warmed-up dinner when my phone rang.

"Jimmy, I have someone with me who might want to talk to you. She says that you promised to help her."

I reached for the wine bottle and poured what was left into my glass. I pushed my chair away from the table and pressed the phone closer to my ear.

"Let me get this straight, Marty. You have Luella in your car and she wants to talk to me. How is this possible?"

"No time for explanations, buddy; just talk to the lady. She's been badly beaten and I'm going to take her to a safe place."

I put my phone on speaker so that Donna could hear our conversation. "Okay, I'm ready."

Luella took Marty's phone with some trepidation. Then, shakily, she asked me if I knew where her daughter might be. I looked at my empty wine glass and grimaced. "I do, Luella; but I can't tell you just yet."

"For God's sake, James. Why not?"

"Because I promised to keep her whereabouts unknown. I... we are trying to get her some badly needed medical intervention, Luella. She does not, as I've told you, act normally. In order to help her, we need to make her feel protected."

"Did she tell you about how I tried to speak to her on the street? She looked right through me, like I wasn't even there! I tried to stop her, but she broke away from me like I was some kind of monster."

"Yes, I know. You're not a red-eyed monster with long fangs, Luella. We all know that. But, we have to convince Madelaine of that. She is stuck in time... that time..." I needed input from Carter, but I had a pretty good idea what we'd be dealing with. I needed to gain and retain Madelaine's trust; if I didn't there'd be no hope. "Can you just hold off a little longer, Luella? I mean, let us do what we think will be best for both you and Madelaine."

There was a long pause before Luella spoke again. Defeated and dismayed, she agreed. "As long as I don't have to go back to my brother's house, I'll do whatever you ask, James." She handed Marty his phone before I could thank her.

"I'm going to ask Fiona to take her in, Jimmy. I don't think she'll be too happy about it; but, hey, won't hurt to ask."

"Okay, Marty. Let me know how things go."

"Yeah, you, too, Jimmy boy... oops, sorry." He hung up and dialed Fiona's number. She answered on the second ring.

"Hello, Marty," she said, testily. "What the hell is going on? I've been trying to reach you. Will you, please, fill me in on this Madelaine disappearance thing? One minute she's missing; then, she's not!"

"I'm heading for your place right now, Fiona. I have with me a certain Mrs. Luella Frazier. I need for you to give her a place to stay for a short while."

"WHAT?!?! You've got to be joking. Be serious, Marty."

"I couldn't be more serious, believe me. I can explain when we get there. Please, Fiona. You owe me a few."

He didn't wait for an answer which could have led to an argument; and, he didn't want to say too much in front of Luella which might railroad his own agenda.

On the way up in the elevator to Fiona's eighteenth-floor apartment, Marty reached out for Luella's hand. "It's gonna' be okay, kid. Trust me."

Fiona opened the door to her posh condo at the Boston Harbor Towers. She wore black skinny jeans, a gray cashmere tunic, and was barefoot. She wore no makeup; her black-rimmed glasses perched atop her hair which hung loosely. Not typically welcoming to uninvited visitors, she stepped back to allow Marty to enter; Luella hung back, trailing slowly taking in the orderliness of the black and white ambiance, the linear leather furniture, the glass tabletops. On the wall hung several large paintings, and although she could not identify the artists, she could tell that they were valuable—art-deco, with large, sweeping brushstrokes of crimson and black. Atop a black enameled side table, a single red rose peeked out from a white ceramic bud vase. Fiona lived in an existential world of right or wrong; of order vs chaos. She owed this opulence to her father, a scion of the ladies' garment industry. Although they argued continually during her adolescence and saw little of each other after college, she did not turn down the huge inheritance he had left her—his only living child—when he died

"Geez, Louise! You look so, um, human!" Marty effused.

"Thank you, Mister Smart-Ass." Fiona knew that, for Marty, those words were meant to be affectionate.

Marty guided Luella into the room and introduced her.

"Luella, this is my friend, Fiona. However negative she sounds, don't believe her; she really is very kind."

Fiona shot him a sharp look. She assessed Luella with a critical eye. "Pleased to meet you… I think. I appreciate that you've had no say in all this, but honestly, as much as I'm concerned about your welfare, I cannot offer you… well, this is not a safe house, you see." Glaring at Marty, she continued, "And he has no business offering my place to you as one."

"Fiona, you're not being the least bit polite. How about a bite to eat? We're famished!"

Swallowing her pride, Fiona said, "Luella, I apologize. Come in, sit down and relax. I'm not much of a cook or a hostess. I can offer you tea, some cheese and crackers… or something stronger." The smell of ginger and soy from discarded cartons of Chinese take-out lingered. A stray chopstick lay on the glass cocktail table. Luella guessed that Fiona ate most of her meals there, watching the huge flat-screen television that hung on the opposite wall.

Luella's body welcomed the cushioned softness of the sofa, a departure from the hard lines of the other seats. "Thank you. As long as you're offerin', I could use a stiff one."

Fiona was just registering the bruised swellings on Luella's face. Here, she thought, was a woman abused, scorned, and berated; a woman who, through no fault of her own, was both reviled and denigrated. Here was a woman who had paid the price for protecting her daughter. She opened her glass cabinet, extracted three tumblers and poured three generous servings of scotch. After handing Luella, a glass, she sat down on a side chair and crossed her long legs at the ankles.

Marty reentered the room, munching on a carrot. He paced as he sipped from his glass. "Listen, all I'm asking for is a week. Certainly, you can grant me that small favor."

Luella interrupted him. "Beggin' your pardon, but, um... I didn't plan on intrudin'. Maybe I should just go back..."

"No!" Marty shouted. "I saw what your brother did to you. No way you're goin' back there; not if I can help it. He'll kill you, Luella!"

Marty's agitation signaled a weakening of Fiona's resistance. "So, can you cook?"

"Yes, ma'am, I can cook, clean, do whatever I have to," Luella replied. She was nobody's fool, guessing that her "qualifications" would win her a refuge. Fiona was accustomed to deference.

"I don't need a housekeeper or a private chef. But, okay, I'll give you one week to find a more suitable arrangement." Again, assessing Luella's visage, she saw a woman who bore scars both inside and out, who did not elicit pity so much as a plea for respect. In an atypical moment of generosity and rare compassion, she declared, "All right, then," she announced, raising her glass, "Here's to one week. But, I insist on paying you. There's a pull-out sofa bed in the spare bedroom; it never gets used. There are sheets, pillows, and blankets in the closet. Help yourself. You are welcome to use the lotions and soaps in the bottom cabinet of the vanity. Just keep it tidy."

Marty hoisted his glass high as if to salute her. Their eyes met and telegraphed a mutual appreciation... and more.

At that moment, a white Persian cat jumped up into Luella's lap, curled up and purred, as if welcoming her. Luella cradled the soft, pink-nosed cat and stroked its snowy fur. "Thank you," she beamed, holding back the tears that a stranger's kindness had evoked.

Chapter 29

*D*wayne returned at sunset, entering his house smelling of alcohol and marijuana. After parking his Harley in the barn, he stumbled into the kitchen, stoned. The house was quiet; the sounds of Penny's T.V. game shows were absent, as was his expected dinner. He searched for Penny on the ground floor but did not find her. Upstairs, he could hear music playing on her boom-box—old recordings he detested. Penny was sitting at her vanity, polishing her nails with a bright pink lacquer. Still fuming from his episode with Luella, he asked, "Where is she?"

Looking distracted, Penny blew on her wet, painted fingertips. "Why? Isn't she in the loft?"

Dwayne ran down the stairs, taking two at a time. He checked the loft, rifling through Luella's spartan belongings. On her bed, lay her workpants, into which she had stuffed Dr. Abbott's prescriptions. Next, he checked the back-storage room, everywhere Luella might have considered hiding. Returning to the bedroom, aflame with fury, he bellowed, "She's not there, Penny. Where is she?" His words, both slurred and menacing, forced Penny to look up.

"I have no idea, Dwayne. I'm not her body-guard, you know."

Nostrils flaring, Dwayne screamed, "Tell me where she is, bitch. You're lying, and I can tell."

"Last I saw her, she was dressed and ready to go to the police station with you. Next thing I know, you're out the door and on your Harley." She got up to turn off the music but didn't get far. Dwayne grabbed her arm, twisted it sharply behind her back, then spun her around to face him. "Tell me where she is, or I'll kill you," he seethed.

"I can't tell you what I don't know. Now let go of my arm." In response, Dwayne threw her onto the bed, ripped off her clothes, turned her onto her stomach and straddled her. He entered and pumped her with a vicious force, as if he were a bull rider at a rodeo; his thrusts were agonizing and unrelenting; yet, she did not cry out. She simply passed out.

Dwayne stumbled to the kitchen, opened the refrigerator door and found nothing prepared. Spying a half-eaten pepperoni roll, he ripped off the outer wrapping and bit off a mouthful, washing it down with beer. Chewing with satisfaction, he suddenly remembered the guy in his store who asked for pepperoni. He stopped chewing, trying to reconstruct the scene. Did he witness the thrashing he gave Luella? Yes, he was certain of that. He had told the guy to forget what he saw. Maybe Luella left with him! He rummaged through his mind, trying to remember the guy's name. Rusty? Randy? It was an "R" name, he thought. He seemed too casual for a stranger, too cool. And, he seemed well-acquainted with the jargon of the drug trade. Dwayne felt a green queasiness in the pit of his stomach, either from the alcohol, the drugs, the pepperoni, or from fear. He made it to the bathroom in time to vomit, continuing until he was drenched in sweat. He lay down on the tile floor; its coolness felt good. He closed his eyes and slept through the night, his head pressed against the base of the toilet.

Dwayne awoke at daybreak, hung over and smelling like spoiled cheese. He rose from the tile floor and stumbled toward the stairway. Descending to the kitchen, he heard Penny scrambling eggs and pouring them into a fry pan. The aroma of freshly brewed coffee filled the air. He poked his head through the doorway, and, as contrite as Dwayne Ricci could force himself to be, murmured, "Sorry 'bout last night." Not waiting for a reply, he turned and, with the help of the banister, struggled back up the stairs to shower.

Chapter 30

*C*arter wasted no time in returning my call; I had said it was urgent. His unflappable professional tone always irritated me; but, considering the circumstances, I welcomed it. We arranged for his visit at eight o'clock the next morning. I had no idea in what state we would find Madelaine; I could only hope that her more positive nerve cells would be working and that she would be amenable to talking to a doctor.

Neither Donna nor I slept. Donna got out of bed several times, once to take a Xanax, then later, some antacids. I feigned sleep, hoping that my stillness would help her fall asleep. No such luck. We watched each hour pass reflected on the face of our digital clock and waited until daybreak to throw off our covers. We could hear Paul calling us from his room. "You first," I offered, meaning the bathroom and shower. I was grateful that it was Monday. Paul would need his morning routine: dressing, tooth brushing, breakfast of granola cereal with banana slices. While Donna showered, I tended to Paul, greeting him with cheerfulness and warmth. I helped him choose the clothes he wished to wear that day. Downstairs, I prepared his breakfast and packed his backpack with the sandwich Donna had made for his lunch: sliced turkey on wheat bread, apple slices, and carrot sticks. Play and Learn had strictly enforced prohibitions against peanut butter; Donna refused to pack tuna or egg salad for fear that the mayonnaise would spoil after the several hours spent in Paul's lunchbox. Peering into his bag, Paul wrinkled up his nose. "Turkey? Again?"

"Don't worry, Sport. You can have whatever you want after school.

"It's not school, Dad," he corrected me; but he accepted my offer and climbed into his seat. "Dad? Is she still here?"

"Yes, she is still here. And, you must remember to keep your promise. Do not say a word to anyone about our house guest. Okay?"

In between mouthfuls of cereal, Paul answered, "I remember. Where's Mommy?"

Donna entered the kitchen dressed in jeans and a hooded sweatshirt. Her hair was still damp. "Morning, Sweetheart." She kissed the top of his head and ruffled his hair. She gratefully accepted the cup of coffee I handed her. The question now was who would drive Paul to daycare and who would remain behind to greet Carter. Donna decided that it would be best for me to stay. "She's comfortable with you, Jimmy. Besides, she seems skittish around me."

Donna was right; Madelaine had always been comfortable around me. Was it because I didn't join in the ridicule heaped upon her when we were kids? Did she really trust that I wouldn't let anyone hurt her? I didn't know the answers; I just had a worry in my gut that when Carter arrived, she would retract into the shell of her other-world. Hugging Paul, I wished him a fun day. "See ya' later, Sport."

"See ya' later, alligator," he laughed, thinking that old rejoinder was as funny as we thought it was when we were his age.

After they left, I heard footfalls on the stairs. Madelaine was making her way slowly and cautiously down to the kitchen. At first, I thought this a good sign; perhaps our encounter at that gravesite would encourage her to remain calm and cooperative. To my utter dismay, she stood in the doorway totally naked but for a towel, loosely wrapped around her body. There was no sign of lucidity in her eyes, just a mystified, vacant glaze. She stood there in total silence and I remained frozen to my seat. Finally, I cleared my throat and spoke

"Madelaine. Can you hear me? You can't come down here undressed. You need to go back upstairs and put some clothes on."

As if transfixed, she turned and ascended to her room, ghostlike. She did not return to the kitchen. At eight o'clock sharp, our doorbell rang. Still shaken by what I had just witnessed, I opened the door.

"Come on in, Carter. Thanks for coming."

Carter removed his leather Ivy cap and placed it on our foyer table. "Good morning to you, too," he said with that edge of sarcasm I couldn't stand.

Leading Carter into the kitchen, beyond earshot for Madelaine, I described to him what had just transpired. He listened attentively, nodding his head and fingering his bowtie. "Yes, yes, I see. Did she make eye contact with you? Do you think she was cognizant of you or her surroundings?"

"I honestly don't know," I answered, scratching my head. "I was so startled by her appearance that I just froze."

"But, she did do as you directed; she reacted with total subservience?"

"Yes, she just turned around and headed back upstairs to her room."

"Well, I think that's where we should go this very second."

"You seem concerned, Carter. Okay, let's go. I'll introduce you as Dr. Simpson."

Together, we ascended the staircase and knocked on Madelaine's door. Not surprisingly, she did not answer. I knocked again and announced that I needed for her to open the door; that she had a visitor. Still no answer. The door was not locked, so we entered. to find Madelaine preparing to jump from the open window. She had one foot on a chair, the other on the sill. She clung to the curtain for leverage. She was stark naked and seemed to wear her nudity without embarrassment, without a sense of self. Early morning sun cast a shimmering, pale light across her body, covering her with a ghostly pall. We ran to the window and grabbed her by the arms, pulling her back into the room.

"Wait, Madelaine!! Stop!!"

With formidable strength she tried to wrestle free from our grasp, a look of abhorrence on her face, defiance in her eyes. I ran to the bathroom and grabbed Donna's bathrobe, while Carter wrestled with Madelaine; she struggled, resisting our attempts to cover her up.

"Put it on backwards, Jimmy, and tie it to the back of the chair". He was thinking straight jacket, I knew. He then unfastened his pant belt and strapped it around Madelaine's waist, buckling it to the chair, as well. It took several minutes for us to subdue this fiercely agitated woman; finally, her thrashing stopped, and she slumped, chin down, in her chair.

"Now what?" I wheezed.

Carter's chest was still heaving, as he sat down on Madelaine's bed and brushed aside damp strands of hair from his perspiring forehead.

"This was, I believe, an acute manic episode, Jimmy. We need to get her admitted to a psychiatric hospital before she harms herself, or someone else."

"She wouldn't harm anyone else," I protested, "but, you're right; she needs professional intervention. Can you make that happen?" I was hoping that Donna would return home quickly from taking Paul to Play and Learn. However convinced I thought I was about Madelaine's not harming anyone else, I could not deny my concern for Paul's exposure to her volatile behavior. I scolded myself for not thinking about that before I brought her to our home. I wanted to help Madelaine; that was my major focus; I just didn't know the extreme odds that we would face trying to accomplish that.

Carter turned to face Madelaine. He cleared his throat and spoke directly to her. I had no way of telling whether she could hear or understand what he was about to say.

"Madelaine, my name is Dr. Carter Simpson. We don't know each other, but I want to be your friend. Will you let me be your friend and help you?"

Madelaine, unresponsive for several seconds, showed no signs of comprehension. Then, in a voice rising from the depths of a vast ocean of sorrow, she lifted her head and whispered:

"Mama."

Carter looked at me, as if to remind me of what he had prophesied at Paul's party. My jaw dropped in bewilderment.

"That's good, Madelaine," Carter said gently. "We will bring your mom to you. But, first, you'll have to agree to being admitted to a facility where they can help you. There are medications out there that are designed for that purpose. Will you agree to this plan?"

To my amazement, Madelaine reached out for my hand and tearfully replied, "Jimmy, help me. Promise?"

I squeezed her hand and moved in closer, so that I could look her directly in the eyes; she did not flinch. "I promise you," I whispered.

At that dramatic moment, I became aware of Donna, standing in the doorway of the bedroom. She had been standing there, listening to this incredible conversation. Seeing her bathrobe wrapped around Madelaine, she understood that something transformative had occurred; she covered her mouth with her hand, stifling a sob.

Carter left the room to call the hospital, using his considerable influence to expedite Madelaine's admittance. I held onto Madelaine's hand while Donna collected some clothing for her to wear. What we all seemed to understand was that time was of the essence; that given Madelaine's mood swings and lapses into withdrawal, we had to keep her compliant and work quickly to have her admitted.

Carter returned, rubbing his hands together. "It's all set; we can leave now. Are you ready, Madelaine?"

We loosened the bathrobe tie and the belt. She stood, clutching the robe to her body. Carter and I left the room so that Donna could help her dress and gather some toiletries into a travel bag. Within twenty minutes, we piled into our cars and set out on our journey for justice. Though reticent, Madelaine was preparing for her own journey, one that would alter her life forever.

Chapter 31

After Marty left them, Fiona and Luella began to chat. Luella described what it was like being married to Edgar and the shock of discovering what he had been doing to their daughter. She told about having to endure the indignities of prison life, fearful of fully falling asleep, terrified that she would be assaulted. She tearfully related how crushed she had felt by her censure in the neighborhood; how no one—not her brother, not her sister-in-law, and most of all, not Madelaine—would testify on her behalf. But, of course, she stopped short of explaining the real reason for what she did; it was a choice she had made and would have to live with. She had been found guilty in the court of public opinion, well before she could plead temporary insanity in a court of law.

Fiona listened intently as Luella detailed her life at her brother's home in Chelsea and how he kept her as imprisoned as she had been before. She was not paid for her work at his store, did not have a driver's license, and she had no way to communicate her servitude in the back-storage room of his grocery.

"So, how did you escape? How was Marty able to get you here?

Luella related the story, all the while stroking the soft, white fur of the cat who indulgently lay in her lap, purring.

Marty returned from a trip to the local market with bags of groceries. He carried them to the kitchen and began to stock Fiona's refrigerator. When finished, he closed its door and rolled up the sleeves of his crisp white shirt.

"This should hold you girls for a while. Luella, stay low until I work out the details for what'll happen next."

Both women asked in unison, "Where are you going?"

"I have to see a man about a horse," he said, grimly.

"Luella, do you know anything about your brother's *other* business?"

Haltingly, she recounted the conversation she overheard regarding delivery or exchange of what she assumed were drugs. "So many creeps coming around late at night. Dwayne was always high on something, and he liked to flash a lot of bills. I never saw any transactions, though. Dwayne was always careful."

"Do you have any idea why he'd keep you 'locked up,' so to speak, and keep watch on James Price's house?"

"I'm guessing, but it might be because of the article he wrote about me. Dwayne wants to keep me out of sight so that no one will come around 'snooping' and asking questions about me. He hates reporters; Sorry, Fiona. James is a threat to his other business, I guess."

"Well, we'll see about that. I told him I'd be back for the "pepperoni."

"But, Dwayne doesn't sell pepperoni," Luella naively asserted.

"Oh, but he does; trust me." Marty hugged both women before leaving. "Lock your door, Fiona. Keep a low profile."

"Marty, be careful." Fiona cautioned.

"Who me? Careful?" He closed the door behind him, grinning.

Chapter 32

a fter showering and shaving, Dwayne returned to the kitchen and sat down on a Colonial-style, maple ladder-back chair. The table, though well-crafted and once costly, was pock-marked and scarred from Dwayne's numerous outbursts. He had jackknifed and gouged the table with any sharp object within his reach. The butt end of his handgun worked best for making his point clear and unmistakable.

Penny served him a plate of scrambled eggs, several rashers of bacon, and buttered toast; then she poured him a mug of coffee; he preferred it black.

Inspecting his plate, he grumbled, "Where's the Tabasco sauce?"

Penny rose wordlessly and removed the sauce from the fridge, then placed it front of him. Dousing his eggs, he asked, "Cat got your tongue?"

Penny remained silent.

"Well, see, here's the story: my no-good bitch sister won't be workin' the back room anymore, so you'll be taking over for her. Lots of deliveries comin' in today." He bit off half of a bacon rasher and chewed with his mouth open.

"But, I've got a haircut appointment this morning," Penny protested.

"So, you'll cancel it, goddamit! Didn't you learn nothin' last night about talkin' back to me?"

Penny glared at Dwayne but said nothing more.

"Sit your ass down and keep me company while I eat. You not eatin'?"

"Not hungry," Penny answered.

"Don't tell me you're on one of them crazy diets again. Ha! You ain't got the will-power to stay on one. Always complainin' that you're fat, never losing an ounce." Dwayne was enjoying his power breakfast. "Warm up my coffee," he ordered.

Penny obeyed with shaking hands, overfilling his mug. Quickly, she ripped off a few sheets of paper towel and began to sop up the puddle in front of Dwayne. He tilted his chair onto its hind legs and smirked. "Can't even pour a man a cup of coffee. Clumsy c..." He stopped short of this last blasphemy, rose from his chair, then slapped Penny on her backside. "Be in the storage room by seven."

After Dwayne left the kitchen, Penny removed the mug she had just filled and poured his coffee down the drain. Her forearms began to prickle with blotches of hives, a reaction to the anxiety from which there was no escape.

∞ ∞ ∞

The deliveries arrived on time with a truckload of dairy products and fresh eggs, breads and baked goods, fruits and vegetables. Penny checked in all the pallets, marking each one off the bill of lading.

179

"Hey, where's the gal with the long puss? Never smiles or jokes with us."

"Oh, she's gone on an errand, Pete. Not one for small talk." She hoped to quash further inquiry. While emptying one of the crates, she found six bags filled with white powder.

"What's this, Pete?" she asked, attempting to extricate the bags.

"Oh, just a little extra pepperoni for Dwayne, a gift from Rocco."

"But Dwayne don't sell meat. I'm confused."

Pete smiled broadly, exposing nicotine-stained and missing teeth. Removing his Boston Red Sox cap and mopping his sweaty forehead with a shirtsleeve, he advised, "Just leave 'em in the box, then. Dwayne will know what to do with 'em. Oh, and tell him that tomorrow's collection day."

"Is there a bill?"

"Nah, he knows what he owes us." Pete replaced his cap and hustled down the wooden stairway to his rig. "Tell that Louse girl I think she's mighty fine!" Laughing, he jumped into the truck's cab, tipped his hat, and backed out of the dirt driveway.

Dwayne entered, as Penny resumed stocking the shelves. Penny pointed to the box containing the six white bags. "Pete says this is a gift to you from Rocco. He said that tomorrow is collection day." Grinning, Dwayne picked up the bags to examine them. "What are they? Pete says pepperoni. That don't look like pepperoni."

Dwayne burst out laughing. "Yeah," he answered between guffaws, "they're a very special kind of pepperoni." He left, laughing so hard he had to press a stitch in his side.

Dwayne waited all day for Marty's arrival, nervously checking his watch, peering out the front windows of his shop. Several customers came and went, each making large purchases and leaving money in the collection jar for the sick child. He dusted and polished the shelves, cleaned the glass doors of the coolers, dusted the necks of soda and water bottles. By four o'clock, he was giving up hope that his "customer" would appear. It was mid-Fall and the days were getting shorter; he didn't like keeping the store open past six o'clock and he questioned whether the guy was going to show up. *Maybe he got scared off by what he saw happen with Luella*, he thought. *What if this guy is a cop?* Dwayne was not used to being the one sweating it out; usually, it was a "client" who owed him money and feared for his kneecaps.

At five thirty, Marty parked his Mini-Cooper around the corner, a few blocks from the store. Just as Dwayne was closing the shades and preparing to turn off the lights, the chimes over the front door announced a visitor. Marty strode through the entryway with the ease and calm of a seasoned con-man. "Glad I could catch you before you closed shop. Now, wasn't today just a lovely day?"

Caught off-guard by Marty's blasé demeanor, Dwayne stiffened. "Yeah, beautiful day. You come for more cheese for your wife?"

"Ah, no, my friend; it's for my mother, bless her heart. She loved the mozzarella and can't wait for the pepperoni I promised to bring her."

Dwayne was feeling uneasy about this smooth talker; still, he couldn't help but admire his nonchalance. He'd done business with people up and down the social ladder, including lawyers, doctors, and politicians. This guy was no ordinary junkie; he was measured and cautious—traits Dwayne sorely lacked.

"Okay, then, pal... um, Randy is it? I keep the pepperoni in the back room—climate controlled, you might say."

"It's Rudy; lead the way."

Dwayne checked to see if the front door was locked, then pulled the shades closed, and turned out the overhead lights. He stole a furtive look out the front window to make sure there was nobody else on the street. "Follow me," he instructed, leading Marty down a darkened hallway. He unbolted the door that opened into the storage room. "I keep it bolted, see, to keep the rats out."

By "rats," Marty understood the reference to addicts.

They entered the back room and Dwayne switched on a single hanging lightbulb. He opened a box containing the white, powder-like substance and handed one package to Marty, who took it with exaggerated appreciation. "Mind if I have a taste?" he winked.

"Nothin' but pure stuff, I assure you," Dwayne replied, hands tucked into the back pockets of his jeans. He leaned against the doorframe, as Marty carefully opened one plastic bag, wet his forefinger, and lightly dipped it into the bag. Touching his finger to his tongue, he felt numbness and was convinced that he had the real deal.

"You're an honest man, my friend. Gonna have some real good pizza tonight! So, how much?"

"Eight "eight balls" or one ounce will cost you twelve hundred. Take what you want; it won't go to waste, believe me. There's more where that came from."

Marty resealed the bag. "Can you hold this for me while I get my wallet out?"

"Sure. You always carry that much cash around with you?" Dwayne asked, surprised to see Marty's wallet bulging with large denomination bills. The outer bills were counterfeit.

"Only when I'm in the mood for Mom's pizza—which is most of the time!"

They both laughed, as Marty paid him. "You got something I can put this in?"

Dwayne slapped Marty on the back and then fished out a brown paper bag from a drawer. He slipped the cocaine into the bag, folded down the open flap, and handed it to Marty. "Enjoy your dinner, pal. Come back when Mom needs more."

He showed Marty out the back door of the storage room. Walking several blocks away, past the black Cadillac, Marty whistled softly. *"I'm gonna' get you yet, bastard,"* he thought.

Chapter 33

Carter worked swiftly and with authority, as he got Madelaine processed and admitted to the psychiatric hospital in Belmont. He insisted on taking over the management of her care, thus giving Donna and me a chance to catch our breaths. When we left her, Madelaine was subdued and melancholy, but Carter assured us that showing emotion was a good sign. We waved good-bye and I winked at her; she did not reciprocate.

"Can't thank you enough, Carter," I said, thinking that I might kiss his hand, as if it wore the Pope's ring.

"This is just the beginning," he cautioned, "there's a long road to haul for all of you; but, she's in the right place, thank God." Donna hugged him and asked that he give our love to Laura.

"You bet," he replied, opening the car door to his Mercedes and settling into the driver's seat. "Get some sleep, you two."

He shifted into reverse, straightened, and drove away. Holding hands, Donna and I returned to our car and drove home in silent exhaustion. We picked Paul up at Play and Learn, drove to our favorite Italian restaurant, Da Lorenzo's, and ate until we could eat no more.

"Are we celebrating, Dad?" Paul wanted to know.

"Yes, son," I sighed. "I guess you could call it that."

"Is that lady still in our house?"

"No, she's in a better place right now."

"Good. I was scared of her." Having been relieved of his concerns, he reached for the largest piece of pizza on the tray.

Fully sated, we drove home. Paul played a game on his youth iPad; we just enjoyed the quiet and relaxed.

$$\infty \quad \infty \quad \infty$$

On Monday, Fiona called us into her office. As soon as we had shut the door behind us, she began a non-stop, detailed account of what had transpired with Luella. She reminded us that she had no intention of harboring her for an indefinite amount of time; she did qualify her conditions, though. She would uphold her part in the arrangement she had made with Marty and not insist on Luella's immediate leaving; and she confessed that having her around wasn't such a bad thing, that she was actually enjoying her company. "I bought her a few changes of clothes to tide her over. And, don't raise those eyebrows, James; I'm a woman and I can change my mind." We were witnessing a side of Fiona we'd not seen before.

"In all seriousness, what do you expect will happen? Has Marty been back to your place?" Donna couldn't douse her curiosity.

"No, but he's called a few times. He said that he was very grateful that I am being "flexible" and asked for just a little more time."

"How is Luella getting on? I mean, have you spoken to her about Madelaine?"

"I wasn't prepared to go there just yet. We're going to need her cooperation. By the way, does she know about the pregnancy? If not, who's going to tell her?" Fiona, for the first time, was not taking the lead. I think she was as fearful as we were to broach that subject with Luella; but, we all knew that it had to be done. It looked like it was going to fall to me and I needed to first work it out in my own mind before telling Luella.

Then, it was our turn to fill Fiona in on our momentous night and day with Madelaine.

"Well, thank Heavens she's safe. How horrible, James. Poor girl."

After work, we scooped Paul up at P and L, ran some errands at the Galleria, and arrived home by eight o'clock. The house was dark, as we had not thought to engage the light timer. Paul and Donna hung back until I could switch on the lights, then they followed tentatively behind me.

"Nothing to be frightened of, Paul. Put your lunch box on the kitchen table and go on upstairs to get ready for story time."

I kicked off my sneakers, grabbed a beer from the fridge, and walked into the living room. Donna had preceded me, turning on more lights. I wondered why I hadn't heard nor seen her. As I entered the room, Donna was standing with her hand over her mouth; pale and shaking, she tried to shield Paul with her own body.

"Welcome home, guys. Helped me self to a beer." An unkempt man was sitting on our sofa, his long legs stretched out before him, holding a can of Coor's. A 9 mm Glock pistol lay on the sofa by his right knee. His eyes were glassy; he appeared to be stoned. His riding boots were planted in our carpet, heel down.

"Who are you?" I demanded, sounding more self-confident than I felt. "How did you get into our house?"

"I'll ask the questions here, bud. Patting his gun, he said, "Sit down, why don't ya'? You, ma'am, leave your cell phone on this here table and get on upstairs with the kid. And, don't do nothin' stupid like calling the police. Your hubby here will get a bullet in the belly before they can get here." Dwayne was gently patting the pistol as he spoke.

Donna stumbled up the stairs, terrified for Paul's safety. I did as instructed; my shaking knees were grateful. He finished the last of his beer and crushed the can in one hand. If this act was meant to intimidate me, it was succeeding.

Leaning forward, his alcohol breath fouling the space between us, he calmly asked, "Where is she?"

Where is who?" I asked, bewildered.

"You know who I mean, Mr. Reporter Man. Luella, my sister. Luella. She's run away, and I mean ta' catch her. You wrote that damned article about her, remember?"

"I have no idea where your sister is. Why would she be here?"

"Because she ain't got no friends—just me who took her in after jail. This is the thanks I get. We were getting' ready to go down to the cops and tell them we don't know nothin' about her daughter's bein' missing. Next thing I know, poof! She's gone. Now, I reckon she's hidin' out here, thinkin' no one's gonna' look for her at your place."

"Look, whatever your name is, I have no idea what you're talking about. I knew your sister a long time ago."

"Name's Dwayne, Dwayne Ricci. And, I don't play games. Hear me? I read that piece in the paper you wrote about having information 'bout her. Well, I'm tellin' you to mind yer own business, see? She lives with me and that's MY business. So, keep yer fuckin' nose out of it!"

"Is that why you've been stalking me in your big, black car? If that's why, then you're wasting your time, Mr. Ricci. I have no intention of invading your privacy. You've broken into my home and invaded mine; that's a felony and I could have you arrested. I suggest you leave quietly, and we'll forget the whole thing." I was grasping at straws, hoping, in his inebriated state, he'd take me up on my offer.

He rose unsteadily, swayed, and leaned on the sofa arm for support. Slurring his words, he said, "If I find out you're lyin', I'll be back." He tucked the firearm into the waistband of his jeans.

"That's a threat, Mr. Ricci; I'll pretend I didn't hear it."

"Pretend all ya' want, smart guy; as I said, I don't play games."

He stumbled out the front door, bumping into furniture and tipping over a lamp on his way. Menacingly, he called over his shoulder, "Don't do nothin' stupid,"

As I closed and bolted the door, I could hear the roar of his motorcycle as he took off at full throttle. I stood stunned and shaken, wondering *how the hell did he get in here?*

When she heard the door close, Donna came downstairs, pale and shaken to her core. She held out a remote phone to me. "Call the police, Jimmy. That man has threatened us again; I for one believe he'll be back. Paul is very upset and scared. We can't let him get away with this."

"He'll kill us, Donna; that much I'm sure of. I'm going to call Marty. I'll go by what he thinks."

Donna wrapped her arms around my neck and I held her tightly. "Jimmy," she cried, "I'm so scared. What does all this mean?"

"I don't think he wants to harm us; he wants to intimidate us, so we'll abandon our plans."

"Still," Donna persisted, "he was armed and threatening. How can we let him get away with that?"

"Let me make that call to Marty." We disengaged, but she clung to my arm as I dialed.

I had to leave voicemail. I was to the point. "Marty," I croaked, "help!!"

As we waited for a return call, I poured each of us a glass of bourbon. If I had a straw handy, I would have sipped straight from the bottle. Our brittle nerves began to settle slightly, but we both worried about what was coming next. I could almost read Donna's mind; she was having second thoughts about our involvement with Luella Frazier and her afflicted daughter. I was having second and third thoughts, ruing the day I read about and saw the images of Luella's release from prison. We were in way over our heads, not knowing how deep the water could be. My family had suddenly become victims, accessories to a crime we had not committed. I should have kept my big mouth shut, not let anyone, including my wife, talk me into—let's face it—a conscience-strapped decision. I had not thought about seeking glory; but, I guess, I was hoping for a tiny scrap of gratitude. Instead, I let Fiona and Donna encourage my so-called "confession" about withholding what I had seen. Had I really done that? Did I really *know* what lay beneath that tiny mound outside the playing field? No one was going to thank me. I was not going to be a hero. If Luella didn't want the world to know what she knew about her husband's dirty deeds, who was I to challenge her?

Throughout my soul-searching, I lost track of time. The ringing of my phone brought me back into the moment.

"Hello, Marty."

"Hey, kid. Got your S.O.S. What's going on?"

I related the events of the night, as he listened intently. "We're scared to death," I admitted, "he said he'd be back."

"Look, Jimmy. I know this bad actor. He's mean and ornery. Crafty son-of-a- bitch."

"So, you've had dealings with him?"

"Yes, dealings. He's a drug dealer who just happened to be involved in my father's murder. What I think you and Donna should do is... nothing. Give me time to get this guy behind bars. In the meantime, go about your business, as usual. And, stay away from Luella. You've come this far with Madelaine, now let the professionals do their job... me included. Fiona has been more than cooperative, but Luella can't stay on with her forever. At some point, we're going to have to inform her about Madelaine's hospitalization."

"She whispered 'Mama' to me, meaning, I think, that she wants her mother to come. I promised her that we would make that happen."

"Let the doctors do their thing, Jimmy. They'll let you know when the time is right."

Sighing, I agreed. "All right. We'll do what you say. And, Marty, um, be careful. He packs a Glock."

"Exactly what I'm hoping to recover. It belonged to my dad."

Chapter 34

*P*ropped up in bed by several pink satin pillows, Penny flipped through fashion and pop-culture magazines. She liked reading about movie stars and television celebrities, fantasizing what it must be like to live in their glamorous world: vacationing on hideaway islands, cavorting on private yachts. Her real world was oceans away from that of the rich and famous, galaxies apart from what she had once believed would be hers. She remembered that her mother had once boasted that she had met Marilyn Monroe and James Dean; of having attended lavish Hollywood parties where she hobnobbed with actors and politicians. "Oh, Penny," she'd enthuse, "you should have seen me, all dressed *up to the nines* in sequined gowns, dripping with expensive jewelry." Her sexual prowess with well-known mobsters bought her entrée to a society perversely rich and equally sordid. Mrs. Callahan, better known as Kitty, sported a thick mane of flaming red hair that accentuated her beauty; her exceptional body was the envy of sophisticated socialites who tried, in vain, to emulate her. It was through her connections on both sides of the law that she was introduced to Dwayne Ricci, son of a powerful "don."

"He's a great catch, Sweetie, in with all the big wigs and important people. By "important" she meant influential and privileged, the movers and shakers who ruled the roost, with destiny at their command. "He'll buy you things you never dreamed of having," she avowed. "He'll light your cigarettes like a gentleman and light your fire like an Italian stallion!" She laughed uproariously at her own joke, then affectionately slapped Penny on her backside. "Just don't get knocked up like me before he says, "I do."

It was of no consequence that Dwayne never finished high school; or, that he had had several run-ins with the police. According to her mother, Dwayne had been "mistakenly identified" as having been involved in the murder of a police Chief. And, to make it clear, she told Penny she was a bastard child with few, if any, choices.

Penny dated Dwayne for six months, and true to her mother's predictions, he lavished all manner of gifts, including a spectacular diamond engagement ring. Never without a wallet bulging with money, he'd take her to fancy restaurants, gala parties, and once, to the Isle of Capri. She was two months pregnant with his child when planning their wedding. "Just a minor inconvenience," his father declared, "we'll just get it taken care of."

Penny agreed to the abortion, knowing that having a child would crimp her style and interfere with her designs on all the things her mother had promised. She and Dwayne were married by a Justice of the Peace and soon ensconced in a magnificent house, just north of Boston, with a swimming pool and maid service.

Life was as good as her mother had predicted, at least for the first two years. She never knew, nor did she ask where Dwayne went or what he did to afford such luxuries; she accepted her good fortune without reservation. When he started coming home later and later at night, reeking of alcohol, and, she could tell, of sex, she knew she'd have to abide by his behavior. Her mother had told her she'd have to pay a price for a lifestyle she never would have had. When Dwayne started to physically abuse her, Mother advised a certain brand of makeup to conceal the bruises and ice packs for her black eyes.

Evoking these painful memories, Penny leaned her head back against the pillows and closed her eyes. Tears trickled down her cheeks, as she recalled Luella's beating. She harbored no ill-will towards her mother, now deceased from emphysema. Silently, she thanked her for the best thing she had taught her daughter: how to hold and fire a handgun.

Chapter 35

For the next two weeks, Donna and I settled back into a more comfortable routine. Our adrenalin levels returned to normal; in fact, we were able to take Paul and one of his friends to a movie, where we shared a large bucket of buttered popcorn. We felt uneasy about leaving him at home with Adriana. We made sure to set some of our indoor lights to come on at dusk and we kept the burglar alarm armed at all times. Paul was having bad dreams, crying out to us in the middle of the night, perspiring and trembling. He worried that someone was going to hurt him, or us. So, it was a relief to see him laughing again and enjoying a Shrek movie with his friend, Joey. As we sat relaxed and comfortable in our theater seats, my cell phone vibrated in the side pocket of my jacket. I had turned the ringer off, setting it to vibrate; so as not to disturb others in the audience. I told Donna that I was going to the men's room. Apologizing, I climbed over ten pairs of little and big feet and headed for the theater lobby. It was noisy, and the snack bar was bustling with activity. I stepped into the ante-foyer. Checking my phone, I saw that I had just missed a call from Carter Simpson. He left voicemail, asking me to return his call whenever convenient; he wanted to bring me up to date on Madelaine's progress. He answered my return call immediately.

"Carter, it's me. Everything okay?"

"I'm sorry if I disturbed you, Jimmy. I'm at the hospital and just finished a consultation with the doctors and nurses attending Madelaine. They've been working hard to make some inroads with her; but, she's gone back inside herself again, not communicating, acting out."

"You mean like how she was at my house?" I was not expecting this disappointing news.

"More aggressive, Jimmy. Throwing things, spewing obscenities, crashing her dinner plates onto the floor. Unfortunately, she's required heavy doses of medication."

"Why do you suppose, Carter? Have you reached a consensus on her diagnosis?"

"Well, it could be severe PTSD, or borderline personality disorder; perhaps, a combination of both. In any case, we may need to consider a more rigorous approach." He stopped, coughed, and let me ask the obvious question.

"By rigorous, you mean...?" I didn't want to put words into his mouth; he was the doctor.

"It's still too early to suggest electric shock therapy; but, we'll have to keep it in mind."

"Did something trigger this behavior? It sounds like she's pretty upset about something."

"That's what we're trying to find out. We'll keep working on it. Just wanted to bring you up to snuff. Sorry."

"No need to apologize. I know she's in good hands with you. Thanks for the update. And, Carter, there is another issue here. Madelaine does not have health insurance of any kind, no disability or unemployment money."

"I know where you're going with this, but don't. We'll worry about that later."

"I just don't know how to thank you, Carter."

"Then, don't. Give my best to Donna. Talk soon."

He hung up before I could respond. Perhaps, his open-heartedness embarrassed him. I made a mental note to research the symptoms of borderline personality disorder that night. I returned to my seat, apologizing again for disturbing the people in our row, sat down, and pretended that all was fine. Donna sensed that the opposite was true, but, for Paul's sake, she just patted my hand. "We'll talk later," she whispered.

I admit that I do not remember the rest of the movie; my mind was preoccupied with what Carter shared with me. I was also anxious to return home and do some research. Could it be that Madelaine was beyond our attempts to "rescue" her? Were our motives merely pie-in-the-sky pipe dreams? The only positive I could take away from this situation was that she was off the streets and in a safe place. It occurred to me that Madelaine may have to spend the rest of her life institutionalized, however much she would hate it.

After the lights came back on and we exited the theater, Paul asked if we could go out for an early dinner at Pizzeria Uno. As much as I wanted to get home, I relented. Paul was having a great day and I didn't want to deprive him of this fun. When we arrived at the restaurant, it was crowded, and we had to wait. While Paul and Joey discussed what they liked best about the movie, Donna leaned in toward me and asked if I could share my conversation with Carter.

"Not here, Honey. Later, for sure. I've got some pressing reading to do tonight."

Bursting with curiosity, she frowned. "Only one story book tonight. Okay?"

"Gottcha,"

After dinner, we drove Joey to his home about two blocks away from ours; his mother came out to the car to thank us and proposed another movie date for the boys which she would chaperone. "Sounds like a great plan," Donna said. We returned home to get Paul ready for bed.

"I'll do the honors tonight, Jimmy. You go ahead and do your research."

"Thanks, Honey. Join me afterward."

I hurried to my computer and Googled "Borderline Personality Disorder." I also looked up "Post Traumatic Stress Disorder." Madelaine's symptoms matched those in an article by the Mayo Clinic: *self- emotional instability, antisocial behavior, feelings of worthlessness, compulsive behavior, hostility, social isolation, anger, guilt, depression, distorted image, or thoughts of suicide.* Wow, I thought, sounds right. I also read that *BPD often occurs with other mental illnesses, making it harder to diagnose and treat.* I then read further about "Post Traumatic Stress Disorder." These were the symptoms I found: *agitation, hostility, social isolation, flashback, mistrust, emotional detachment or unwanted thoughts. It's described as a condition triggered by a terrifying event—either experiencing it or witnessing it.* The Mayo Clinic article went on to describe *difficulty experiencing positive emotions, feeling emotionally numb,* and others, as well. I understood why Carter would need more time to diagnose Madelaine's illness. The encouraging news was that both conditions appeared treatable over time.

Donna joined me and leaned over my shoulder to read the descriptions on my computer screen. She stepped back and sat down on the carpet next to my chair. Rubbing her chin, she rationalized, "It's clear that we've saved Madelaine's life. We can only hope that she'll recover."

"I agree; but what do we tell Luella? And, do you think I should tell her about Madelaine's pregnancy?"

"I'm not sure," Donna pondered, "she should at least know where her daughter is and why—although the why is pretty evident."

"Okay. Let's set up a time with Fiona when we can stop by her place to talk with Luella. This isn't going to be pretty."

"We can ask her tomorrow at work; she'll be able to talk more freely if Luella can't hear her."

"Right. I'll be up in a minute; just want to think about revising my article. I'm sure people are wondering what's become of my investigation."

"Okay. Maybe I'll read a bit, distract myself enough to make me sleepy."

Donna pecked me on the cheek and left for our bedroom; I revisited my article, reread it, then leaned back in my chair to think. Within ten minutes I was in a deep sleep having a sweet, serene dream about my mother. In it, I was a little boy, snuggled up next to her on our worn living room sofa; we were having hot chocolate together. She was stroking my hair, telling me how much she loved me and how she envisioned great things for my future. "Jimmy," she said, "always do the right thing, no matter what people throw in your path." Years ago, she had done the "right thing" by defending Madelaine in the school yard. I would do the "right thing" now. I awoke to Donna's gentle nudge on my shoulder.

"Come to bed, Jimmy. Tomorrow's another day."

Chapter 36

*H*aving delivered the bags of cocaine to police headquarters where they were secured and labeled as "evidence," Marty decided to pay a visit to Dwayne's store. Slipping his old police revolver into the back waistband of his pants and donning a leather jacket for cover, he set out on his mission. Late autumn afternoon sunshine dappled the changing colors of the oak and maple trees along his route to Chelsea. He rued that this was going to be a waste of a beautiful day, given what he was about to do. He selected a CD of classical music that would soothe his jumpiness. His father, a man exposed daily to the vulgarities and dissonance of his job, sought inspiration from the three B's: Bach, Brahms, and Beethoven. He believed that there was a higher nature to man, one that would elevate rather than debase him. He taught his son to seek out the beauty and genius from these masters of men's souls. Today, Marty chose the Violin Concerto in D major by Brahms; it brought him to greater heights, despite what he was about to do. As he rounded the corner and parked his car within walking distance to Dwayne's shop, he reluctantly turned off the music and headed for the entry. It was almost closing time and Dwayne was straightening items on the shelves and preparing to lock up. There were no customers in the shop. The overhead chimes announced his entry, and Dwayne looked up in surprise.

"Hey, man. Back so soon?"

Marty took a few steps closer to Dwayne and looked him in the eyes. He was calm, yet direct.

"Your stuff's no good. In fact, it's so cut no one wanted it. You cheated me, pal and I want my money back."

"No way, Jose. That stuff is pure. Who the hell are you, anyway?"

Marty had anticipated the outrage; in fact, his intent was to create it.

"You must think me some kind of goat, my friend. Well, when my 'associates' tell me it's no good, it's no good."

"You're pushin' me, mister, pushin' too far. Nobody comes here and calls me a liar." Dwayne's face had turned scarlet; his upper lip curled into a sneer. Get outta' here while you still can walk, or I'll mop the floor with your ugly face."

Marty sidled in closer, his hands in the side pockets of his black jeans. "You know, punk, I've been waiting for this moment for a long time."

"Oh, yeah? For what?" Sensing Marty's deliberate confrontation, he turned to the doorway and yelled, "Penny, get my Glock outta' the bedroom. Now!!!" He had just revealed that he was unarmed.

"Do you think, in that little pea-sized, warped brain of yours, that you got away with killing a police Chief?"

"What's that got to do with you? Penny!!"

"What I'm getting at, pal, is that you were involved in my father's murder. You ambushed him outside a floral shop, shot him in the head, and left him to die with the dozen white roses he had bought for my mom. My mom hates your mozzarella."

"You can't pin that on me. You're bluffin'! Who are you, anyways?"

"I told you, dimwit, I'm that man's son. I'm turning you in to the authorities for pushing drugs."

Dwayne, begging for time, laughed out loud. "You got nothin' on me; besides, I know all the right people. They'll laugh you out of the station."

He kept looking at the doorway, expecting Penny to appear.

"On the contrary," Marty said, "I've got you nailed for pushing drugs; your fingerprints are all over that bag of "pepperoni" you were so kind to give me."

Dwayne was panicking, desperately eyeing the doorway, shifting his focus from there to Marty who inched closer and closer, until their noses were just inches apart. Suddenly, Dwayne lunged for Marty's throat, pressing hard against his windpipe with both thumbs, his fingers digging into the sides of his neck. Trying to fend off the attack, Marty kicked Dwayne in the groin; he flinched but did not loosen his grip. Marty tried to reach behind him for his revolver, but he could not reach it. Barely able to breathe, he dropped to his knees. Dwayne increased the pressure until there was little resistance from Marty. He then spotted the gun tucked into the waistband of Marty's pants. Crazed, he released one hand from Marty's neck, grabbed the gun and cocked it. Marty caught his breath, but slumped onto the floor, choking. Dwayne stood over his prostrate figure and pressed the gun barrel into Marty's right temple.

"Thought you had me, huh, asshole. Thought you could outsmart ol' Dwayne here. Ha! So, now I'm gonna have to kill ya'. You're a cop, right? Well, you already know what I think of cops." Dwayne spit on the floor.

As Dwayne was about to pull the trigger, a shot rang out from the doorway. The bullet found its mark between Dwayne's snakelike eyes that, in an instant of disbelief, recognized the shooter. Penny's arm hung by her side; in her hand was Chief O'Brien's 9mm Glock.

Marty rose unsteadily, unsure if Penny intended to shoot him, too. He stepped over Dwayne's exsanguinating body, his punctured head resting in a pool of sticky blood. Gently, he removed the gun from Penny's hand, carefully wrapping it in his shirttail. Penny stood in dazed silence; not a tear glistened in her eyes.

"You saved my life," Marty spoke hoarsely. "I'll see to it that the charge against you will be justifiable homicide. But, you'll have to come downtown with me when the police and the medical examiner get here."

Penny nodded that she understood. Marty made the call to headquarters, and both of them waited, sitting on the lid of the cooler where Dwayne had kept the mozzarella.

Chapter 37

*M*onday morning served up a platter of new issues. Fiona had agreed to meet with us to work out a plan for a visit with Luella. She informed us that, despite the awkwardness of the situation, day-to-day living with Luella had been going well, and, that she rather enjoyed coming home after work to a well-prepared, hot meal and a spotless apartment. The two women, having nothing in common, seemed to have bonded. For the first time in years, Luella was beginning to trust. Fiona was looking into securing a job for her as a seamstress in an upscale bridal atelier in Boston. "I think she's ready to venture out," she declared. "She knows a lot about stitching and sewing." Fiona seemed pleased with herself for suggesting this idea to Luella.

"There is some business that we still have to get through," I told her about our hope to visit with Luella and to bring her up to date vis-à-vis Madelaine's diagnosis. "We think it would help Luella to know that Madelaine is being treated for a serious illness; and, that there is hope."

"Yes, of course, James; she has a right to know." Examining her manicured fingertips, she reflected; her mood darkened, and she sighed. "Luella is a strong woman," she stated, "but, there has been a new fly in the ointment."

Donna and I exchanged glances, wondering what new hurdles we'd have to jump over.

Fiona cleared her throat, approached the large windows that overlooked the gardens below. The flowers that had been artistically planted there in the spring had looked like an embroidery in silk from above. With the first frost of the season, however, they now lay exhausted, their fine threads awaiting disposal.

"I got a call from Marty this morning," she began, vigorously rubbing her forearms for the courage to proceed. "He called from police headquarters where he had spent the night."

Donna looked at me with a mixture of concern and a hint of irritation. Her blue eyes scanned my face for reaction; but, I remained inscrutable. "Go on, please, Fiona," she urged.

Turning from the window to face us, she said, "Marty's been on Dwayne Ricci's case for a while now, trying to get his illegal business shut down, while following his every move to your home. Dwayne tried to kill him last night; his wife, Penny, shot him as he was about to pull the trigger. He won't be bothering you two anymore, or pushing drugs; but, he is—was—Luella's brother. We'll have to tell her as soon as possible."

"There's no love lost there," I commented.

"Perhaps not. It was Marty who rescued her and brought her here. I suppose she'll have a great deal of empathy for Penny."

"Marty almost got himself killed. How horrible." Donna had curled into a ball on her seat and tucked her legs under her.

"One ironic takeaway is that Dwayne wanted to kill him with his own father's gun. Luckily, Penny got to it first."

After a few moments of reflection, Fiona sat down at her desk, opened the middle drawer, and extracted a manila envelope, and slid it across to us. Donna and I hunched together to inspect the contents and found enlarged pictures of Penny, semi-exposed, sunbathing on Revere Beach. There was another photo of the black Cadillac Dwayne had used to intimidate us.

"Marty wanted me to hold on to these, thinking that if anything untoward happened to him, these pictures would serve as corroborative evidence that the car belongs to the Ricci's."

"So, what do you do with them now?" I asked, rather naively.

"My guess is nothing at the moment. Penny saved his life by shooting someone who was about to kill him. Legally, that is considered justifiable homicide. Originally, I guess, he thought to use Penny's picture to infuriate Dwayne. The guy didn't need help in that department. So, maybe, he'll just burn them."

Folding her hands tent-like and leaning forward on her elbows, Fiona decided that we might as well lay it all on the table for Luella, as soon as the weekend.

"Come to my place for lunch on Sunday. I'll prepare her for your visit. Just one thing, though; check in with Dr. Simpson to ascertain Madelaine's present condition and ask him about the advisability of Luella's visiting her in the hospital."

We agreed to the plan. Smiling grimly, Fiona rose, placed her hands palms down on her desktop, and said, "James, if I might make a further suggestion?

"Sure."

"Perhaps it would be wise to reconsider furthering your initial plan to divest yourself of certain knowledge regarding Madelaine."

"You mean OUR initial plan," I corrected her. "Yes, Fiona, I've already given that a lot of thought. At this point, what could be gained?"

"Exactly," Fiona agreed, brushing off the correction. "Well, back to work. The world hasn't stopped spinning yet, as far as I know."

Closing the door to Fiona's office behind us, we walked, shoulder-to-shoulder. "Let's have lunch at Scully's. We'll talk; or, better still, we'll listen."

"So, are you thinking what I'm thinking?" Donna asked. "I believe that Fiona sees this drug dealer killing as a much more interesting story than your so-called confession." She added, never word-wasteful.

"Exactly," I agreed. "There's no way she's going to keep this one under her hat. Remember, her job is to sell newspapers."

"Well, she can't keep it out of the news; the press will be all over it and she'll want to be the one to break it."

"Right. Especially the part about Dwayne's being Luella Frazier's brother. That puts her in the spotlight again, just as she was getting her life back together."

Donna digested this and made a sour face. "We're forgetting about Marty. How will the press treat him?"

"Fiona will make him sound like a hero, of course; he did, after all, risk his life confronting Dwayne. What Fiona shouldn't divulge, of course, was Marty's real motive for going after Dwayne."

∞ ∞ ∞

Scully's is a neighborhood bar and grille within walking distance of the Globe offices. It is dimly lit, with a wide, wrap-around, highly polished, oak-hewn bar. Low-hanging lamps with dark green shades lend the bar an air of intimacy and, at times, intrigue. The bar is a favorite among lawyers, journalists, and news hounds, who gather for the purpose of overhearing gossip or a shared confidence.

A more private corner table is a certain target for eavesdroppers. Whispering, hands cupped over mouths, darting eyes suspicious of being overheard, are the preferred modes of communication while ears work as antennae for whatever gem of news they might detect. You might ask why we would choose such a place for our own confidential conversation. Our whispering was sure to draw the attention of anyone who knew us, especially reporters from rival newspapers who recognized us. One such person, Ben Sawyer, approached our table, seemingly affable, but nonetheless trolling for a hot scoop. Ben is a tall, beefy guy with a thick neck, acquired during his years playing defensive tackle in college football. A full, wiry, salt-and-pepper beard partially obscured his face; his eyes fiercely vigilant for a "tackle."

"So, Jimmy, what's the big reveal? How's that investigation coming?" Outwardly congenial and easy-going, Ben possessed extra-sensory olfactory ability; he could smell obfuscation with a sniff; one miscue or feint on the field, he pounced.

"Nothing to report, yet, Ben. Still working on it." I demurred.

He raised one bushy eye-brow, questioning. "Well, don't let too much time pass without a follow-up, eh?" His hazel-green eyes lingered on my wife's blouse for seconds more than they should have. "Nice to see you again, Donna. Looking as fine as ever." He smiled, knowing that his presence was annoying. Donna didn't acknowledge the compliment. "Take care, Ben." He handled her dismissive response with his usual aplomb.

"Sure, see ya' kids." He strode off with the same casual confidence he had learned to execute when walking off a football field.

"Bastard," Donna whispered.

Once served, we ate our lunch in relative quiet, listening intently for an inadvertent slip of the tongue, any reference to names or police activity from the preceding night. We were almost through, when Donna heard clipped words: drug dealer... Chelsea... shot.

"They know, Jimmy," she said, worried.

I nodded my head in agreement, closed my eyes and ears to the din surrounding us. Our questions had been answered and we knew who leaked the story. Luella would soon learn the gruesome fate of her brother.

"Maybe," I hedged, not wanting to think it, "but, why?"

On our walk back to the office, Donna posed the obvious question: "Do you suppose Fiona advised a call to Carter as a delaying tactic?"

"Maybe. But, again, why?" I scratched my head, flummoxed. "I can't imagine why; but, we'll call him tonight and see how Madelaine is doing."

When we returned to our office, Fiona was not there. Her desk top was disorderly with folders, pens, papers, left in disarray. Our colleague, Mike, informed us that she had left rather precipitously, "Like her pants were on fire?" he joked with a wink.

"I'm going to look for her," Donna announced, emphatically, a note of concern in her voice. "She couldn't have gone far."

"What if she's in a meeting with the top brass concerning the shooting? Maybe she lost track of time, what with all that's been happening?" I was determined to minimize Donna's fears, bowing, however, to her usually incisive assessments of human behavior.

"Look," Donna said, pointing to Fiona's office, "her handbag is still slung over the back of her chair; that could only mean that she is somewhere in the building."

Donna bolted out of the room. First, she checked the ladies' restroom at the end of the hallway, calling out Fiona's name and eyeing the shoes of those who were occupying the six stalls. From there she peered into the upper glass portions of several conference rooms, all of which she found deserted. She ran down to the cafeteria still bustling with the lunch crowd and scanned the tables, as well as the counter along the far wall. Fiona was not there, either. Then spying the heavy side door that led to the garden courtyard, she ran to open it. There, huddled on a green wooden bench, arms wrapped around her, Fiona sat, distraught and shivering. The once lushly verdant plantings with their profusion of vibrant colors, had lost their struggle against the frost; they lay limp and wilted, heads bowed to earth in surrender. Fiona, too, appeared defeated; her shoulders slumped, and her head, too, was bowed. Until Donna approached, she hadn't noticed that Fiona was crying. She cleared her throat, not wanting to startle.

"Are you okay?" she asked, softly.

When she got no response, Donna tried again. "Fiona, please speak to me. What's wrong?"

Fiona raised her head, revealing a stream of tears running down her flushed cheeks; her eyes were red-rimmed.

"Can I sit down next to you?" Donna asked, tentatively.

To her surprise, Fiona inched to her right and made room on the bench for Donna to sit.

"I don't mean to intrude; I'm just very concerned. Can I help you?"

Still shivering, Fiona looked into Donna's eyes with a forlornness uncharacteristic of the sturdy-souled, no-nonsense, take-it-on-the-chin boss Donna thought she knew. Fiona's silver streaked hair had come undone from the bun she wore at the nape of her neck. She dabbed her eyes with wads of balled-up tissue. "I'll be all right, dear. Not to worry. Just some old memories have got the best of me." Laying cold fingers on Donna's hand, she said, "Thank you for your concern. Go on back inside where it's warm."

Obstinate when she thought it suitable—and often when it wasn't—Donna persisted. "No, I'm not leaving you like this. It may not be any of my business, but please tell me what's wrong."

The late October sky had become overcast; dark clouds hung low and lugubrious. Despite the chill in the air, both women remained fixed in place. Donna waited for an interminable few minutes before Fiona began to pull deeply seated roots from well beneath the surface of her being.

"I was not an only child, as I've told you in the past." Here, she took a deep breath and willed herself to continue. "I had a younger brother, Blake--we called him 'Buddy.'" A tiny smile escaped from the corners of her lips as she conjured up his image. "Buddy was a fair-haired, handsome boy, lanky and lithe. All the girls adored him, especially when he suited up and bounded onto the gymnasium floor; he played point guard for our high school basketball team. He was at home on the court, eyes always sparkling with anticipation." Fiona stopped, wiped away more tears.

"Go on; I'm listening." Donna urged.

"Well, everyone idolized him, as I said, except my father. Buddy was not a good student; he narrowly passed from one grade to the next. Teachers issued him passing grades as a favor to his coach— Mr. Donnelly—who convinced them that my brother was the most valuable asset on the team. He was the crowd-pleaser with his outstanding athletic prowess and agility. My father, however, had absurd visions of Buddy's becoming a successful businessman, like him. Buddy did not have the aptitude nor the interest in my father's absurd visions; he wanted to go to trade school, learn a skill. The ladies apparel business did not interest him in the least, and this refusal to follow in my father's footsteps infuriated Dad. So, he set out to destroy him. May father detested sports of all kinds, mainly because he had a clubbed foot—a congenital deformity—which negated his ever playing anything more than chess. "Basketball is not a profession, boy," he'd say. "You'll never amount to anything in this life throwing a ball and galumphing up and down a parquet floor. You're a spectacle in a circus act, and people come to see you perform just like they do trained seals."

Donna could not help but cringe, thinking how these venomous words must have stung.

Fiona continued now without more encouragement; she was opening the door to her darkest childhood memories, letting them escape from the boundless well of her animus. "My father taunted and goaded Buddy every day, berating him for his poor scholarship and lack of common sense. Buddy took the abuse and suffered silently. Then, one day, my father let the guillotine's blade fall. He forbade Buddy from playing the sport he loved and in which he excelled. He had been lying in ambush until the week of play offs; Buddy's team was destined to win the league championship. "As of this week," my father declared, a malicious grin on his bloated face, "you'll not play another game."

"But, Dad," Buddy protested, the team needs me; I just can't quit at the most critical time."

"Don't bullshit me, boy. No one is indispensable. That's my final word. Cross me, and you'll find yourself out on the street, disowned."

It was getting dark, and Donna knew I'd be worried about her absence. She withdrew her cell phone from her pant pocket and texted me that she had found Fiona, to just wait.

"Go on, Fiona."

Predictably, Buddy's team lost in the playoffs and the championship. Buddy was devasted and felt personal responsibility for the loss. His subsequent depression was unbearable for him, and for my mom and me to watch. Both of us had tried in vain to convince my father to allow Buddy to play out the season. He screamed at us, reminding us that he was the man of the house and we were just emotional women."

"Fiona," Donna begged, "why don't you finish telling me your story inside, where it's warm?"

"No, I want to sit here and hurt, just as Buddy had. I tried to comfort him, but there was nothing a little sister could do to assuage his terrible pain. Weeks passed, and Buddy began skipping classes, started to hang out with a bunch of undesirable kids; he couldn't face his teammates. He often came home with alcohol on his breath. One day, I found a bong in his jacket pocket. It didn't take long for Buddy to turn to opioids, cocaine, heroin, the works. My mother tried to get him help, but he brushed her off. And then... and then, we got the inevitable visit from the police telling us that Buddy was found dead under a train trestle in Roxbury—a familiar campsite for shooting up. My mother collapsed into herself and could not escape her grief; she wound up spending the rest of her days in a psychiatric hospital." After a very long pause, Fiona finished her story. "After Buddy's funeral, I packed my bags and ran away to my aunt's house where she allowed me to stay until after graduation. She helped me with my applications to college and paid my first year's tuition."

"Oh, Fiona, what a tragic story," Donna sniffed, then wrapped her arms around Fiona in a warm embrace, hugging her tightly. Lifting her head to meet Donna's tearful gaze, she ended, "This whole business with that scumbag Dwayne Ricci, the violence, well, it brought back that terrible time. You know, memories are like shrouds that bind our souls; when they fall away, we are naked, exposed, and vulnerable."

Donna wanted to ask what happened to that dreadful father but didn't have to. "I hated my father and we didn't speak to each other after that. He left me a large inheritance, not because he loved me, but because he hadn't. What he did was unconscionable, and I would not forgive him. The money was his attempt to assuage the guilt a gutless man like that can suffer."

"Let's go inside," Donna pleaded.

211

Fiona relented, rose stiffly, and, with Donna's arm around her shoulder reentered the cafeteria.

I was waiting for them with two cups of hot coffee to warm their hands, if not their spirits. We headed back to the office, collected our belongings, and spoke with lowered voices. In the parking garage, we offered to drive Fiona home; but, she declined, assuring us that she was fine enough to drive herself. "I'll deliver the news to Luella. Thank you both for..." her voice cracked, and she didn't finish her sentence. We bade farewell and agreed to talk more in the morning. Fiona left ahead of us and we followed at a safe distance to assure ourselves of her steadiness behind the wheel.

Heading towards Cambridge via Memorial Drive, we passed university students walking to their dorms, shoulders raised, and heads nestled in the collars of their winter jackets; some wore knitted caps pulled low to their brows. An early frost had visited us. I raised the thermostat in the car to coax some warm air for Donna who was still shivering.

"I'm thinking that Marty and Fiona are more than good friends, and I suspect that his calling her first about Dwayne would bring her some peace."

"How so?"

"One more scumbag drug dealer off the streets. I guess he didn't figure on the news upsetting her."

"You were a great support for her tonight. She trusted you with very intimate information."

"I think she's relieved that Marty survived. We all are."

∞ ∞ ∞

Paul was cranky when we arrived home; he had looked forward to sharing his day's activities and discoveries with us, not with Adriana. We forestalled calling Carter and placated Paul with the promise of three bedtime stories. We all had mac and cheese for dinner.

Around nine o'clock, I was feeling antsy. As exhausting as the day had been, I couldn't put Madelaine on the back burner. I remembered Donna's concern regarding Fiona's breaking the story and its appearance in the morning headlines. I couldn't blame Fiona for wanting to be the *official source* of the breaking news; she was doing her job. Hoping that Carter hadn't retired for the night, I phoned him. In a lowered voice, Carter answered on the first ring; Laura had already gone to bed.

"Carter here."

"Sorry for the lateness, Carter. It's been a hectic few days."

"No problem; I was just going over the most recent reports on Madelaine."

"Is she making any progress?" As I waited for Carter's response, Donna brought me two fingers of scotch.

"Two steps forward, one back. The good news is that she has been responding to two female doctors on staff; they report that Madelaine has been talking to them, but she's not giving up much in the way of critical information. She doesn't act out much now and hasn't needed restraints. Some days, however, she just disappears into that inner other- world where she feels safe."

"Any idea as to when she might be up to a visit from her mother?"

Carter was less than enthusiastic. "So hard to say. Behavior is unpredictable. Anything could set her off, you know."

That wasn't what I wanted to hear. "I mean, she did whisper 'Mama.'"

"Jimmy, that could mean one of two things: she may be terrified of seeing the mother who killed her father; she fled from their encounter on the street. Or, she might be calling out for her. There's just no way of knowing at this point; we run the risk of further traumatizing her."

I could hear the clink of an ice cube in an empty glass. "I do remember your promising to bring her mother to her if she agreed to go with us willingly." I was pressing Carter and feared that I'd ruffled his ego-feathers.

"Okay. I'll ask the two doctors she's worked with to run a trial balloon. They might agree to play a recording of a lullaby or a song that her mom sang to her as a young child. Ask Luella for a suggestion. Sometimes, childhood melodies evoke memories of happier times. Music is a phenomenal therapeutic tool."

I was feeling hope; I had something I could hold onto as a possibility, even if it was ephemeral. I wanted so much to forge a new bond between Luella and Madelaine, however fragile. Was I on a quixotic crusade, tilting at windmills? "Can't' thank you enough, Carter. Tell me, how do you deal every day of your professional life with so much sorrow? Doesn't it sometimes get you down?"

"I'd be lying if I denied it. But, every now and then I may affect a breakthrough; when that happens, when someone's seemingly hopeless existence can be resuscitated, pulled from the brink, I'm certain that I was right to choose what I do."

"And, when all your efforts fail? You must feel dreadful."

"Devastated is the word, Jimmy. But, it's then that I realize my limits; that I'm not God, and there are many things totally out of my control. 'Man plans, and God laughs.'"

Well, let's hope that with your efforts and God's help, two broken people will be mended."

"Amen to that."

I had caught Carter at a rare, humble moment; I much preferred this other side of his humanity to the one I'd known.

"Good night, Jimmy." He sounded tired.

"'Night, Carter."

"Not such a bad fellow, after all," I said to Donna who had sat down next to me, listening to our conversation. I drained the last few drops of scotch from my glass.

"Adversity brings out the best in all of us, I guess."

"Adversity? Carter's had adversity?" I wouldn't have guessed it; now I sounded fatuous.

"Laura and Carter lost a child to cancer, Jimmy. I thought you knew. Shit happens to all of us."

Donna rose from the sofa, returned our two glasses to the kitchen, turned out the lights, and held out her hand to me. Together, we ascended the stairs to our bedroom. I stepped into Paul's room and kissed his cheek.

Chapter 38

$\mathcal{F}$iona drove around town for an hour after she had left the garage. She had phoned Luella to tell her that she would be a little late; that she had an errand to run. Luella did not sound agitated, and Fiona assumed from Luella's calm voice that she had not been watching television or listening to the radio. Tired of fighting Boston traffic, she found an empty parking space in front of Scully's Bar and went in for a drink. As always, it was bustling with an after-work crowd of young professionals, their shirt collars unbuttoned, their ties stuffed into their jacket pockets; many of the women had removed their red power-jackets and hung them on the backs of their chairs. The atmosphere was relaxed and convivial; music blared, adding to the upbeat rhythm of the lively crowd. Fiona took an unoccupied seat at the bar and ordered a Manhattan. "Light on the vermouth," she instructed the bartender, "no cherries." While she waited for her cocktail, she extracted a notepad and pen from her purse. Tapping the pen against her cheek, she tried to conjure helpful words with which to inform Luella about her brother. Luella had killed Edgar in a moment of unprecedented rage; surely, she would understand Penny's breaking point, as well. She debated whether to share her brother's story and the contempt she felt for Dwayne who, she believed, was complicit in Buddy's death. Dwayne had kept Luella as much a prisoner in his house as she had been while in jail. The motives for his generosity in providing Luella a place to live were entirely self-serving and counter-intuitive. His rationale, if one could call it that, was simple: she was "family."

Fiona's drink arrived promptly, but with two red cherries bobbing at the bottom of the glass; she fished them out with her fingers, placed them on a napkin, and gave the bartender a withering look.

"Oh, sorry, ma'am. Would you like me to make you another?" he apologized, whisking away the offending cherries.

Fiona dismissed him with a back-handed flip of her wrist, took a sip of her drink, and put the glass down on the bar. She tried to concentrate on her task, but the loud music distracted her. She had an additional problem: when and how to convince Luella that a face-to-face encounter with Madelaine might yield a positive outcome. She had no proof that such a meeting would be wise; she would have to wait for the doctor's approval. She jotted down some workable phrases such as "in her best interest," or, "a potentially life altering event," but none of these rang true for her. She wondered how much rejection poor Luella could withstand, especially since there would be no guarantees of a successful outcome; it would be a crap shoot, at best, and Luella had already suffered immeasurably from the previous face-to-face. She crossed out her notes with a big X, closed the pad, and returned it to her purse. Frustrated, she tossed back the remains of her drink and signaled the bartender for her check. At that moment, a large, burly man with a wiry red beard took a seat beside her.

"Can I buy you another?" he asked, offering his beefy hand in greeting. "I'm Ben Sawyer."

Ignoring Ben's gesture, Fiona replied, "I know who you are, and no, thank you; I was just leaving."

She raised her forefinger to again summon the bartender; he appeared to be ignoring her.

"Say," Ben said, eyebrows arched. "Aren't you Fiona Moran, one of the big guns at the Globe?"

Placing a twenty-dollar bill on the counter, Fiona attempted to slide off her stool. A heavy hand landed on her knee. "Hey, no offense. Stay a while."

"Mr. Sawyer," Fiona warned, her voice menacing, "remove your hand or I'll scream, and have you arrested for assault."

With a hearty, mocking guffaw, Ben did remove his hand from her knee, but not before giving it a hard squeeze.

Fiona fled for her car. Ben turned to another patron at the bar and said, "That's one feisty bitch."

Chapter 39

*R*iding the elevator up to her eighteenth-floor condo, Fiona still fumed over the incident with Sawyer. In retrospect, she chided herself for not swiping his beefy hand away from her knee and remonstrating more affectively. But, she reasoned, she would have made her situation worse by insulting him; that he would, of course, stir up the crowd's sympathies, hurl invective at her. He would probably claim that she flirted with him; that she encouraged him with innuendo, that her long, silky legs had rested invitingly on the bottom rung of his barstool. The more she replayed the scene in her mind, the more agitated she became. The elevator chimed to announce her floor and the doors opened. Exiting, she fished her key from her purse and inserted it into the lock. To her surprise, the door was unlocked—a broken hard and fast rule that Fiona had nearly branded on Luella's brain. Cautiously, she pushed the door open with the toe of her shoe. Inside, she found Marty, sitting on the white leather sofa, his arm extended around Luella's shoulders, comforting her. Luella was dabbing tears from her cheeks with Marty's white handkerchief; neither had heard her enter; both were shocked to see someone else in the room. More relieved than annoyed, Fiona cleared her throat, took Luella's measure, then casually set her purse on the glass-topped parson's table by her door. She removed her shoes, noting that Marty had not complied with yet another of her rules. Annoyed, she took a seat opposite the twosome. Sitting back in her chair, she crossed her legs, and gave Marty a nod. "I'm so sorry, Luella. I assume that Marty's filled you in with all the details."

"He was not a good person," Luella sniffed, "but, still, he was my brother."

Ah, family, Fiona mused.

"You won't have to live in fear of him anymore; that should count for something, dear." Was she being callous? No matter. She was thinking of her father, as she said this.

"I don't blame Penny," Luella sighed, "'cuz I know how it is; I've been there. But, still..."

Fiona slipped into her all-business mode. Commiseration was not her forte; its effects were helpful for just so long and it sometimes interfered with the job of moving forward.

"If it's any consolation to you, I've been able to secure that job for you at the bridal salon. You can stay here with me for as long as you need to."

As Luella brightened, Marty, rose from the sofa, relieved that he had accomplished his mission. He looked overwhelmed with tiredness, his face wore a haggard, hang-dog expression. Deep creases of abject sorrow lined his mouth and brow. The adrenaline rush had dissipated.

Fiona uncrossed her legs, leaned forward and said, "Marty, you're welcome to stay the night." They exchanged a tender look. "If you've got a beer in the fridge and some left-overs, I'd be mighty obliged, Ma'am."

Luella had stopped sniffing; she wiped the tears from her cheeks and forced a weak smile. "Anyone up to some left-over lasagna?"

Marty cringed at the sound of that word, but he said nothing.

∞ ∞ ∞

Marty dozed on the sofa, nestled beneath a warm, downy blanket, his head on two puffy pillows. He awoke around midnight and listened for any sounds, assuring himself that Luella had fallen asleep. He slipped out from under the covers, clad in a T-shirt and blue checkered underwear. Quietly, he padded toward Fiona's bedroom door; it was slightly ajar. Upon opening it, he was delighted to discover that she had expected him. In the scant illumination of the bedroom night-light, he could see her slender figure, propped up on silken pillows, her silver hair loosened and cascading onto her bare shoulders. She drew back the covers and beckoned him to join her.

"Are you sure?" Marty asked.

"That's not a question I ever ask myself. Just get in."

Marty smiled, lay down beside her, and opened his arms to her. Fiona slipped down into his embrace, thinking, *there is nothing equal to the joy of being wanted.*

In the early morning light, on her way into the kitchen, Luella noticed the unoccupied sofa; Marty was not under the blankets, but his shoes and socks were neatly tucked underneath. Not surprised, she smiled and began preparing breakfast, this time for three. Marty emerged from Fiona's bedroom, hair rumpled and face unshaven. Espying Luella, he bashfully informed her that he would not be staying; that he needed to "tidy up" at his place before joining Penny at her preliminary hearing.

"Will you tell her for me that what she did, well, she saved others from dying, and that I forgive her?"

Buttoning his shirt, then zipping his black jeans, Marty replied, "I will do that, Luella; that's very charitable of you. Like you, Penny has no one to support her; your doing so will mean a lot"

"Well, she has you, too." Nodding, Marty acknowledged Luella's distinction that her having been spurned was not equivalent to Penny's.

He finished dressing, leaving his tie hanging loosely around his neck, and was out the door.

Luella brewed a fresh pot of coffee, toasted an English muffin and set out a small dish with whipped butter and raspberry jam. Into two small bowls, she scooped Greek-style yogurt and sprinkled blueberries on top. As Luella was extracting two coffee mugs from the cabinet, Fiona fluttered in, as weightless as a butterfly, and took a seat at her table. A carefully arranged chignon lay at the nape of her neck, from which a hint of Chanel #5 perfume scented the air. She greeted Luella with rare jauntiness.

"'Morning."

"'Mornin' to you, too," came the reply.

Neither asked if the other had slept well. One did; the other did not.

Fiona sipped her coffee slowly, then buttered one half of her muffin. Luella watched, as Fiona chewed. There was a twinkle in her eyes and an undeniable upturning at the corners of her mouth.

"Delicious coffee, Luella. So much better than Starbuck's." She wiped crumbs that had fallen onto her skirt, dabbed at her mouth with a paper napkin, then rose to check her appearance in the hallway mirror. After applying fresh lipstick, she grabbed her briefcase and handbag from the parson's table and rummaged for her car keys. "Don't forget, now. Saturday morning, nine o'clock, you'll be starting at the bridal boutique downtown. I'll drive you over, okay?"

"You're so kind to me," Luella said softly. "Once I start making some money, I'll be able to contribute... a small amount, I know, but it will make me feel like I'm not a burden."

"Nonsense. You're not a burden. I kinda' like having you around. By the way, if they require you to fill out an application that asks if you've ever been arrested, say "yes." I've already explained to Miss Kaiser, your new boss, that you were unfairly sentenced. See you later." Leaning against the door frame, she slipped into black, sling-back shoes and reached for the doorknob, then added, "And, please remember to keep this door locked at all times"—a not-so-subtle reprimand for the previous night's negligence. Before boarding the elevator, she listened for the click of the dead bolt. *Can't be too careful,* she thought.

Once Fiona had left, Luella poured herself another cup of coffee and sat down at the kitchen table, pondering what was just said. *Why would she say, "unfairly," and just how much does she know?*

Chapter 40

*A*fter weeks of high tension and drama, Donna and I decided to wait a while before visiting with Luella. Respectfully, we thought it best for her to have time to grapple with her brother's killing. We also wanted to wait for what we hoped would be more definitive news from Carter about Madelaine's progress. In the meantime, we agreed to focus on our daily work.

Fiona was late in arriving. She glided past us with a jaunty gait, her demeanor remarkably blissful. As she made her way into her glassed-in- office, she wiggled her fingers in a greeting to her minions—her way of saying "hi."

Assured that she was out of earshot, our co-worker, Jake, ventured a guess and sniggered, "There's only one good explanation for that."

Chrissy, seated directly across from his cubicle, glared at him. "Chauvinist!" she retorted, then rose from her swivel chair to attend to an imagined task. Donna and I exchanged looks of disbelief, her eyebrows raised in arcs of wonder; my jaw had dropped in equal curiosity. Behind her glass enclosure, we could see Fiona, black glasses perched low on her nose, concentrating on developments regarding Dwayne Ricci's shooting, as well as the updates on Penny's forthcoming scheduled court date. Oblivious to our continued gawking, she ignored our furtive glances.

Around mid-day, she rose from her desk and beckoned me with a crooked forefinger and a less than assuring look. Marshalling my composure, I smiled and rose from my desk chair. Donna watched uneasily from her own desk, her blue eyes conveying a sense of foreboding.

"Sit down, James. Something to drink?" Fiona was being casual, but her manner often presaged something more ominous. The breezy, bouncy air she had displayed in the morning had obviously dissipated.

I sat down, leaned back, crossed my legs, and tried not to look cowered. "Something up?" I asked nonchalantly.

"Well, yes, James; as a matter of fact, there is." She walked over to the window, gazed at the now defunct gardens below, arms crossed over her chest. She massaged her elbows, kneading them between her thumbs and fingers. I waited, steeling myself for what I suspected would be inevitable, bad news. With her back still to me, I could see her slender shoulders rise and fall with each deep breath she took. Finally, she turned and looked at me kindly.

"I've been reading dozens of letters to the editor relevant to your article about Luella Frazier. Every one of those letters questions why you haven't provided further information on what you 'withheld.' Your readers have been waiting for the promised evidence that you have not yet produced. They want to know why you led them on."

I squirmed, readjusted myself in the seat, sitting upright. "You know, Fiona, that's not true. After all that's happened these past few months, how can I possibly expose Luella to more scrutiny, maybe censure? And, with Madelaine in a psychiatric hospital, the last thing I want to do is make matters worse."

"Yes, I understand, James. But, we're talking readership here. If people think they've been duped, they're not going to be happy with this newspaper." She paused, sat down, and looked me straight in the eye.

"You're going to have to write a retraction."

"That will make me look like a fool, Fiona! It makes me look like I'm still hiding something." My ire was getting the best of me.

"Well, James, in truth, you are. Luella is about to start a new job on Saturday and I want her to succeed. She's paid her debt to society and deserves to be left alone."

"You didn't feel that way when we decided to run the piece," I countered. I intentionally included her in the "we." Our intentions were well-meaning and beneficent. I have nothing to apologize for." I could feel my face burning red.

"You're talking out of both sides of your mouth, James. You can't have it both ways. Either you come forth with the truth of what you know or find a way to obviate your having misinformed." Fiona's stare was intense. "My superiors will expect nothing less from you."

"So, you're implying that I should lie; that I should confabulate?"

"Memory error that is fabricated, distorted, or misinterpreted without intention to deceive is exactly what is required here. It's the only way to save your ass, bluntly speaking."

I felt as if I were sucker-punched. Fiona was giving me no choice; I had to compose another article that made my original one appear naïve, or worse, disingenuous. In short, I had to bury my knowledge alongside the tiny grave in the schoolyard thicket. "All right, I see your point. I'll work on it tonight." I rose and, though not excused, let myself out the door. Donna could tell by the color in my cheeks that things did not go well. She approached, paused at my desk and suggested that I take a walk to cool off. I agreed, grabbed my jacket and went for a walk outside, hoping the crisp November air would help clear my mind—and my conscience. I exited the Exchange Place complex at 53 State Street and headed toward Faneuil Hall, just a two-minute walk. The iconic marketplace was bustling with activity: holiday shoppers, tourists, youngsters playing on the outdoor courtyard, parents wheeling baby carriages or strollers, young lovers walking hand-in-hand. I spied the unoccupied Red Auerbach bench and sat down, enveloped by the gaiety around me, but also cloaked in a cloud of dismay. Although I felt much calmer than when I left the office, my thoughts returned to Fiona's insistence that I retract my "misleading" article. I understood the necessity, given the current circumstances; but, how in the world was I going to confess that I had made a premature declaration of knowledge that I didn't have? I concluded that knowledge is like a fickle mistress; she can bring you to unimagined heights of ecstasy or drag you down to levels of deceit you never dreamed yourself capable of. She can make you feel sorry you ever courted her and wind up owing her your soul. But, in all honesty, I never **chose** to know about Madelaine's plight; somehow, it seems as if it were preordained. So, I have to ask myself which is worse: to say that you have knowledge about something you don't; or, to pretend that you don't know something when, in truth, you do? Do I disgrace my "mistress" by exposing her; or, do I live with the guilt of my own complicity and betrayal? Is this what is meant by moral turpitude?

As I sat there, deep in my well of wistfulness, I felt a tugging at my jacket sleeve. I opened my eyes to find a young, lanky teen-ager watching me quizzically, concerned.

"Mister, you okay?" he asked, his dark, deep-set eyes observing me with caution. He wore baggy green long pants with a white stripe running down the sides and green high-top sneakers. Under his arm he held a basketball. Awakened from my reverie, I blinked twice to reacquaint myself with my surroundings. "Oh, yes, yes, I'm fine," I sputtered, "thanks for asking."

"Who's the statue guy with the cigar? he inquired.

I leaned forward and rested my elbows on my thighs. "He's Arthur "Red" Auerbach, son, the legendary coach of the Boston Celtics. He helped them win 938 games and 16 NBA championships. Toward the end of each game he was sure of winning, he would light up a cigar. Boston fans admired him so much they had this bronze statue made in his likeness." I guessed I was showing off a bit because my young friend's eyes were wide with awe. I had shared something worth knowing.

"Wow!" he exclaimed.

"Do you watch the Celtics on television?"

"Uh-huh. I watch all the games with my Dad. I wanna' play ball when I'm old enough." He removed his basketball from under his arm and started dribbling, pivoting, feinting, then pretending to shoot. His skills were undeniable, even for his young age.

"Very impressive, young man. I hope you get your wish. Just remember, education first."

"Yeah, that's what my Dad says." He looked down at his sneakers, then brightened. "Thanks, Mister. Glad you're okay." He trotted off, dribbling his basketball, the sounds ricocheting off the brick pavement. I looked at the statue and said, "Thanks, Red; you've made my day." I was ready to return to the office, hoping the youngster would get his wish and that he would grow up never having to think of knowledge as a burden.

I retraced my steps to the Exchange Place complex and rode the elevator up to the Globe's offices. I could almost hear Donna's exhalation of relief on seeing my recovered composure. Her shoulders, which had been hunched-up, hanging out around her earlobes, visibly relaxed. I approached her desk and kissed her on the forehead. "Looks like I have some work to do tonight. Maybe you can help me figure out a way to twist the truth and still keep my credibility."

"We'll find that way, Honey. I'm beginning to believe that honesty isn't all it's cracked up to be."

For the rest of the afternoon, I thought about what Donna had said. Maybe she was right; maybe there's a downside to truthfulness; maybe sometimes it can be do more harm than good. Fiona remained in her office, ostensibly buried in a workload of important matters; she never looked in my direction. As we cleared our desktops, shut down our computers, and prepared to leave at 5 p.m., we still hadn't made eye contact, not even to say, "Good evening," or "Have a great weekend." Was she feeling guilty or was she angry? Maybe, she was angry with herself. Who knows?

Later that evening, after dinner and Paul's bedtime routine, Donna and I sat side-by-side on the sofa, feet propped up on the ottoman we shared, each of us with pen and a pad of paper in hand. Fortified by a bottle of Bordeaux, we jotted down our thoughts, searching for the most palliative words we could conjure. After an hour had passed, we were able to construct a believable explanation of "unforeseen circumstances" that precluded further inquiry—a kind of nolo-contendere—which expressed regret without admitting wrong-doing on my part. I submitted that it was my duty as a reporter to protect the privacy of those whose lives would be adversely impacted by my pursuing further investigation.

When we finished the draft, we clinked our now-empty wine glasses, lay our heads back on the sofa, and closed our eyes.

"The dastardly deed, done," I quipped.

"Shall we get some sleep, Cassius?" Donna asked, taking my hand and leading me up the stairs to our bedroom.

∞ ∞ ∞

My article, which appeared in the Monday morning edition, was subsequently received with mixed reviews. Some saw it as gratuitous; others wrote in to say that they were grateful for not having to trudge through the muck of salacious speculation. Still others, were indignant, feeling that my so-called confession was merely a ploy to stimulate readership. It was this last category that Fiona had fretted over and hoped not to alienate. In the end, it was I who was condemned to shoulder the burden of cowardice born long ago. Despite my falling out of favor, I kept telling myself that there was still the hope of reuniting Luella and Madelaine; that we could achieve something positive, or, at the least, restorative. All would depend on Madelaine.

Chapter 41

The strained atmosphere in the newsroom abated when Fiona felt assured that she wouldn't be serving my head up on a platter to her bosses. A sense of normalcy returned to our relationship, although it never quite rebounded to its original state of bonhomie. So many times, I was tempted to ask point-blank what was niggling at her but resisted that urge, settling for a cordial, though listless relationship. She was always a private person, but not detached nor prone to intrigue. In time, I figured, she would snap out of her indolent behavior and act more like her old self.

For the next two months, we co-existed with the utmost of caution. Donna and I worked diligently on our separate projects, aware of the scrutiny under which we performed our tasks. For her part, Fiona tried to minimize the chill that had developed between us, emitting a gracious, yet reticent scent. One day, and for several days thereafter, she failed to show up for work. We tried reaching her on her cell phone, but to no avail; all we got was her voicemail. When we inquired of her bosses, we were told that Fiona was taking an extended leave of absence; that she had asked to be relieved of her responsibilities—at least for the time being. They professed to knowing nothing more than "personal issues." We scratched our heads, trying to comprehend the suddenness of her departure, as well as the weeks of strange behavior that preceded it. As a last resort, we called and reached Marty O'Brien. He said he was not available for comment.

"But, Marty," I persisted, "surely you can understand our concern. Is Fiona ill?"

"No, my friend, she's not ill. Let's just say, "burnt out." What I can tell you, though, is that it has something to do with Luella."

"Is she still living with Fiona?" I pressed.

"No, she moved out to her own place last week."

"Do you know where she moved to?"

"I'm not at liberty to say, Jimmy boy."

"So, how is it you know all this, and we don't?"

"We've become um... good friends. She confides in me. Let's just say that she's tired. Fed up. Sick of being asked to cover everyone else's ass. She doesn't mean to be hurtful, Jimmy; she just needs space."

"Okay, Marty; I get it. When you see her or talk to her, please wish her our best. And, Marty?"

"Uh-huh?"

"Would you please ask her to let us know how to reach Luella?"

"Sure. I can do that. Thought you might like to know that I've been working hard on Penny Ricci's case. Looks like the prosecutor is satisfied with justifiable homicide and she'll be let off."

"I'm glad for her, Marty. Take care, now." I hung up feeling totally confused and left out of the loop. I had been waiting for Carter's phone call for some time and wondered why he wasn't connecting with me. I dialed his cell phone number with the taste of bile in my mouth. He answered on the second ring, after he could check his caller ID.

"Carter here. Hi, Jimmy."

"I was hoping you could bring me up to date on Madelaine. Is there any hope?"

"I've arranged a twice-a-week visitation for Luella at the hospital; she shows up punctually, goes home deflated."

"How so?"

"After each attempt on our part to bring the two into some kind of dialogue, Madelaine recoils and refuses to participate. However stinging Madelaine's rebukes have been, Luella does not give up trying."

"How about your request for a childhood song, something to jog her memory?"

"Luella could not comply. She told me that she never sang to her baby, never played games with her. As Madelaine grew older, she began to distance herself; Luella thought this was predictable teenage behavior. She told me, quote, 'Madelaine was never normal; Edgar saw to that.'"

"How were you able to get Luella to agree to the visitations?"

"It was before she moved into her new place. Fiona Moran told her how to get in touch with me, and she did."

"Carter, is there any chance I can be present during her next visit? I really need to talk to her."

After a long pause, Carter agreed. "It's against protocol, Jimmy, but I'll do it. Her next visit is scheduled for tomorrow at 2 p.m. We usually meet in the cafeteria beforehand to go over the week's treatment sessions and to discuss the feasibility of rapprochement. Between you and me, I'm not optimistic."

"Thanks, Carter. I'll be there tomorrow. Luella isn't one of my biggest fans, but I think she'll talk to me."

"We'll see. Just don't expect much."

"Okay. Until then."

After we disconnected, I went into the kitchen and sat down. Laid out on the tabletop were several of Paul's school drawings; he had mentioned his work at bedtime, but, preoccupied, I had forgotten to view them. Donna stood at the sink, hands clasped in front of her.

What I saw made me gasp. There in Crayola vividness, was a crude drawing of a man sitting on a couch; next to him, in stark black, was the unmistakable depiction of a gun. "Oh, my God," I moaned, raking my fingers through my hair. "We never thought... I mean, we..."

"Don't, Jimmy," Donna advised. "We'll talk to him, help him get over his fright. He must have been haunted by that awful man's getting into our house. We'll have to work on it." She laid her hand on my shoulder and gave it a gentle squeeze. "I just can't believe what an awful mess this whole business has become." She sighed, then walked away, leaving me to sort out my priorities. Later, I told her about my intention to visit with Luella at the hospital.

"Quite frankly, Jimmy, I'd rather not have to think about her right now. I'm sorry I ever got you into this cockamamie thing, this absurd idea that we can undo or rewrite the past. You go; I'll keep Paul home tomorrow and try to calm things here."

Reluctantly, I agreed to Donna's suggestion. I, too, was growing tired of Luella Frazier. One thing troubled me, though. How did Fiona know about Carter? Had I shared that information with her? I must have told her about the night Madelaine nearly jumped out of the bedroom window. Sure, I consoled myself, that must be the answer. I went to sleep wishing I had never known Madelaine Frazier.

Chapter 42

I arrived twenty minutes early for the scheduled meeting with Carter and Luella and chose a table near the sidewall. On the pale, yellow walls hung framed paintings of full-blooming hydrangea, peaceful magenta-hued sunsets, and ocean tides receding or ebbing. There was something to suit every taste. Lunch hour was over, but many visitors lingered at their tables, some head to head in whispered conversations. I studied the deeply lined faces, the tightly pursed lips, and the sadness in the eyes of the people around me; I wondered what effect the mental illness of their loved ones had had on their lives. As I studied the visages of these total strangers, I could not help but absorb their sorrow. Within minutes, I was alerted to the presence of Luella Frazier, as she entered the room and sought out Carter's table. Dressed in a lovely emerald green sweater and heather gray slacks; a paisley scarf hung loosely from her neck and she carried a tweed, woolen coat draped over her left arm. She eyed me with surprise, then advanced, carrying her leather handbag over her shoulder. I wouldn't describe her demeanor as diffident, but rather as confident.

"Why, James," she inquired, "what brings you here?" Her tone was rather proprietary, as if I had invaded her territory.

"Hello, Luella." I rose and pulled out one of the red plastic chairs. "Please have a seat. Carter will be here momentarily." Though off-put, she acquiesced, and sat down, arranging her coat and bag on the back of her chair.

"Can I get you some coffee or tea?"

"Well, yes, that would be lovely. Thank you." Luella had taken on that false air of sophistication commonly acquired from the genteel clientele she served in the bridal boutique. "No cream or sugar, please."

I strode over to the coffee station, filled two cups with steaming coffee from the gleaming urns, paid, then headed back to our table. In my absence, Carter had joined Luella and greeted me kindly. I offered him a cup of coffee, too; but, with a wave of his hand, he declined.

"Nice to see you, James. Luella and I were just about to discuss Madelaine's... um, situation. I'm afraid that I do not have good news to share with you. Madelaine is still vehemently opposed to a face-to-face encounter with her mother." He sat back in his chair, removed his shelled half-glasses, fidgeted with his polka dot bow-tie, and waited for Luella's response. Several moments passed before she spoke; when she did, her voice was both controlled and measured.

"Doctor," she began, "I'm convinced at this point, that Madelaine will never agree to meet with me. She hates me, maybe rightfully so. But she is a very disturbed woman, as you've told me, and no amount of *intervention,* as you call it, on your—or my part—is going to change that."

Carter pulled his chair in closer to the table and leaned forward; his eyes bore into Luella's, emitting steely darts. He folded his hands on the table top to keep from shaking. I had a sense that I was about to witness a bomb shell exploding right there on the table before us. "Luella, it's time to stop this pretense. You show up for each visitation, knowing that Madelaine will not meet with you. It's time to cut this bullshit and tell us why."

You know, there are times when truth smacks you on the head like a rubber mallet, demanding that you open your eyes and see through the fog of your own dissembling, your unwillingness to believe in the evil that lives in the heart of another. I had fooled myself all along. I knew I was out of line in crossing the boundaries of Carter's domain, but suddenly, rage grabbed me by the neck and jerked me to a standing position. Carter knew what was coming; he buried his head in his hands and rocked side-to-side. He didn't try to stop me.

"You knew!!" I screamed. "You knew!! For how long, goddammit, did you look the other way?" I was spitting my fury, my spittle falling on her clasped hands. She made no attempt to move them. How like her brother, Dwayne, she looked at that moment: cold, vengeful.

"James, let's go," Carter urged.

"No! I'm not gonna' go until I'm finished here."

By now, all conversation in the cafeteria had ceased. It was as if time itself had stopped and all of us were frozen in place.

"How could you? Answer me, bitch!" My anger knew no bounds.

Luella dropped her coffee cup onto the table; her eyes grew wider and wider as the liquid spilled onto the floor. She clutched her neck, then, with a clenched fist, pounded her chest. Tears streamed down her pale cheeks. She looked up into my eyes, aflame with revulsion, my knuckles, pressed white against the table. She reached for a napkin and tried to blot the puddle of coffee. Then, she inhaled deeply and hit me with cold contempt.

"When you know deceit first-hand, James-and, believe me, you **will**- you won't be so... holier than thou. When you are betrayed— and you **will** be-you won't be so high and mighty. I'm surprised it took you so long to figure this out. After all, you were the one who found the... the..." she couldn't continue.

"How the fuck do you know about that? I shouted. "So, that's why you didn't want me to investigate!" I could hear my heart pounding against the inner walls of my chest. I felt dizzy and had to hold onto the tabletop to keep from falling.

Sitting ramrod-straight, she explained. "Before she passed away, Viola Sandakis wrote to me in prison. She told me that Madelaine had divulged the shameful secret to her. She hoped that I would rot in hell."

"But, why? How could you possibly do this to your daughter?" I was dumbstruck by her answer.

"I thought about that every day I was in prison. I guess the only answer I came up with was that I never really wanted a child; it was Edgar's idea. I blamed Madelaine for my wretched life and my meaningless existence."

"So, you punished her for being born?" I didn't quite understand.

"Madelaine betrayed me, and I hated her for it. She lured Edgar away from me and I resented everything about her. I don't know why she thought I wouldn't notice that she had skipped two periods. It finally reached a point—that dreadful afternoon—when I just couldn't stand it anymore." She waited, gathering her strength to continue. "He thought **I** was his precious "porcelain posy"—that's what he called **her**—lying beside him."

"She was a child, for God's sake!! You let him do that to your little girl?"

Looking me square in the eye, Luella whispered, "You knew about the baby James, and you didn't say a word to anyone. How come?"

"I'm as much a coward as you are, Luella. I'll take the blame for that; but, you... I hope you'll never see Madelaine again for as long as you live."

Never before had I felt such anger. Never before had I experienced the impulse to harm anyone. Overcome with rage, I reached for the metal napkin dispenser on the table and raised it high over Luella's head. She did not flinch. Carter leapt from his chair, knocking it over. He grabbed my wrist and held it tightly, until he could feel my muscles slacken. Prying the dispenser from my grasp, he beseeched me, "No, Jimmy. Don't!" I hung my head, suddenly enveloped by sheer exhaustion. And then, I understood how naked, unbridled rage can turn an otherwise rational person into a murderer. Luella sat perfectly still; a single tear trickled from her downcast eyes.

"God in Heaven," I moaned, "what a fool I've been, thinking that your twelve-years sentence was too harsh! No, they should have kept you locked up and thrown away the key!"

"Viola was right," Carter told her, "you should rot in hell. Come on, Jimmy, I'll walk you out."

We left Luella sitting by herself, not caring if she sat there forever. Let the night janitor throw her out with the rest of the trash.

On the way out, Carter hung his arm around my shoulder. "At least, now we know why Madelaine won't look at her mother. We'll continue to treat her as best we can, James, and hope to get her transferred to a half-way house at some point. Jeez, I could sure use a drink. Shall we?"

Carter and I made our way outside and down the street to a local bar. We sat at the counter and drank scotch until the shock of what we had heard slowly ebbed from its source. We shook our heads in dismay, never quite believing that Luella had been the silent partner in Edgar's heinous crime.

"So much for my "confession," eh, Carter?"

"Yeah, so much."

"Tell me, Carter, did you suspect anything like this?"

"Well, in all honesty, it confused me why Madelaine begged for her mother that night we caught her at the window and then, adamantly refused to see her. I think she was trying to tell us something but couldn't put it into words; that Luella was complicit in this sordid story."

"And, do you think Luella knew about Dwayne's drug dealing?" I was certain that she did but had no real proof.

Carter replied, "Who knows? One thing I do know, though, it that: "Heaven has no rage like love to hatred turned/ Nor hell a fury like a woman scorned." He recited Congreve's 17th century poem, as I drained my glass of scotch and placed it on the bar. I wasn't used to drinking liquor that early in the day and was feeling tipsy.

"Let's get some fresh air," I suggested.

"Yeah, fresh air. Sounds good."

We walked around the block several times, arms wrapped around each other's shoulders, each absorbed in his own thoughts. When both of us had regained our equilibrium and could walk unassisted, we headed back to the hospital, our jacket collars turned up against the chill. I took several deep breaths of cold air and exhaled slowly. I didn't know what would become of Luella Frazier and, quite frankly, I couldn't have cared less. If she had a conscience, she would have to live with it.

Driving home, I decided that when, in the future, I should find myself wanting to right a perceived wrong, I should remind myself that not all damaged souls can be mended; that there are no repair shops for broken hearts. I should recall what Carter had said, "Man plans, and God laughs." And, I should remember what my mother told me and the boys on Eighth Street years ago, "Mind your own business."

Photo by Patty Whitehouse

About the author:

Georgene Weiner was born and raised in Waterbury, Connecticut. She received her Bachelor of Arts degree from Boston University and taught Spanish in Boston-area schools. In addition to her novels, Ms. Weiner has authored poetry and short stories. A devotee of classical music, she is a pianist and singer. She lives with her husband Allen, near Cape Cod, Massachusetts.

Follow the author at: amazon.com/author/Georgene.Weiner

48621450R00145

Made in the USA
Columbia, SC
09 January 2019